DO NOT REMOVE
CARDS FROM POCKET

I Never Had a Best-Seller

I Never Had a Best-Seller

The Story of a Small Publisher

by

Jacob Steinberg

Founder, Twayne Publishers, Inc.

HIPPOCRENE BOOKS
New York

Library of Congress Cataloging-in-Publication Data
Steinberg, Jacob, 1915-
I never had a best-seller : the story of a small
publisher / by Jacob Steinberg
    p.   cm.
Includes index.
ISBN 0-7818-0049-8
1. Twayne Publishers—History. 2. Publishers and
publishing—United States—History—20th century.
I. Title.
Z473.T9S74   1993   92-36851
070.5'09747'1—dc20   CIP

For information, contact:
Hippocrene Books, Inc.
171 Madison Avenue
New York, NY 10016

This book is printed on acid-free paper.

Printed in the United States of America

To my grandsons Brian and Matthew,
who once wanted to know
"what was so special about Grandpa."

Contents

Introduction 9

I. Autobiographical Sketch 19

II. The Early Years — 41
John Ciardi and Other Editors

III. Sylvia Bowman and the 107
Authors Series

IV. Literary Diplomacy 135

V. Tsurris 185

VI. Author-Publisher Relations 219

VII. The Subsidized Book 229

VIII. The End of Twayne, Inc. 237
and Thereafter

Afterword by 249
Thomas T. Beeler

Index 269

Introduction

ESSENTIALLY, THIS IS THE STORY OF A SMALL PUB-
lisher who found a special niche in the world of
books. The firm grew and prospered eventually
on small editions with never a best-seller to mar
its twenty-five-year existence as an independent
house. But many of the Twayne titles sold well for
a small house, year after year, and the accumulated sales of a title could exceed 25,000[*] or more,
a respectable total for any trade house. We did a
survey one year and found that sixty-nine per cent
of our annual sales consisted of backlist titles.
Some readers of the manuscript thought my title,
I Never Had a Best-Seller, somewhat misleading
in view of what I have just written about sales
over the years.

What I had in mind with the proposed title was
to point out that it was quite possible to succeed
in my field without a best-seller and to convey a
sense of the disruptive impact on a small firm of a
book suddenly taking on the dimensions of a best-
selling title. A best-seller dictates its own imperi-

---

*I may have underestimated. Tom Beeler, who succeeded me
at Twayne, informs me that Warren French's *John Steinbeck*
reached sales of more than 45,000 five years ago.

ous course: promotion and advertising well beyond the small firm's means; print runs that are ruinous should the book suddenly stop selling. The book business is peculiar in that books are always subject to return if unsold, under the terms of the publisher's announced returns policy. As a consequence, cautionary tales circulate about well-known authors' books, such as Sinclair Lewis's later titles, for example, where enthusiastic salesmen placed first printings of 25,000 copies in stores, encouraging second and third printings of equal quantity or more to keep the sales momentum going, only to find these printings fresh off the presses colliding with the flood of returns of the first printing from the bookstores.

That is why when Herbert Tarr offered me first crack at *The Conversion of Chaplain Cohen* with his assurance that the book would be a bestseller, I replied that that was what I was afraid of. Of course, that was not the way I started out. In the beginning, I, too, like most fledgling publishers, wanted the lightning to strike the way it had with Will Durant's *Story of Philosophy* for Simon and Schuster as I heard M. Lincoln Schuster describe it. But by the time Tarr visited me, I had learned the hard way what Twayne could and could not do.

Twayne Publishers, Inc., was founded by me in January, 1949. Its capital, some of it borrowed, was $8,000, a hopelessly inadequate sum. When it became a part of the G. K. Hall & Co. of Boston (It is now a unit of Macmillan in New York City.), as a result of a merger with ITT in early 1973, Twayne had published more than one thousand titles, with 100 plus in 1972 alone, during the last year of its independent existence, according to the publishing record. So, one can assume a satisfying growth over a twenty-five year period.

The original intent of the firm was to publish translations of Chinese classics, a consequence of my being then a graduate student majoring in Chinese at Columbia University.

The name "Twayne," a variant form of "twain," was my wife's suggestion. Claire, who played an indispensable role in the proceedings I describe, thought it would indicate our commitment to the idea that East and West could meet, at least at 42 Broadway in New York City, our first address where we rented desk space. At the time, despite the fact that we were more greatly indebted to Rudyard Kipling for our name than to Mark Twain, the latter's heirs were vociferous in objecting legally to the use of "Twain" in any shape or form, hence our change of spelling, which owed something to my course in Old English at Brooklyn College. Mark never did object. We were probably too small to make a difference to his heirs, or they assumed we were an old English firm setting up a branch in the United States, as I was assured we were by a book buyer in a West Coast department store some years later. It is interesting to note, by the way, that the author generally regarded as Mark Twain's unofficial literary executor, Charles Neider, had his first novel, *The White Citadel*, published by Twayne.

More troublesome at this time than Mark Twain's heirs' possible objection, but equally flattering, was an early rumor that John Ciardi, then our poetry editor, encountered in Boston to the effect that we were mounting a Chinese Communist propaganda effort with the founding of the firm. John was then on the Harvard faculty and sufficiently upset by this to ask his friend, Fletcher Pratt, the well-known military analyst and historian, to check the story out with his Intelligence contacts. I never did learn what Pratt found out — presumably that we were a completely indigenous, if indigent operation. But the facts must have been reassuring, for Pratt wrote a few books for us later on.

I thought at the time that the fact I had studied Chinese while in the Army in World War II might have had something to do with the rumor. And, of course, the time was ripening for this kind of speculation, no matter how far-fetched. Senator McCarthy was shortly to charge Owen Lattimore with leading the Communist penetration of the State Department and being thus responsible eventually for "our" loss of mainland China.

It is true that some years later two of my war-time fellow students[*] became actively involved

---

[*]I include in this category not only those who studied Chinese with me at Cornell University but another group from Harvard. Both groups wound up together at a Signal Corps training center in Virginia, where we became 808J's, cryptanalysts of Japanese codes and ciphers. We had been studying Chinese with the expectation that we were to serve as liaison non-coms with Chinese forces when General Joe Stilwell assumed overall command of the Allied forces in China, a sound strategy that might have changed the course of history in China. Chiang Kai-shek eventually vetoed the idea, Stilwell was recalled, and our Chinese studies came to an end. The military decided our Chinese studies made us ideal 808J material. Scheduled to participate in the planned invasion of Japan, but not in the first waves because of our security classification, we set up house in Oahu. There, in barbed-wire installations as befitted our top-secret clearances, we practiced breaking intercepted messages that, ironically, had appeared in the Honolulu *Star-Bulletin* weeks if not months before.

with the Chinese People's Republic. Both wrote books about their experiences and were to cross my path later in my publishing career as I detail at some length. But others became teachers and translators, members of the United States diplomatic corps, and other government agencies, including one who admitted publicly to espionage in China for one of these agencies, when he was released from imprisonment by the People's Republic.

But I have gotten ahead of my story. Twayne's first book was to have been *Dream of the Red Chamber*, an 18th-century work by Tsao Hsueh-chin, regarded by many as the greatest of all Chinese novels. Chi-chen Wang, a professor of Chinese at Columbia University and my teacher, was to do the translation. Some twenty years before, he had done a much shorter version for Doubleday that had sold well, and there was a good deal of interest on the part of a number of publishers for the expanded edition. We were therefore very hopeful that the new translation would get us off to a flying start with a profitable first book and prominent reviews. Wang had invested in Twayne, which accounted for his willingness to entrust this work to the new firm. Despite his good intentions and our great expectations the book was not to appear until 1958, ten years after the founding of the firm. What were we to do? With a mounting sense of urgency and despair I cast about for ways to keep afloat personally and corporately.

To keep our meager publishing capital intact, I continued with freelance editorial services for which I found a considerable demand. In addition, I set up a book production unit, Bookman

Associates, with Joel E. Saltzman. Joel had sold printing before, had a varied business experience in addition, and was affable and well liked. This venture required very little of our own capital since it derived income from services rendered. After a year or so, Joel joined in the enterprise full time. When Wang decided to sell his Twayne shares at an appreciable profit in 1957, Bookman became a unit of Twayne. Its imprint was used for the publication of scholarly and specialized studies, many of which were subsidized in part, but which did surprisingly well in sales to college libraries and are still in print today.

The owners of Twayne then and continuing to the merger with ITT were: Jacob Steinberg, 50%, president and managing editor; Mary Silverman, my sister, 25%; and Joel E. Saltzman, 25%. Joel handled production and sales and the business functions of Twayne until his death in 1967, after which I assumed many of his duties. His widow, Hilda, elected to continue with Twayne as a shareholder. Morris M. Silverman (Moe), Mary's husband, was essentially Twayne's attorney and accountant, though a number of other practitioners handled those activities over the years, my brother Aaron being the first Twayne accountant. It was Moe's law office at 42 Broadway that provided our first address.

In casting about for a literary replacement for our *Dream*, I came upon an article by John Ciardi, then a young poet with a mission and Briggs-Copeland Assistant Professor of English at Harvard University, on what American poetry needed. It needed, wrote Ciardi, more responsible publishing opportunities. I wrote to John about our new firm and suggested we might be able to implement his ideas. And thus was born the first of many Twayne series, The Twayne Library of Modern Poetry. The project did much to establish the imprint on a solid literary footing. The *N.Y. Times Book Review* reviewed most, if not all, of these volumes of contemporary poetry, generally favorably, and frequently excerpts would also appear in the well-known columns of J. Donald Adams in the Sunday *Book Review* section.

In addition to serving as poetry editor, Ciardi gradually took on more ambitious tasks, becoming in effect Twayne's executive editor. It was under his direction that books by Thomas Hart Benton, Sidney Bechet, Donald Hall, Harry T. Moore, Fletcher Pratt, Wallace Fowlie were issued, and the first illustrations by Edward Gorey appeared to illustrate the sonnets of psychiatrist Merrill Moore, M.D., which we published. Ciardi remained with Twayne until 1960 or so but on a considerably diminished scale after he joined the *Saturday Review* in 1956.

One of the early projects that Ciardi passed on was the possibility of Twayne joining forces with Grove Press to publish an unexpurgated edition of *Lady Chatterley's Lover.* Ciardi's Harvard friends felt that there was "not a ghost of a chance" of the postal authorities allowing the *Lady* anywhere near the mails. Barney Rosset of Grove, who contacted Twayne and other publishers, never went near the mails, shipping the best-seller by truck and by Railway Express. He made no money on the publication because of the lawsuits involved but his shippers made a fortune. All they had to do for their 5% shipping charge was to slap labels on the book cartons as they came from the bindery. I know because the firm set up to do our warehousing wound up doing the bulk of Grove's shipping on the title.

Another project that Ciardi was dubious about turned out to be the one that led us on to fortune. In January of 1958, Sylvia E. Bowman, then on the faculty of Indiana University at Fort Wayne, wrote to us about publishing a "series of pamphlets...which I should like to organize and edit...about American poets and novelists." She proposed to use as a model for the series, *Writers and Their Words* published by Longmans, Green for the British Council and National Book League. Ciardi responded on January 30 from *The Saturday Review* that he was "intellectually enthusiastic...but fiscally pessimistic. With books of poetry selling so badly, it is almost inevitable that pamphlets about individual poets should be a bookkeeper's nightmare." He continued, making reference to the possibility of foundation support, about which he would talk to me, and that he "would be more than delighted to see such a series in print." Nothing was to come of the idea at the time but this was the opening for what was eventually to become a famous open-ended series of critical studies. TUSAS (Twayne's United States Authors Series), TEAS (Twayne's English Authors Series), and TWAS (Twayne's World Authors Series) attempted a critical survey of the world's literature, both past and present. It was a most ambitious undertaking, breathtaking in its scope, envisioning more than two thousand titles, and enlisting many scholars from other countries in the project. The first books devoted to American authors (TUSAS) were issued in 1961. Thereafter, in roughly two-year intervals, followed the English Authors Series, and the series (TWAS) devoted to the writers of some twenty other national literatures, including the USSR and Eastern Europe, China, Latin America, and the British Commonwealth countries as well. Still going strong but considerably modified, the Twayne series is by far the largest critical survey ever launched. In 1991, Twayne became an operating unit of Macmillan in New York City.

How a relatively small publisher successfully managed this large publishing program is detailed hereafter. Readers may also find some of my adventures in literary diplomacy worth while.

Hopefully, too, my comments on author-publisher relations, legal literary problems, hidden censorship, and what I call the "creative conversion of *tsurris* (trouble)" will provide food for thought as well. It would be my hope, too, that some young aspiring small publisher would find my experiences helpful.

I have already made mention of a number of authors, editors, and associates who contributed importantly to my story but there were others who shaped my enterprise amd helped immeasurably. Among these, my first assistant at Twayne and now publisher of New Amsterdam Books, Emile Capouya, whose early affiliation with Twayne provided even then an assured literary touch to the proceedings; George Blagowidow, author, publisher, and friend, who deemed this septuagenarian not too old to head one of his enterprises; Walton H. Rawls, accomplished art editor and author, whom I tried vainly to keep at Twayne when he left for greener fields; Professor Hans L. Trefousse, distinguished historian, author, and editor; the late Harold U. Ribalow, who tried in vain to make me rich and famous; the late Dr. Cecyle S. Neidle, who became editor of The Immigrant Heritage of America series; Erik J. Friis, whose knowledge of the Scandinavian world of letters was of tremendous assistance in this area. These and others that I mention in the pages that follow supported my endeavors. But, of course, the errors in judgment and the missed opportunities — "those ships that leave our ports everyday," as Tom Beeler, my successor at Twayne who became the head of G.K.Hall, put it — are mine, all mine, and I clutch them fiercely to my chest. I am grateful to Dr. Beeler for writing the Afterword, which brings the Twayne account to midyear 1991.

I wish to thank Eileen Rosner and my grandson, Brian Steinberg, for their assistance in the preparation of the manuscript.

A good deal of the early Ciardi-Twayne correspondence can be found on deposit with the Library of Congress. Sylvia Bowman's files are with Indiana University. The Arents Research Library at Syracuse University also has some Twayne materials. All of the letters, however, to which I refer are from copies or originals in my possession.

I

Autobiographical Sketch

WHAT KIND OF PERSON BECOMES A SMALL PUB-
lisher? I can't speak for the other obsessives,[*] but
books as objects of veneration held a fascination
for me from my earliest days. I recall the trips I
made to the Stone Avenue children's library in
Brownsville in the company of my sister Mary or
my brother Aaron, who introduced me somewhat
later on to the Liberty Boys, Nick Carter, and
Frank Merriwell, whose adventures I read avidly.
Perhaps I was most impressed by the careful scru-
tiny given my hands by the checkout librarian
before she entrusted me with the books I had
selected. And it was not a perfunctory check, for
I remember at least once having to forego the
pleasures of my choice because I could not pass

---

[*]Emile Capouya, editor and publisher, who wanted to publish
this book, used the term "passionate" to describe my involvement with books. Perhaps that was the other side of my coin.

inspection! On the next trip my chapped hands were scrubbed to the quick and thereafter subject to home inspection before I left for the library.

Brownsville then was the Jewish ghetto of Brooklyn, N.Y., and I lived at 446 Rockaway Avenue, between Pitkin Avenue and Belmont, both distinguished streets; Pitkin being the broad avenue for my first remembered parade after World War I — I was four years old then, having been born on January 31, 1915. Belmont was Pushcart Alley, full of pungent odors and all kinds of fascinating mysteries.

My mother and father were literate but with no opportunity to become lettered in their struggle for survival. They had the usual Jewish parental aspirations for their offspring as participants in the American dream.

Along with attendance at P.S. 84, we all went for Hebrew lessons and religious instruction to the Stone Avenue Hebrew School where my sister and brother attended advanced classes. I wasn't an outstanding student, probably compelled to attend classes despite the greater street attractions that clamored for my attention.

I recall no traumatic events connected with my early years in Brownsville, but there was great excitement in the streets: my brother's fight with Fats _____ , for example, with me trying to even the odds by jumping on the back of my brother's bigger adversary. We lived cheek by jowl with young friends who were to make a name for themselves as writers, scientists, or criminals.* My

*Alan Lelchuk's recent (1990) entertaining novel, *Brooklyn Boy*, categorizes headliners from Brownsville and other

brother's opponent, for example, wound up years later in the electric chair for a murder he had committed. But Fat's younger brother was a friend of mine, and his sister was a lovely young lady. Their mother did me out of the balance of a $20 bill I had found on Belmont Avenue, but not before my friend and I had gorged ourselves on goodies we had purchased. When I told my mother about my good fortune and loss, she decided to do nothing about it. Fat's mother was a formidable lady, rumored I later learned to be in the "frauen" business, as a madam or procurer. But I didn't know what that was all about, though I recall with affection a young girl-friend that I was paired off with by virtue of our family friendship. I met her again when we were young adults, but the magic was no longer there.

The carefree years were soon to end. My father in his early forties was stricken with what eventually was diagnosed as Bright's disease, then a fatal malady. At the outset, his doctor suggested that he pursue a more tranquil existence and so he was forced to withdraw from a pants manufacturing partnership he had set up in Brooklyn. My mother's younger sister, Aunt Bessie, persuaded my parents to move to Albany, New York, where we purchased a small grocery with living quarters in the back and an upstairs apartment for rental.

My father's illness lingered for four or five

Brooklyn neighborhoods: Danny Kaye, Shelley Winters, Sam Levinson; Abe Reles, Bugsy Siegel, Lepke Buchalter, *et al.* of Murder, Inc.; Dr. Jonas Salk, Dr. Isador Rabi; and many others, some of whom were my contemporaries.

years when he died of apoplexy in August of 1926.
The fatal stroke occurred early one morning as he
was lying next to me in bed; perhaps he had a
premonition of what was to come and wanted to be
near his youngest child. He had opened the store
as usual, my mother said, but had complained of
not feeling well, and she had taken over, urging
him to lie down for a while.

He was not afraid of death, though I was at the
time. I recall his comforting words to me when a
young friend passed away. I was immediately
stricken with similar symptoms to those I had
overheard described, of course. My father's
words, strangely comforting, did not pooh-pooh
my fears. He addressed himself to the fact that
death was a part of living that had to be faced by
all God's children and mentioned his experience in
the Russo-Japanese War of 1905. My mother attributed his illness to his wartime tribulations, a
particularly horrendous occurrence centering on
his being penned down in a ravine, wounded and
unable to move and near freezing for many hours
next to a mortally wounded comrade whose con-
gealed blood matted with his own.

For many years after my father died, I felt that
I was to follow in his path to an early death. For
years my blood pressure registered much higher
readings than normal, a reaction attributable, I
am now sure, to the memory of my father's experiences when his pressure was taken while he was
ill at home and which I witnessed. It was not
until I reached and passed my father's age that
my fears left me. I realized that my father's death
did not come from a genetic cause but from envi-
ronmental circumstances, and that, more than

likely, I had inherited my mother's long-lived genes.

She was a wonderfully stubborn Jewish lady, who passed away at ninety-six, just a month or so after a family Passover seder for more than twenty of her children, grandchildren, and their offspring. Left a widow in her early forties and in poor financial circumstances, she could say "no" to God — to borrow an expression I heard Elie Wiesel use — and dedicated her life to keep her family together. She was unfailingly drawn to the underdog and her attachment thereto was permanent, never subject to alteration even when the status of the unfortunate one changed to greatly favorable circumstances.

My mother usually found something affirmative in negative things that happened to her. When, for example, she broke a tooth in her late eighties, she marvelled at the fact that it was only half a tooth, and that she could still get along quite well with what remained.

My memories of Albany are not too pleasant. It was there that I had my first encounter with anti-Semitism and other unpleasant manifestations of man's inhumanity to man.

We lived at 134 Lark Street in a house that is now demolished. It was a moderate-to-low income area, just on the outskirts of a ghetto area populated by working class immigrants. The public school I attended was just past a parochial school whose hours seemed to lag those of my school by fifteen minutes or more. Since there were so few Jews in our neighborhood and only two in my school, I was easily identifiable. My brother and sister were attending high school in another section of town and couldn't accompany me to face my tormentors, and my father was ill. The juxtaposition of the schools made it mandatory to run the gauntlet day after day. Since I was not a good runner I became very handy with my fists, but there were times when I had to retreat.

The young people in the immediate vicinity of my home reflected some of the prejudices of their elders but allowed me to participate in their games, their fights, their pleasures. I recall how thrilled I was to be identified with my friends when a neighbor chased us out of her back yard with the injunction "and take that fat little Irishman (me!) with you."

At Christmastime, I was invited by some of my friends to their homes to share in the warmth of the season, to play with the games and the toys. When I incurred their wrath, however, their anger took on overtones of the prejudices they felt. I shall never forget the feeling of overwhelming shock when the one I treasured as my best friend turned on me with an epithet I remember to this day. But I remember with affection another of my friends, Pegleg, so called because of a limp he acquired as a result of infantile paralysis. He taught me how to sneak into the movies, insisted on boxing with me despite his infirmity which resulted in affirming my prowess as a fighter.

This reputation was not without its perils, however. I recall one such incident with trepidation even today. The challenge came in the form of a reluctant gentle giant from the adjoining ghetto who had been egged on by small fry eager for the sight of my blood! I had known my opponent, only a few months earlier it seemed to me, as someone of my height and, in the haphazard way evaluations took place in youthful circles, rumored to be decidedly inferior in fisticuffs to Pegleg, whom I had so handily defeated. But my challenger had grown two heads taller since I had seen him last, and I would never have agreed to face him had I been aware of his formidable appearance. But here I was and I wouldn't run. I would not, however, make the first move, and, thank goodness, neither would he. So, after staring at each other for what seemed to me to be an eternity, I walked away, gratefully intact.

Pegleg was, I think, gifted with an optimism and a curiosity that should have stood him in good stead later in life. He went to Hebrew school one day with me, at his insistence, assuming the *nom de guerre* of Morris Goldberg! Pegleg must have felt he was penetrating enemy lines. I don't think my teacher was taken in — Pegleg was a handsome Irish lad and looked it. He was a lovable fellow, in the mold of Penrod or Tom Sawyer, I think.

In retrospect, I can understand the prejudice I encountered at the hands of the young and the ignorant. They were behaving in conformity with what they encountered everyday then in their religious catechism.

One other recollection of Albany remains seared in my memory; it concerns my first encounter with yellow journalism. The event was tied up with the Sacco-Vanzetti case, which took place at a time (1927) of virulent anti-Communism in America. Many Americans believed the two anarchists had been wrongfully sentenced to death, and sentiment pro and contra were the stuff of headlines.

Into this atmosphere, my uncle, the husband of Aunt Bessie, gentle but determined that a wrong had to be righted, set out in a rented truck with broadsides calling attention to a protest meeting to be held the next day. The police hauled him off for doing who knows what without a permit. An hour or two later he was released without a charge. In the meantime, however, the local yellow sheet had come out with an extra, headlines screaming about the Sacco-Vanzetti plot that the Albany police had uncovered! Of course, the name and address of my uncle, Isidore Brooks, was given, along with his business affiliation — he was in the dental supply field — and his livelihood destroyed. No charge, no arrests, just a screaming headline, and a family wiped out. My aunt and uncle, and my three cousins, Miriam, Eleanor, and Dorothy left for California in a few months, and my uncle died there some years later, still fighting for what he believed to be right. He was a gentle person of great courage.

After my father's death, we returned to Brooklyn, where I completed grammar school and graduated from Thomas Jefferson High School* in 1932. I was an honor student, particularly good in English, but not among the leading student literary lights — the poets, the editors of the school publications, and the like. Possibly, this was because my mother had bought a small candy store which required a lot of my time, so that I

---

*It was not then one of the city's worst schools, as a *N.Y. Times* article of February 28, 1992, described the once distinguished secondary school in East New York, after two students were shot to death by a fellow student, the third such killing in a year.

could not volunteer for these extra-curricular activities. Despite my valiant efforts to eat up all the profits, the store managed to see us through the desperate years of the Depression.

I entered Brooklyn College, from which I graduated in January of 1936. I was fortunate to have as my instructor in Freshman English, Maurice Valency, who went on to Columbia University and became a well-known critic and writer. He taught me the importance of terseness in expression and felt that I should be encouraged to develop what he thought might eventually turn into talent. I never lived up to the promise he thought I had. But I enjoyed the hours I spent in writing chores, and, as I have indicated elsewhere, put my small talent to work at 40 cents an hour, pretty good pay then, writing poetry for hire, not one aspiring poet declining the immortality I conferred.

Despite a "D" in College Algebra, charitably bestowed by an instructor who recognized my hopeless incompetence as a mathematician, I graduated from Brooklyn in three and a half years, *cum laude* and with a major letter in boxing, the only sport in which I seemed to have any ability.

After Brooklyn College* I went on to Columbia University for my first period of graduate studies in English, taking the History of the English Language as my major concentration. I had so greatly enjoyed my courses in Anglo-Saxon and Chaucer

---

*Later, I was able to show my high regard for the college by publishing *Against the Running Tide* by President Henry D. Gideonse, *The Brooklyn College Student* by Gladys H. Watson, and *A Commitment to Youth* by Abraham S. Goodhartz, none of them best-sellers.

taught by Professor Neumann at Brooklyn College that I thought a continuation of these at a higher level would be equally interesting. Despite the reputation of the professor at Columbia as a scholar, he turned out to be a poor teacher.

But Columbia proved helpful in adding to my editorial and publishing skills. Just out at the time was the first edition of the one-volume *Columbia Encyclopedia* under the editorial direction of Claude Ainsley. I was hired as an NYA student — a depression era project — at forty cents per hour, later increased to fifty, and given various checking chores. Before long I started to turn up proofreading errors, inconsistencies, and the like, attracting some attention from the editors. As a consequence, I was recommended to the Mesdames Eugenia and Lucie Wallace, who were preparing all of the book indexes for the Columbia University Press, and did similar work for other firms. What followed was a couple of years indexing, copy editing, proofreading — all skills that were to stand me in good stead some ten years later when I established Twayne.

The income this activity engendered supplemented my earnings as a per-diem teacher, first as a teacher-in-training at $4.50 per day and then as a substitute teacher with a license in English at $7.50 and $8.50 per day. The only regular jobs available were at the tougher schools, and I managed to keep myself permanently employed at East New York Vocational High School in Brooklyn — first at the Annex, a renovated Telephone Company building — where the students were most reluctant scholars. They were simply marking time till their sixteenth birthdays when they could legally leave school. A few of them had already run afoul of the law and were out on probation or awaiting trial. We had more than our share of problems, including physical injury to the faculty.

My first year there was a horror story, coming as it did after a year of sheer enjoyment at Abraham Lincoln High School in Brooklyn, where I was a teacher-in-training in the English Department. My students in the second and third year there were bright and kept me on my toes. Perhaps the contrast was what made East New York so dismal an experience. I came there after the school year had begun and the students had literally run off several of my predecessors with such dramatic techniques as setting fires in the classroom. They regarded my presence as a challenge to find a prompt method of dispatch. And what they dished out would have been more than I could take were it not for the fact that I desperately needed the job. We had sold the store by then for a few hundred dollars, and I was the principal support for my mother in maintaining a small apartment, my brother and sister having married.

Since teaching English or any subject was really out of the question, at least initially, I resorted to stratagems to at least maintain a semblance of order. When signs of restiveness set in, I would lead the class in shoulder roll exercises. Since those days were not too far from my prime as a boxer, I was able to outlast them. After a few hundred rolls, I had control of the class, and they were willing to sit back and relax their aching muscles, and, of course, they must have realized I was not as soft a touch as they had perhaps thought.

One other incident contributed to my eventually getting control of the class. Because of the lack of adequate facilities, our building was on late session, and our school day ended after dark during the winter months. The faculty generally departed as a group. One Friday, however, as we left the building, the assistant principal in charge of the Annex with us, we encountered an unruly group of students just outside the building. It was apparent that carnage was about to take place.

I expected the assistant principal to take charge, to ascertain what was wrong and to disperse the group, but he did no such thing. He walked on with some vague admonition to the group in general to get away from the building. Somehow, I could not walk away and I found myself alone with the students. They were not hostile but they were obviously expecting some dramatic, perhaps bloody encounter, and they did not want to be deprived of their entertainment.

The principal antagonists were clearly indicated. The argument was over a dollar bill that the smaller, better-dressed student claimed his mother had given him. The other, much taller, insisted that he had lost the dollar, and that it was his. I asked the two to re-enter the building with me so that I could separate them from the others and asked the bigger one who looked lean and mean if he would be satisfied with recovering half his loss. When he responded reluctantly but affirmatively, I took a half-dollar out of my pocket and gave it to him, making sure, however, that his smaller adversary, whose story I believed, had a few minutes headstart. By that time, the crowd had dispersed, and I left too with the one remaining contestant. His opponent was no longer in sight. I had defused the situation at small cost. When I returned to school after the weekend, the story had spread and I had no trouble thereafter maintaining discipline. In confronting the students' problem, I had solved my own.

But teaching still continued to be impossible. How could it not be when I had students in the graduating senior class of high school who could not read nor write?

With the building of a new structure to house the high school and a gradual change in the student population to include those capable of future college work, the student body improved considerably, so much so that by the time I was drafted for military service in 1943, I was enjoying the teaching profession again but it was still far removed from the challenge I had faced at Lincoln High.

Prior to my induction into the army, however, Claire (nee Bernstein) and I were married on January 31, 1943, my birthday. Our son Michael was born on March 14, 1944. He died in 1986, a talented and caring physician.

When I reported for my medical examination prior to army induction, I was pretty sure that I would not be accepted for I had recently been turned down for life insurance, black-listed as a matter of fact, because of my blood pressure readings. This at the age of twenty-eight and despite my Board of Education physical which I had passed some years before. It was a hell of a situation for a young man about to be married, as I reported to Claire, my beautiful fiancée. The draft board medical staff, however, refused to be intimidated by the initial readings. The physician in charge told me I was to be detained for an indeterminate period — perhaps a few hours or a few days and that the sooner I relaxed, the sooner I would be released. After three or four readings conducted an hour or so apart where the pressure remained in a satisfactory range, I was told I was physically fit for service in the army, though on limited service because of my nearsightedness.

My initial army service was as a military policeman, and I was sent to Fort Ontario, N.Y., for training. Aside from the snow that still saw two to three feet in May, it was not a period of difficult adjustment. Most, if not all, of my fellow GI's had some sort of disability. I had hoped that my background would place me somewhere in the army book world but this was not to be.

After the snows of Ontario, we were assigned to an M.P. unit at Whippany, N.J. Most of my outfit wound up doing guard duty aboard ships docked at the New York piers, a deadly monotonous task. A few others and I were spared and assigned to the 66th Street Armory from which we were dispatched to the Penn Railroad trains on the Washington to New York run, and the N.Y. Central going as far north as Syracuse.

I rode the trains for the better part of six months. It was not unpleasant except for the occasional problem, mostly with inebriates who were on furlough after overseas tours of duty. We also drew assignments in New York City proper, and I recall one call involved a giant of a drunk in uniform whose wife wanted him arrested for abusing or threatening her. It was a walk-up tenement and would have required the two of us on duty to carry the drunk down the stairs. He was too inebriated to move on his own. I thought the better part of valor lay in persuading the soldier's wife that we would all be better served if she allowed him to sleep it off. I pointed out that he was in a stupor, that he was in no condition to bother her, and if in the morning she still wanted him incarcerated we would be able to oblige her. Thank goodness I persuaded her.

Most of the MP's loved the N.Y.-Syracuse evening run because after the initial hour or so of walking up and down the train asking the military aboard to show their passes or identification, the balance of the long hours could be passed in sleep. The run back got into Grand Central about 12 noon, leaving one with a whole day off, usually.

Occasionally, too, when our return came in the early A.M. hours, I would not return to the Armory but would with some trepidation wrap up the impressive looking Colt 45 (I think that's what it was) in its holster in newspapers and carry it home with me, returning later that day for duty. Travelling the IRT subway to Brooklyn before dawn was not the fearful experience then that it became but it was comforting to have my wrapped-up companion as I walked the empty dark streets home from the last stop on Flatbush Avenue.

Memorable, too, was the time I found Eleanor Roosevelt in a hot, dusty car without air-conditioning in mid-summer, all alone. No one else wanted to sit there apparently. But she obviously wanted to be left alone, and I did not intrude though I wanted to. The job of M.P.ing was occasionally hazardous, as when we were called out because of a riot in Harlem or when on guard duty at the entrance to the Armory, where a novice literally took to heart the instructions he had received, and killed a hapless civilian inebriate who persisted in his efforts to gain entry to the building after being ordered to halt and desist.

Once a month, we had to visit our home base, the West Side piers, to collect our pay and register our presence. It was on one of those visits that I applied for the Army Specialized Training Program (ASTP) in foreign languages. I qualified in German as a result of two years study in high school and three years in college. But to my amazement I was assigned a program in Chinese language instruction at Cornell University. As luck would have it, I was ill in the hospital with the flu when it came time to report, but aside from this rocky beginning a few days late, I got along swimmingly. I could not believe my luck! Here I was attending classes at a school that I never could have afforded privately. At twenty-eight, married, and soon to be a father, I was completely aware of my good fortune. There were a few other "seniors" who relished the opportunity but most of the younger men took full advantage of the coeducational aspects of the university facilities to the detriment of their studies. But I enjoyed every minute of the learning process, becoming increasingly fascinated by the Chinese, both the language and the people.

We were to learn how to speak and understand Mandarin in nine months or less. And, amazingly, those of us who were truly interested in attaining this goal, and not tone-deaf, were able to achieve fluency in that period of time. The top student, however, Aaron Marc Stein, a writer of superb mysteries under the *nom de plume* of George Bagby, could not master the tonal qualities and had to be dropped, despite the fact that he was in comprehension so clearly ahead of everyone else in the class.

I was no match for Marc in his overall grasp and in his ability to spend so much time studying — he was virtually indefatigable in this — but I was nevertheless a top student and my yins (tones) were always correct. At the end of our nine months I was among those chosen to make a 15-minute recording for broadcast to China, and I could speak extemporaneously on the everyday matters I was likely to encounter as an American soldier serving as a liaison non-com with Chinese troops under the overall authority of General (Vinegar Joe) Stilwell, which was our rumored assignment.

Using methods of oral Chinese language instruction that had originated at Yale University, our instructors or tutors — one for each five or six students — were all native speakers of Mandarin with little grasp of English. We could communicate only in Chinese. Mastery of the phonetic system we used to duplicate the Chinese sounds was a fairly simple task. Thereafter we were given scripts to memorize, covering virtually every situation imaginable. And lo, after a few short weeks, we were actually able to speak the language, our tutors correcting our faulty tones and pronunciations.

Day and night, while waiting in line for our meals or for injections or inspection, or whatever, we would memorize from flash cards, one side of which gave us the Chinese character, pronunciation and meaning, and the other, the numbers of stroke sequence in writing the character. While mastery of spoken Chinese was the desideratum, we were also given courses in reading and writing Chinese, and history and other cognate lectures.

But when Chiang Kai-shek refused to go along with the American game plan involving Vinegar Joe, our studies came to an end. The army decided that since we had mastered one Oriental language, we could be helpful in breaking Japanese codes and ciphers. We were to become 808J's, Japanese cryptanalysts.

This was, however, a top-secret classification, and some of us were weeded out. One of the no-no's seemed to be affiliation with organizations identified with the far left. Another seemed to be deliberate omission of such affiliation. As a teacher, I had belonged to the Teachers Union, then generally identified with the liberal left, but had left the organization when it flip-flopped on the war issue at the time the Soviet Union signed the short-lived non-aggression pact with Hitler. For the record I duly reported my affiliation, along with the fact that I had once been arrested, though not convicted of any criminal charge. I suppose whoever was running the clearances was impressed by my candor, and I was accepted.

We went through a period of basic training in the new field at Vint Hill, Virginia, and shortly after were alerted for overseas duty. Before that, however, I had to hit the target and the dirt in simulated combat. I had no trouble with the latter, but I did have difficulty with the target, which

I couldn't see clearly. But, finally, even that obstacle was overcome somehow. The solution was, I think, the gunnery sergeant acting as *deus ex machina*.

Three weeks later we were in Oahu, Hawaii. The two-week trip from Seattle on board a converted Liberty freighter was a nightmare. We seemed to be alone, without escort, for the greater part of the journey. Early on, the toilet outlets were either plugged by design to avoid enemy detection or became clogged, and we were reduced to washing or showering with one eye alert to the floating feces everywhere.

Oahu was not hard to take. Our days were spent in a building behind barbed wire. There we were initiated into the mysteries of breaking encrypted Japanese messages, the contents of which had been reported in the public press months before. But, of course, these were practice sessions. The scuttlebut was that we were to take part in the invasion of Japan, but not in the first waves because of our security clearances and when an attempt was made to rescue five of us by another branch of service for China duty it was turned down on the ground that we were "indispensable," obviously a term of elastic definition.

Eventually, my outfit, the 3793 Signal Intelligence Service Detachment, moved on to the Philippines. But by then the war in Europe was over, and those of us scheduled for early discharge stayed on. When my outfit departed, I and two other sergeants (My rating as a T-3 was equivalent to that of a staff sergeant.) were billeted at an abandoned camp on the outskirts of Oahu. There our duties consisted of sun-bathing and taking care that no injury came to government property. A first lieutenant was in charge of this array. His duty seemed to consist of merrymaking at night with fellow officers and a number of assorted ladies from town. But we didn't bother him and for the most part he left us alone. It was an idyllic "live and let live" situation. I was also able to continue teaching in Oahu public schools. There was such a shortage of manpower that the army permitted us to moonlight in certain occupations including teaching, which I did for the better part of a year.

My military career came to an end after nearly three years of service when I was discharged on January 29, 1946. Shortly thereafter, I enrolled at Columbia University again, this time for graduate studies in Chinese. After my first semester, I applied for a fellowship. This, plus an opportunity to teach two classes of basic Chinese in the School of General Studies, seemed to offer a way to keep going with my studies. Unfortunately, the fellowship, applied for in May was not approved until September. In the meantime, I was offered the princely sum of $70.00 per week to work for Edward Uhlan, a vanity publisher with a number of imprints, the most notorious one being Exposition Press. Uhlan's book, *The Rogue of Publishers' Row*, an *apologia pro vita sua,* is a fascinating read, but it is a classic example of the devil quoting scripture. Later on I discuss the problems involved in vanity and subsidized publishing. I did very well for Uhlan but it meant working on books that should not have been published. And when I occasionally came across a title that merited publication but where the author would not provide a subsidy, Uhlan would veto my recommendation. This went on for the better part of two years when I left to set up my own firm. My wife and her parents, particularly my mother-in-law, were very supportive. They opened their home to us rent-free, offering to lend me money should we need it.

II

The Early Years— John Ciardi and Other Editors

DURING THE FIRST YEARS, THE CIARDI PRESENCE was central to Twayne's achievement. John Ciardi (1916-1986) joined us early in 1949. He was then on the Harvard faculty, an ambitious and energetic young poet with two books of poetry published and yet to achieve his mark in poetry, but even then a superb and mature critic. He had written an article on contemporary poetry for the Sunday supplement of a Chicago newspaper. What American poetry needed, he wrote, was a publisher who would publish it regularly and publish it responsibly, supplementing the limited publishing opportunities for poets then available from New Directions, the Yale Series of Younger Poets, and a few other specialized imprints. I was at this time, as I have indicated earlier, seeking desperately for a book project to replace our perennially postponed *Dream of the Red Chamber*, the book that was supposed to provide a solid financial basis for our enterprise. I wrote to Ciardi about his article and suggested that our new firm might be able to implement his ideas. We met and agreed to set up The Twayne Library of Modern Poetry, which embodied his plan. The Library, with Ciardi as editor, was projected to issue five books of poetry a year, one of which had to be a "first book," selected by what we called the Twayne First Book Contest. The contest brought in hundreds of manuscripts interesting, as I recall, May Swenson and other young poets of comparable stature. The winnowing was done in-house, and we were fortunate to have at the time Emile Capouya as a part-time editorial assistant to supplement the other low-cost talent that was then available, including mine, to screen the manuscripts.

The winning title, in addition to $100 advance against royalties, was to carry a preface written by a distinguished critic. The first winner was Marshall Schacht's *Fingerboard* and F.O. Matthiessen of Harvard wrote an appreciative preface. The winner the next year, 1951, was Rosemary Thomas's *Immediate Sun* for which Archibald MacLeish wrote the preface.

In 1951, a description of the Library on the back of the dust jacket for one of the volumes carried the following:

THE TWAYNE LIBRARY OF MODERN POETRY
To Serve the Poet, To Serve the Audience

In 1949 TWAYNE announced a full scale program devoted to contemporary poetry. In an era when volumes of verse issued by the major publishers are few and far between, the Twayne project has been recognized as a significant force in modern letters, and a distinct contribution to American culture. The publishers have derived a good deal of satisfaction and encouragement from the support of such distinguished literary figures as William Carlos Williams, Melville Cane, Archibald MacLeish, Mrs. Francis Biddle, David Morton, Dudley Fitts, Robert Frost, Bernard De Voto, Howard Mumford Jones, and others who are numbered among Twayne Library subscribers.

Discriminating publication, frequent publication, — these are services a publisher can render to the cause of poetry. But the success of any such program rests ultimately with the reader, for there is no league to support poetry but the fundamental league of book buyers.

The Twayne Library of Modern Poetry means to publish the best poetry available and distribute it at the lowest possible prices by means of its subscription plan...

Special Subscription rates are available.

The following titles are now ready.

1. THE DOUBLE ROOT. John Holmes, $2.50
2. THE CATCH. T. Weiss, $2.25
3. THE CENTER IS EVERYWHERE. E. L. Mayo, $2.50
4. WHERE THE COMPASS SPINS. Radcliffe Squires, $2.25
5. THE DAEDAL IMAGE. George Zabriskie, $2.25
6. IMMEDIATE SUN. Rosemary Thomas, $2.50
   (*Winner of 1950 First Book Contest, selected by Archibald MacLeish*)
7. HORN IN THE DUST. Selwyn S. Schwartz, $2.00
8. FINGERBOARD. Marshall Schacht. Preface by F.

O. Matthiessen, $2.25
(Winner of the 1949 First Book Contest)

9. ADDRESS TO THE LIVING. John Holmes (3rd Printing), $2.50

10. CLINICAL SONNETS. Merrill Moore (Third Printing), $2.50

11. WALK THROUGH TWO LANDSCAPES. Dilys Bennett Laing, $2.00

12. ILLEGITIMATE SONNETS. Merrill Moore, $2.75 and

13. MID-CENTURY AMERICAN POETS. John Ciardi, Ed., $4.00

Subscribers will be kept informed of additions to the list as they are selected. No reader interested in modern poetry will want to forgo these titles.

Subscriptions to the Library were solicited by mailings to the Poetry Society of America and similar groups, including libraries, but we had not yet established our presence and the Library never became self-supporting. It had, however, among its subscribers a number of distinguished members as the book jacket description indicates. It was abandoned after a few years, Ciardi concurring. The subscription approach, however, proved an invaluable experience, and I was able to utilize it much more successfully some twelve years later in promoting Twayne's United States Authors Series (TUSAS), whose first books were released in 1961. Ciardi tried valiantly but vainly to persuade some of the poets in *Mid-Century American Poets* — our first major success — notably Richard Wilbur and Theodore Roethke, to publish their poetry in the Twayne Library.

In a letter to me dated January 21, 1951, he

wrote from Salzburg, Austria, where he was participating in a seminar in American Studies:

> I'm especially anxious too that you don't trade me off on this: we should do the Faulkner [a symposium on Faulkner's achievement] and bid for Roethke. I'm thinking of futures in this, Jack. Ten years ago you could have picked up Auden for a song: his books were remaindered. In '38-39 I bought for $.19 for $.29 and for $.49 Auden, MacNeice, and Yeats items (among others) that are worth $20 and $25 apiece right now. They hadn't made it yet. Now their publishers are making a very ripe thing from these poets, not only in sales but on their cut of anthology permissions. Roethke in ten years and in less than ten years is going to be one of the people that count, and heavily. Wilbur is another one....

He also enclosed his letter to Roethke, which he asked me to forward after making a copy for my files:

> Dear Ted:

> A long drift toward time since Yaddo, and a rich time since, a time largely spent in reviewing the collected works of all the people in the *Mid-Century* Anthology in preparation for the course I've been giving here at the American Seminar. I've come out of these last few months with an increasingly powerful conviction about your writing. I can put that conviction into three words: *This is It*. Let T.S.Eliot and Jarrell back Lowell, let Matthiessen back Shapiro, and let sauve qui peut back Peter Schmiereck [Viereck], I'll back Roethke.

> Which is not pure blurb, though it is pure sentiment. What I'm getting at is this: I want you on my Twayne Library of Modern Poetry list. I began this list in order to publish the best poetry I could find. I think we've made a good beginning, but what the hell is the use of a list dedicated to poetry if we can't

touch the top work that's being done. I want the new book you were working on at Yaddo, and I don't expect to have it for free. I know you're quite happy at Doubleday, but you belong on our list.... Finally I'm ready to back it with money: how much advance do you want?... I'll pledge myself to meet any reasonable advance you may ask for even if it means digging into my own pocket....

My response, on February 7, 1951:

About Lewis book....contract received. Certainly worth a $50.00 expense nut.

There most certainly will be other Faulkner symposia. Commins of Random House is Faulkner's editor and according to him several projects are under way....If you'll tell me how and where I can reach Lewis with a $50.00 check, which I hope I'll be able to write when this week's bills are paid, I'll send it along.

I read the *Times Literary Supplement* article on *Mid-Century American Poets*. It's certainly stimulated sales in England and on the Continent but as far as the home trade is concerned, no stir as yet. Still we're quite puffed up about it and I have personally saluted ye poetry editor with 5 cups of coffee today. Great doings, John!

About Roethke...the spirit is willing but where in hell's name are we going to get that kind of money for an advance? By all means make the bid for the guy if he's that good... but isn't there something else we can offer him instead of cash?...I honestly don't see how we can go more than $100.00 in cash advance. We just don't have it to offer. So, let's not kid ourselves or indulge in wishful thinking...our cash reserves remain very much a problem....Tell me, John, what publisher holds titles for 10 years for futures? For two hits he's got to warehouse, store, insure 200 other misses. What I think you need is a couple of months of rassling with production...and the thousand and one horses' asses that you run into in this business....

I have no reservations about your abilities, John. And for public consumption, I attribute the fame and glory of Twayne to John Ciardi more than to any single or combination of figures we have, and I think with some business seasoning, there is absolutely no reason why you should not make a brilliant editor, but once in a while you hit me with a $500.00 advance for a book of poems! *You want we should go broke?...*

Roethke's answer must have put an end to the matter, for John never brought it up again. In retrospect, I think what we should have done was to enlarge our efforts on behalf of the unpublished poets, rather than trying to attract those who were already well on their way. For $500.00 advance to Roethke we could at the time pretty well cover the production cost of a 64-page book of poetry and give some unknown a push to recognition.

Mid-Century American Poets, the anthology edited by John Ciardi, was probably the most prestigious volume published (1950) by the Twayne Library. It was widely reviewed. William Carlos Williams in the *N.Y. Times Book Review* gave it a terrific sendoff: "The result is a treatise on the poem that should be of the greatest interest to the student as well as the curious reader who has begun to wonder what all this pother about modern verse signifies... an excellent book for teaching... a collection which contains some of the ablest work of our day. Read it all." The *New Republic* review described the purpose of the volume: "An honest, useful book, its simple principle being to gather together poems reasonably representative of the best work of a generation of poets, and to have each poet preface his poems with a guide to the reader's better understanding of his work and intent..."

The volume received a new lease on life, as did many of our books, when it was put on all the recommended college library book lists in the late 1960's. It is still regarded as one of the outstanding anthologies of poetry in the 1950's.

On the strength of its early prospects, Ciardi suggested that we follow up with a similar volume for French poetry and one for British poetry. We were fortunate to get Wallace Fowlie to undertake *Mid-Century French Poets* which appeared in 1950. It was a bilingual edition, and Fowlie translated the poetry so that the French and English versions were on facing pages. This too enjoyed good sales and was paperbacked eventually by Grove Press. Professor Fowlie's volume was also included in most college library recommended book lists.

The third volume, *Mid-Century British Poets*, ran into problems. Originally, Stephen Spender and John Lehmann were to collaborate as co-editors of the anthology. Spender withdrew, but the volume still remained viable, one of the attractions being Lehmann's publishing affiliation, which promised the possibility of placement of a part of the edition. When the manuscript arrived, however, Lehmann had given up his publishing connections and the manuscript itself did not impress us as being on the same level as the Ciardi and Fowlie anthologies. We abandoned publication plans and returned the manuscript.

Despite the end of the Library subscription plan, we continued, however, to publish poetry, both under the Twayne imprint and that of Bookman Associates which, as I have said, had been established for the release of limited and largely scholarly publications. Ciardi had to approve the poetry released by Twayne. We disagreed occasionally, however, and this explains, for example, why *The Selected Poems of Claude McKay* appeared under the Bookman imprint. Other prominent poets such as Alfred Kreymborg and Norman Rosten were also published by Bookman. The authors, however, had been attracted to the firm by the growing reputation of Twayne in the poetry field.

In our effort to continue publishing poetry, we resorted to various stratagems. One such effort, Norman Rosten's pitch for prepublication sales on his book, *The Plane and the Shadow*, is a classic and deserves to be memorialized. It was quite successful, more than reaching its goal, and inspired Eve Merriam, who received a copy of Norman's appeal on our stationery and wrote to John Ciardi because she had been told that Twayne wasn't publishing poetry any more. He got in touch with me, assured me of Eve's outstanding poetic qualities, and she came up with a superlative sales pitch as well. It worked, and we published her volume in 1953. And there were others from time to time.

Norman's letter follows:

Dear Friend:
As you know, the decline and fall of American

poetry has been going on for a number of decades now, alarming practically no one.

Some attribute this state of affairs to the death of iambic pentameter (a serious blow), the absence of rhyme or meter, and the general feeling of hostility toward the short line. Some, frankly, give it no thought whatsoever.

The standard publisher's attitude toward poetry is:

> We've read your little volume,
> And it has thrilled us all;
> Shall we send it back by mail,
> Or would you rather call?

A publisher called Twayne (blessed be the name!), with a refreshing sense of responsibility toward the poet, has been trying to solve this problem, which involves defying the law of diminishing returns.

Being a gentleman, he cannot ask the poet to pay for printing his book. He wouldn't get very far if he did!

Being a realist, he says he would like to publish the book if he could be sure of a pre-publication sale of 200 copies, which of course doesn't cover his costs but does cushion his fall.

Which brings us to the denouement:

You are either known to me or you have been suggested as a possibly friendly native. For the price of $2.50 sent in now, you will receive an autographed copy of my new volume, *The Plane and the Shadow* in the Spring of '53. It will contain about 80 pages of my recent poetry which I hope you will enjoy.

Never has so much been offered for so little with such controlled desperation.

Claude McKay's volume was one of the most profitable books of poetry to be released by us, thanks to the popularity and attendant permission fees for use of "If We Must Die" and other memorable McKay poems that were mandatory for any anthology of Black poetry in the heyday of Black literature in the 1960's and thereafter.

Of historic interest is Winston Churchill's use of McKay's stirring "If We Must Die," without crediting the Black poet, to rally his countrymen in World War II. Neither did *Time* Magazine in its account of the Attica uprising, when it commented on the poetic talent of some unknown inmate for these "crude but powerful lines." I was able, at least, to rectify that omission with a letter to *Time*. We also received a permission fee for *Time*'s one-time use of the sonnet. According to *Time*'s letter editor, hundreds of other letters, including one from Pulitzer prize-winning poet, Gwendolyn Brooks, also called *Time*'s attention to the rightful author of those immortal lines.

McKay was five years dead when we published his poetry in 1953 and so I never met him but I did meet his daughter, Hope McKay Virtue, and advised her about getting funds from the USSR for a trip to Russia. McKay had been lionized by the Communists in the 1920's and I thought the USSR would be willing to pay for her stay in the Soviet Union using the blocked funds in royalties that should have accumulated to McKay's account for the use of his poetry. She succeeded in this. I wasn't so successful, however, with *What Happened at Pearl Harbor?* edited by Professor Hans L. Trefousse, a documentary that the Soviets circulated without regard for copyright status in the years before they agreed to participate in copyright agreements.

Another African-American poet published by

Twayne was my friend, Melvin Beaunorus Tolson. I thought he was a great poet but Ciardi had some initial reservations, though he approved the release of the volume, *Libretto for the Republic of Liberia,* in 1953 and did everything he could thereafter to help Tolson gain recognition as a major voice in American poetry. He nominated Tolson for a permanent Bread Loaf Fellowship,* calling him "the most rocket-driven poet we have published" and continued: "The one thing about Tolson is that he is incapable of writing a mediocre line; it's either tremendous or it's nothing." And I think Ciardi supported the American Academy of Arts and Letters poetry award to Tolson for 1966, the year of Tolson's death. Karl Shapiro was also in Tolson's corner, a very powerful supporter, at the time.

The writing of the *Libretto* had been commissioned by the Liberian government in 1947 when Tolson became the official poet laureate and was asked to write a poem to celebrate the centennial of that country's founding. When it appeared, with a preface by Allen Tate, a leader of the Fugitive group along with Donald Davidson, John Crowe Ransom, and Robert Penn Warren, it created a sensation because of Tate's endorsement. "... For the first time...a Negro poet has assimilated completely the full poetic language of his time, and by implication the language of the Anglo-American poetic tradition." Tate continued: "...I found I was reading *Libretto*...not because Mr. Tolson is a Negro but because he is a poet, not because the poem has a 'Negro subject' but be-

---

*Cited by Joy Flasch in *Melvin B. Tolson,* TUSAS #215.

cause it is about the world of all men and this subject is not merely asserted, it is embodied in a rich and complex language and realized in terms of the poetic imagination." It was reviewed widely and well but the critical consensus was that the book was ahead of its time. John Ciardi wrote in *The Nation* "...the blast of language and vision is simply too overwhelming for first judgments"; Selden Rodman in the *N.Y. Times Book Review,* "...opens vistas undreamt of by the English-speaking poets of his race and by few poets of other races." Presumably these "few poets," Tolson's peers, were T.S.Eliot, Hart Crane, and William Carlos Williams, with whose works Tolson's poetry is compared. And Karl Shapiro writing some twelve years later in his "Introduction" to Tolson's *Harlem Gallery* notes it is still "too early for the assimilation of such a poem, even by poets."

But one of the sad and unfortunate effects of the *Libretto*'s publication with a preface by a well-known Southern critic was to infuriate the ethno-centric critics who obviously felt that Tolson should have catered primarily to a Black audience. The resentment of the Afrocentrics was to reach a crescendo with the publication of *Harlem Gallery: Book I, The Curator.* Tolson had planned the work as a five-volume epic, telling the history of the black man in America, present and past. Had he lived to realize his dream, I think there would have been no doubt as to the eminence of his poetic stature. As with the *Libretto*, the critical reception was wide and overwhelmingly favorable. It was prompted by Karl Shapiro's "Introduction," which focused critical attention in much the same way as Tate's preface to the *Li-*

bretto But, again, Shapiro was a white critic and Jewish to boot, which did nothing to mollify the ethnocentrics. And so Tolson became "controversial," a reference that still clutters the way to objective appraisal of his achievement. But surely this great man did not deserve the epithet "Uncle Tom" that I heard hurled at him publicly by a small-bore critic seeking self-aggrandizement at Tolson's expense. Tolson's vision was a world vision, and he reached out to a readership that would not brook the limitations of race or ghetto. I am appalled at "Uncle Tom" being applied to a man who dared the lynch mobs in South Texas in the 20's and 30's to preach a message of hope and human rights!

Joy Flasch's important introductory volume[*] on Tolson points out "His vision for America, however, was never a separation of peoples but a multiracial culture composed of many kinds of American artists, each preserving the qualities of his particular race for the enlightenment and appreciation of all men." Tolson himself put it this way in *Harlem Gallery*

White Boy,
Black Boy,
freedom is the oxygen
of the studio and gallery.
What if a chef-d'oeuvre is esoteric?
The cavernous By Room, with its unassignable
variety
of ego-dwarfing
stalactites and stalagmites
makes my veins and arteries vibrate faster

---

[*]Op. cit., p. 135.

as I study its magnificence and intricacy.
        Is it amiss or odd
        if the apes of God
    take a cue from their Master?

In *Melvin B. Tolson...*, a meticulously researched volume by Robert M. Farnsworth, published by the University of Missouri Press in
1984, the author sums up the attitude of the
1980's. Tolson, alas, is not widely read but still
holds the critical esteem voiced by Tate, Gwendolyn Brooks, Ciardi, and Shapiro as a poet
greatly ahead of his times.

Ciardi was also responsible for Sidney Bechet's
autobiography coming to Twayne. Unfortunately,
that great jazz musician would not or could not
cooperate in providing the additional material
Ciardi requested, and the volume languished,
though it wasn't for lack of effort on Ciardi's part
as the correspondence eloquently confirms. In
December 1951, when I met with Bechet at the
Twayne office he was on his way back to Paris and
complaining about the severe pain his ulcers were
causing. In addition to his illness, a dispute had
broken out as to the auctorial role of Joan Reid
Williams in the writing of the book. Bechet
claimed that she was largely a secretary to whom
he dictated his story. According to Joan, however,
she was to a considerable extent co-author. An
agreement between Bechet and Joan Reid, dated
May 8, 1952, was notarized and signed by the two
parties: on September 10, 1953, by Bechet in San
Francisco and June 20, 1952 by Joan Reid. This
gave Joan 10% of all royalties due Bechet from the
publication of the book.

At any rate, with the passage of time we had become disillusioned with the property and its problems. Nothing happened until 1957 when Desmond Flower, a director of Cassell and Company, became interested as a result of the efforts of our British agent, Mark Paterson. Flower, however, felt the manuscript had to be drastically overhauled. I wrote to Ciardi about this, querying him as to whether he wanted to get involved. He responded that he did not, but wished us well with the revised manuscript. Finally, by July of 1958, Paterson wrote that despite the fact that Flower had "rewritten 95% of the manuscript, he does not wish his name to be on the title page... the book should stand as Bechet's own work..."

Treat It Gentle finally appeared in early 1960. Flower had been successful in getting Bechet's cooperation, adding the events of nearly twenty years more to the earlier account. Hill and Wang published the book in the United States under license from Twayne. Bechet died on May 14, 1959, and never had the pleasure of seeing his autobiography in print though he knew that it was well under way at last.

In September of 1950, Ciardi wrote enthusiastically about his meeting with the artist, Thomas Hart Benton, in Martha's Vineyard. In a lengthy communication he described a number of projects with Benton that he thought suitable for Twayne.

The first of these concerned the possibility of a limited edition, an outsize volume, containing Benton's collected lithographs with commentary by the artist, along with some preliminary sketches and about 2/3 original size of 9" x 12" of the lithos. Ciardi thought that the University of Kansas City in Benton's home territory ought to be willing to lend its name to the release of the Benton projects. President Clarence R. Decker, a Benton enthusiast, eagerly agreed and wrote to the artist on October 20, 1950, conveying the agreement of the University to the idea. On June 16, 1951, the Kansas City *Star* carried a 17" story about "A University Press in Kansas City," a laudatory account of Twayne and Ciardi's leading role, and the plans and editorial set-up for the new university press as a cooperative venture with Twayne.

A revised and enlarged edition of Benton's *An Artist in America* with an introduction by Decker was also to appear, along with two new extra-large lithographs, 12" x 16" available in limited quantity. These were "The Hymn Singer," a characterization of Burl Ives and "Photographing the Bull."

The collected lithographs volume posed a problem. It required the cooperation and permission of Associated American Artists Galleries. A copyright search undertaken by us for items listed for the year 1944 by Benton, as a sampling from the list of 71 lithos enumerated in a handwritten letter to me, indicated that the copyright had been registered in the artist's name *and* Associated American Artists. Aside from any other agreement that may have existed between Benton and Associated, this clearly indicated that we would need approval and cooperation. But that was not forthcoming, as a letter from Reeves Lewenthal, president of Associated, clearly stated.

On November 22, 1950, he wrote to Benton that

he would not grant permission nor cooperate to make this project possible. He was not very complimentary to Twayne, questioning our ability to finance such an undertaking. He was right on target concerning our meager funds, but I thought we could adequately handle such a commitment and wrote to Benton to this effect. Despite Lewenthal's caveat, Benton and his attorney seemed anxious to cooperate with us. David L. Sheffrey wrote to me on January 17, 1951 in response: "I am delighted with your letter of the 15th...the promise of a wholesome experience for Benton means more than I can tell you."

Benton confirmed this in another handwritten letter to me on January 19. Most of Benton's letters to me were written by hand. They were quite legible but I found his scrawl almost as inimitable and characteristic as the artist's paintings. One can immediately and unerringly recognize a Benton work of art, I think.

I never did learn directly from Tom why he had fallen out with Reeves Lewenthal but there were references to the disagreement in his and Ciardi's letters. In his autobiography, Benton speaks very highly of Lewenthal, crediting him with mounting success in the marketing of Tom's paintings. He says there were some minor disagreements but that basically his decision to leave Lewenthal's organization was that it was no longer concentrating on American art and artists. A minor disagreement may have been the one Ciardi voiced in his letter to me of September 16, 1950 when he broached the subject of Twayne going into the lithograph business:

Benton has had a tiff*with Associated American
Artists. They were supposed to be pulling no more
than 500 copies of a litho from each stone. He found
they were pulling 800 and putting a pencil-stamp of
his signature on them....He raised a stink...and now
they are at odds. He still proposes to do at least two
lithos a year, however, but he needs a distributor...I
suggested we might be able to handle his distribution...

Perhaps it was with this experience in mind
that Benton made sure in our agreement that he
alone retained control of the number of lithos pull-
ed of each subject. He proposed, and we accepted,
that he would initiate and become editor of a litho
project. Presumably, like the Twayne poetry program, it would seek a balance between well-
known artists and those just coming to the fore.

This is the way it shaped up: Twayne was to
finance the litho series. Benton was to select the
subject and the artist and supervise the processing of the lithos. And we were to split the profits
after the cost of production was recovered by
Twayne. Benton proposed to get the project off
the ground by using four of his own subjects. He
planned to use George Miller, a noted lithographer, to prepare two stones for the first two subjects.

On May 3, 1959, he wrote: "I have finished two
lithographs. They are now in the hands of George
Miller, the printer....**If you can get the time I

---

*See Benton's remarks about this on page 67.

**In other letters, Benton cautioned against using the term
"printer" in connection with the lithograph projects. "Never
use the words 'print, printed, printer.' Describe the process
as 'pulling.'"

think it would be well to pay him a visit and look over the impressions. Titles are "Photographing the Bull" and "Hymn Singer." I suggest that you mention George Miller's name in your advertising....We will sell these lithos at $10.00. Publicize them as 'extra large' — they are."

I wrote back about a week later, indicating that I had picked up the proof but that Miller was away on vacation. I also added that I was delighted to learn that we could charge $10.00 for the lithos to make up "for the lean pickin's in poetry — a little, at least."

Benton wrote again on May 7, suggesting that we meet on June 2 and informed me that the subject of "The Hymn Singer" was Burl Ives, who had no objection to our publicizing that fact. I replied that June 2 would be Benton day as far as Twayne was concerned.

Again, on May 12, Benton wrote. "In preparing your announcements of the lithographs don't forget to have a note about the printer, George Miller. It might be good to say 'impressed on the finest French paper by George Miller, noted lithographer who has made impressions for such famous artists as George Bellows, Arthur B. Davies, Grant Wood, John Curry and others.'" In the same letter Benton concluded: "Let's get the old book [*An Artist in America*] and the lithos going. The latter may mean a little dough."

In the meantime, Benton had added an additional chapter for his autobiography. The addition was controversial and restated his unflattering view of the art establishment controlled by the Eastern seaboard critics — "museum boys" — as he referred to them in plain-spoken

hostility against "the concentrated flow of aes-
thetic-minded homosexuals into the various fields
of artistic practice..."

We also suggested to Benton that we use his two
famous nudes for the jacket, his "Persephone" and
"Susanna and the Elders." "Persephone," the
model for which was reported to be Rita Benton,
Tom's wife, was sold in 1987 for $2.5 million to the
Nelson Atkins Museum of Art of Kansas City. I
cleared the jacket suggestion with President
Decker of the University of Kansas City, who
somewhat hesitantly wrote of the proposed use:
"...at least one should go on the jacket, perhaps
both if you are persuaded that two will not give
the publication a too sensational send-off. With
this caution, we leave the final judgment to you."

Benton had no reservation concerning the
jacket illustration. "Let the 'good taste' go by —
the sales are what we want" and he went on to
sketch an original drawing of what the jacket
should look like. Sidney Solomon, our book designer, had no trouble utilizing the design and our
edition carried the two famous nudes as the
jacket. I met with Tom on June 2, as planned, and
we did clear away a number of problems, including the question of discount on the lithos to the
University bookstore, the focal point of sales in
Kansas City, as well as projecting the future of the
Benton-edited litho project. I wrote, rather opti-
mistically as it turned out, to President Decker on
June 11:

"There is small doubt but that we can sell the
original lithos — they're extra large, 12" x 16" —
for the full price but since the U.of K.C. Press-

Twayne imprint is issuing the lithos it would be queer not to have them at the bookstore.

"If we are successful in moving these, we would like very much to expand in this direction. Tom has assured me that it would not be very difficult to get the biggest artists to come in, particularly on the basis we propose: a share-the-profits deal which ought to yield the artist several times the customary artist's fee....The idea ought to attract as much favorable attention in the art world as did the Twayne Library of Modern Poetry in the literary." Tom wrote on June 21 approving the bookstore discount and indicated that he had ordered another stone from George Miller for two additional lithos. He added, "If I had thought of it in time I would have suggested that you advertize these lithos as the beginning of a new series. This would help to let people realize that we are in a permanent business. Keep in touch."

On the 25th of June he wrote about changing some pages of the material he had sent me for his autobiography.

> After a discussion with Tom Craven I have decided to change this Grant Wood episode. The story is true but most people would feel that I was taking advantage of the fact that I am still alive....Also Craven thinks that the line we discussed on page 16 "You can't play with corruption..." is too risky. So change that also. No use in getting in trouble for one line.

My letter to President Decker of July 24,1951 provides some additional information concerning progress on the Benton projects and responds to a suggestion about publishing a collection of short stories by Frank Brookhouser, a popular Philadelphia columnist, who had come into the University of Kansas City orbit via John Ciardi.

We have sent out a mailing of 12,000 circulars on the Benton projects, largely to libraries. If you can use any of these for the bookstore, I can have them made up in any quantity. Tom has agreed that we ought to let the bookstore have lithographs at one-third off list. Miller, the lithographer, is out of town but these should be ready soon.

We've run into a bit of unexpected difficulty with *An Artist in America*. It seems that when McBride went bankrupt, the rights to the book were assigned to one of the Crown outlet houses. Fortunately, we hadn't gotten very far with the type-setting when we made the discovery. At any rate, what looked like a piece of bad luck is turning out quite well. The original color plates are available. While, of course, we will have to pay for the use of them, the results will be a much more handsome production.

I'd like to give the Brookhouser book some thought. Books of short stories are poor sellers usually...almost as bad as poetry. In this instance, there probably would be a return of our investment and some good publicity at least. But this has been a terrible book season and I should have to see what the financial prospects are before making a commitment. Is there any chance of the University participating in the costs?

On August 10, 1951, I wrote:

Dear Tom,

Hot as hell here but at last the Benton projects are nearing completion. I will have proofs of the additional material for the new edition of *An Artist* shortly.

I also enclose the Twayne Fall list which carries a prominent notice of the volume and the lithos. We are also placing an ad in the Fall Announcement Issue of *Publishers Weekly.*

Bill from Geo. Miller informs us that the lithos have been completed and are, presumably, in your possession. Is that right?

Will you be good enough to return them after you have the signature affixed to

    ZINNS   Att. Twayne Publishers
    55 West 16th Street
    New York, N.Y.

They are the people who will do the matting for us. We will then affix our authentication there. These should be sent via Railway Express, collect, and insured for as much as they will let them be insured for. (I don't think we can collect the face value if — God forbid — they are lost in transit.) Please let us know when they go out from your place.

A rather nice news item in the N.Y. *Times* last week about the U. of K. C.-Twayne/Benton project. I don't have the exact figures handy but we have sold quite a few lithos already. And, of course, once they are available, the flood should be on...

On September 25, 1951, I sent the following letter to Norman Cousins of the *Saturday Review.* I had written to Tom about the possibility of placement of the new material, and Tom had taken the opportunity of a visit to New York to discuss this with Cousins.

Here is the portion of Tom Benton's *An Artist in America* which he discussed with you. Unless I mistake the signs, there is every reason to suppose that the appearance of this in the form of a lead article will set off the same kind of response that accompanied Robert Hillyer's article on obscurity in modern poetry.

At the same time, it provides a pretty good background for understanding the Regionalists in American art and the outstanding proponents thereof.

Mr. Benton has asked me to take care of the matter of placement for him. I should, under the circumstances, like a reasonably early decision since I have had some expressions of interest from other periodicals.

On October 6, I wrote to Benton that Cousins had decided to use the article and was going to have it responded to by his art editor, James Soby. The items were featured and did stir controversy. Benton acknowledged this a number of times and added that it had led to a number of lectures and sales of his paintings. But, of course, Twayne derived no income from that. In a letter dated January 9, 1952, he remarked about a State Department sponsored international broadcast as a result of the exchange in the SRL, writing, "I'll give you a reply but I don't think there is one chance in a thousand that SRL would let me piss on their boy. Give them a chance, a damn short one, and then try some one else — *New Leader* or maybe one of the paying sheets." He continued: "I'll get at two more lithos. Perhaps we'd better limit these to 300 impressions. How about it? I've heard the art market is dead as hell." He concluded with the interesting observation that, what with all this God damn writing, talking flood relief and river control meetings, he hadn't done a bit of painting. And now he was mixed up in a "knock out Eisenhower campaign" for which he was going to have to write and talk again. The worst thing the U. S. could do, he wrote, would be to put a military man in the White House — no matter how upright and honest.

Benton sent me his reply to Soby but I was unable to place it. In the letter accompanying the article he had this to say about litho prices: "Don't like the idea of raising litho prices. The point in making them is primarily democratic circulation — 'people's' pocket book circulation. Extreme limitations on editions put them in the very 'exclusive' class I'm running from."

In February, I wrote suggesting a 250-edition of a two-color litho, which Margaret Lowengrund of the Contemporaries gallery had been urging, offering to cooperate and to provide the stones free. I also added the information that Twayne's address was now 34 East 23rd Street, about double the amount of space for the same amount of rent we had been paying at 42 Broadway. The building had been the Schermerhorn family mansion and our offices in what must have been the conservatory floor and servants quarters in the back had an attractive personality of their own.

I told Benton that reviews of *An Artist in America* "have surprised me, both as to quantity and overwhelming approval of the book and the man. A few of them have also gone out of their way to praise the general appearance of the book." I added, however, that sales had not kept up with the reviews and that I thought his reply to Soby of the *Saturday Review* fell far short of the piece in the book, but that I would try to place it with one or another of the various periodicals he suggested.

He responded in a letter addressed to John and to me that I return the manuscript and that he would try to whip it into shape. On the subject of lithos, he added, "...well, turn them over to the retail folks if we can't make sales otherwise.

Never can tell about lithos — Lewenthal, you will remember, sold out two whole (500 impression) editions before they were even signed a couple of years ago but it is impossible to tell how much accident, and the peculiar popularity of the pictures, had to do with the success..." Again he complained of too little time for his painting because of the demand for his time elsewhere, adding again that he was getting calls for lectures as a result of the SRL exchange, but in which, of course, we did not share. He added "anent color lithos — I'll have to talk with George Miller about the process — but no more than a two-color job. I'm agreed on smaller editions — 300 say."

In March, Benton wrote that he had just returned from Martha's Vineyard where he went to attend his mother's funeral, "long expected and in fact a relief." He thanked me for returning the unsatisfactory manuscript and the notations I had made concerning it. Then he added:

> The two retrospective exhibitions out here, Omaha and Wichita, proved finally to have been well worth while. Very substantial sales have come out of them — both museum and private. The museums always seem to want Bentons when I begin questioning their place in a creative world — as if to give personal proof of my wrongheadedness.

He also reported that the color lithographs would have to wait until he replenished his stock of pictures but that he would go ahead with this. And, in his non-painting time he would try to collect the essays which would reflect his "philosophy of art, life, and politics" which we had indicated an interest in publishing.

In June I wrote to indicate again poor sales on

the autobiography and on the lithos as well which still had not recovered costs. I sent him copies of a couple of ads for our Benton projects and reported on poor results from another mailing of 5000 circulars to local art museums, art associations and/or contributors.

I had a friendly letter from Tom in October of 1952 commenting on an excerpt from *An Artist* appearing in the *N. Y. Times* and reporting his own very good sales as a continuing result of the SRL exchange.

In February of 1953, I sent him a copy of a Twayne book suggesting that he consider reviewing it for the Kansas City *Star*. The book, *The Great American Parade*, a report on America by a French journalist, Duteil, had been translated by Fletcher Pratt. Benton replied that he could not review it.

> I would have to quibble a lot, work up a sort of fictitious disagreement to be able to say anything. By and large the book makes a true picture to my mind. As a matter of fact most of it seems to lean over backward to be "nice," more nice than necessary.
>
> What Duteil says about America's position in the arts I have been saying for twenty-five years. The Irish stuff is pure prejudice but how many times in my contacts with officialdom have I had the same prejudice arise. The Negro stuff is rough, but, perhaps, coming from a Frenchman may have certain beneficial effects. Because, the truth is, that in spite of many repressive conditions, more is done to advance the Negro in America than is done anywhere else in the world. A realization of that just might help, rather than hurt, our racial difficulties.

Of course Walter White will stand on his head over the chapter but I can't do so.

Benton went on to say that he was turning the book over to a reviewer for the *Star*.

I can find no additional letters from Benton though there were a number of events celebrating the artist's achievements in which Twayne cooperated. But I did get a phone call nearly ten years later from Tom in response to an offer we had received to purchase all the Benton lithos on hand. Apparently, the intervening years had brought a sharp increase in the value of the Benton lithographs of which we were unaware because we had not been selling them despite the initial considerable effort on our part. Tom agreed to pay us $5.00 for each lithograph, F. O. B. New York. I wrote to him on April 17, 1962:

Dear Tom:

I was glad to get your call the other day and to agree to your proposition. We can appreciate that you can get from $40.00 to $50.00 the lithograph, which is more than we can get for them. We wish you all success in selling them.

I then went on to say that we would like to reprint a new edition of *An Artist in America* and that we had also had an expression of interest on the part of a paperback publisher. I concluded, "Please speak to your attorney and see if the release from Crown cannot be arranged so that we may proceed with this project. I am not happy with the way the previous edition was handled and feel that we can do a better job now, if our hands are not tied, as is the case with no clear-cut control of rights..."

I received no answer to this.

Nor did I receive an answer to an inquiry concerning the safe receipt of the lithos in June of 1962.

Finally, on July 18, Rita Benton responded, addressing her handwritten letter to my associate, Joel Saltzman, who had inquired as to why we had not been paid. She answered in part:

> I was shocked by the size of the shipment. I did not realize that there were so many remaining lithos when I asked you to send these to us, to protect our prices. Neither Mr. Benton nor I remembered the size of the editions. Lithographs bring good prices only when they become rare on the market. We will have to lower our sale prices a great deal for the lithos you sent. There are just too many of them, and it is going to take years to dispose of them. Because of this I think you should lower the price we pay you.

She concluded: "I do not want you to lose money on this business but I do think we should readjust our arrangements about it."

A reply from Joel indicated that her suggestion that we lower the price was not welcome and concluded: "Since you and I seem not to see eye to eye at all in this matter, I would suggest that if Mr. Benton still feels he has made an unwise purchase, he communicate directly with Mr. Steinberg, so that the matter may be settled between the two principals involved..."

Despite several additional requests there was no response, and I finally wrote on December 21, 1962 voicing my distress at having to write about this. To this letter I received a response, not from Benton but from his lawyer, explaining that the delay in payment was attributable to him, not to Benton. Our charges were for $3300 approximately. He offered $2300, including in his deduction payment for lithos that had disappeared, attributable I think to the art collectors in our warehouse masquerading as shipping clerks and warehousemen! This amounted to a 9.1% shrinkage of the lithograph editions, and I shall have something to say about inventory theft, an unpleasant fact that plagues all publishers — the more attractive the item, the greater the problem. I also concluded that the deduction should be regarded by us as a reasonable artist's fee for the lithos Benton had contributed to our failed venture, though our agreement said nothing of inventory shrinkage being attributable to the publisher.

In retrospect, I would say that the trouble with the Benton projects lay in the fact that we could not sell the lithos in the early fifties, no matter how hard we tried, and the record indicates that we did try valiantly. Even the University of Kansas City bookstore could not sell more than a handful in Benton country. And, when we finally did get a customer for all of them, it was ten years too late. Today, the extra-large lithos that we were offering at $10.00 retail ($6.00 to the stores) were being sought at $600.00 for *The Hymn Singer* and $1000.00 and more for *Photographing the Bull*. Rita Benton's fears about having to lower the prices for these seem not to have been realized!

I enjoyed my exchanges with Benton, Missouri's most controversial artist. Had we been successful with the lithos, Benton assured us entree to prominent American artists who would have been glad to join our artistic adventure. We didn't do too well with his autobiography either, finally having to remainder the beautiful limited edition in buckram and marbled edges which we had been encouraged to issue. Many of the dealers felt the book was really a reprint with only one additional chapter and introduction. But it got good review coverage, and the SRL argument sold paintings for Benton as he freely admitted, but not books or lithos for us.

Ciardi was also responsible for a number of books on D.H.Lawrence published by Twayne, including Harry T. Moore's *Life and Works of D.H.Lawrence*, which helped establish Moore's reputation as a leading scholar in the area. Moore also edited a collection of essays by Lawrence, *Sex, Literature and Censorship*, which was cited in the judicial decision permitting publication of the Grove Press edition of *Lady Chatterley's Lover*. As I have previously indicated, Twayne was one of the companies that Grove contacted in the search for a co-publisher of that work.

Another Moore attracted to the Ciardi-Twayne orbit was Merrill Moore, M.D., the world's champion sonneteer. Merrill had been an original member of the Fugitive group at Vanderbilt University and had maintained his friendship with Robert Penn Warren, Allen Tate, John Crowe Ransom and other well-known and respected figures. And, as a psychiatrist with a literary or poetic avocation, he had quite a number of patients famous in the literary world who sought his help. I think Robert Lowell and Joshua Logan were two who acknowledged their doctor-patient relationships but there were many others. He not only became a Twayne author but he tried to befriend me. Knowing of our financial difficulties he attempted to interest some of his rich patients, one of whom owned a chain of theaters and motion picture establishments into lending us substantial sums of money... to no avail, I hasten to add. He enjoyed promoting his books of poetry: *Clinical Sonnets, More Clinical Sonnets, Illegitimate Sonnets, The Hill of Venus* and *Case-Record from a Sonnetorium* sending out thousands of circulars to his special lists. He gave Edward Gorey, then a graduate student of Ciardi's at Harvard, an opportunity to further his career by commissioning illustrations for several of Moore's poetry titles. These were very early Gorey but even then they are unmistakably vintage Gorey.

Merrill frequently dropped in on the Twayne office when he was in New York, inviting me to lunch occasionally with people like Louis Untermeyer, the anthologist. I particularly recall one such visit. He assured me of success if I continued to stick to the main business of our enterprise: the making of books not the making of money. He was right, of course, but though he was only confirming my own thoughts on the subject, I welcomed his sage advice. He was a good and generous friend to the end. He died in 1957 but I think of him often as I peruse his letters.

Science fiction and fantasy literature constituted another area of Ciardi interest, and he attracted writers like Fletcher Pratt, Sprague de Camp, Fritz Leiber, H. Beam Piper, James Blish,

Judith Merril and other well-known sci-fiction writers to do books for us. *World of Wonder*, an anthology edited by Pratt, sold well for us.

Leiber's *Conjure Wife* — originally included in our *Witches Three*, a collection of three individual novels by Pratt, Blish, and Leiber — was issued as a separate title both in cloth and paper. In our contract the author had conferred motion-picture rights but when an English film "Burn, Witch, Burn" appeared, using *Conjure Wife* for the story, it turned out that motion picture rights were controlled by Universal Pictures and had been given as early as 1943. The story had first appeared in a shorter version in the magazine *Unknown*. So, what we thought was going to be an unexpected financial bonanza didn't turn out that way. Still, we did well enough on the title. A TV treatment of the story appeared in 1960 and did bring in some revenue. The title was frequently paper-backed, every two or three years by different firms. It's a terrific story. Damon Knight called it "...easily the most frightening...of all modern horror stories...."

The Petrified Planet was the first of a series embodying another interesting sci-fiction idea: a triple-header in which a distinguished scientist draws up the specifications of an imaginary planet and three top writers work out independently the fictional problems of that environment.

Financially, the sci-fi program was an "iffy" proposition, some of the items contributing substantially to the red ink which was plentiful in those days. *Tales from Gavagan's Bar* by Fletcher Pratt and Sprague de Camp was one of the latter.

The fantasy books in the program, which I enjoyed most, just wouldn't sell. Gradually, as more and more publishers were drawn to the genre, the number of books completely inundated the field, and we got out of this area.

But all of us at Twayne were then in the learning stages, and Ciardi was casting with a very large net. Not all of the catch was edible, at least not for us then. He made no bones about the fact that he was hoping for the time, in the near future, when publishing could be counted on for a substantial portion of his time and income. The Briggs-Copeland chair at Harvard was untenured and for five years only and time was up.On September 7, 1952, he wrote: "By May of next year I've got to make a serious decision as to whether I should accept one of several quite lucrative jobs in the middle or far-west (which would inevitably mean giving up the Twayne connection) or of taking a part-time (and low-pay) teaching job here in the East and putting in most of my time on Twayne. I would much prefer the latter, but in that case I should have to depend on Twayne for a substantial part of my income and with some regularity....If I can't count on a little now [We had fallen behind in our schedule of payments to him.] how can I count on more later?...This is, you see, more a letter of concern than of complaint. ...And let me have your thoughts on all this, yes?"

My "Dear John" letter of September 9 responded to his concerns: "I realize that I must make it my personal responsibility to see to it that your check goes out promptly the first of every month..." I continued:

Joel has undoubtedly told you that we have had tough sledding these past two months, not only because of tardy remittances but also because our publication program is by far the most ambitious we have yet undertaken. All of our books are in production and this in turn has meant that we have had to go to other than our usual suppliers where credits are not as liberal.

This should be the best season we have ever had. The salesmen are delivering advances which would have seemed unbelievable only a year ago. As soon as these books are paid for, money should be in plentiful supply.

The thoughts you have been having are not strangers to me! I, too, have had words with Joel about differences as to who and what should be paid. Short of stepping into a financial muddle where I would be completely out of my depth, however, I can see no alternative save to accept his estimate of the situation. I sense a congenital reluctance to let go (the hallmark of all good guardians of the exchequer) but until the coffers are full I have no choice except to go along.

I think, however, you need have no fears of collecting whatever is due you. We have managed to pay off far greater indebtednesses than that and I am sure that whatever we owe you will be paid....Let me end this phase of the letter on the note of complete recognition of your identity with the firm and our mutual interdependence....

The cash shortages were to plague us again and again, and Joel, as controller, came in for more than a fair share of blame and abuse. He had to pay our suppliers or we would be out of business. Authors, he felt, had to share our own tribulations. Too often we had to postpone our salary checks. But everyone got paid... eventually.

Despite a number of such contretemps, Ciardi

continued with Twayne activities, much more loosely after he joined the *Saturday Review,* until 1961.

Aside from the books that Ciardi sponsored directly, there were a number of other Twayne titles originating elsewhere that Ciardi edited. Among these were *La Cucina*, an Italian cookbook by Rose L. Sorce. This sold quite well over a number of years, eventually going to Grosset and Dunlap by license. *Explorations in America Before Columbus* by H.R.Holand was another title he handled, which sold quite well. *The American Sexual Tragedy* by Albert Ellis was another Ciardi editorial project. The *N.Y. Times* refused to accept advertising on this title and eventually the book wound up with Lyle Stuart after we remaindered our edition. Ellis credited Ciardi with a superlative job of editing. Despite this, we were not successful with the title, nor was Lyle Stuart, judging from our share of royalties derived from the sale of his edition.

The *Harvard Advocate Anthology* was another Ciardi undertaking. It seemed a terrific idea to me when Ciardi brought it up. Here was a book providing the first or early writings of a number of famous men. How could it miss? Alas! It missed badly despite the famous contributors: E.A. Robinson, Wallace Stevens, T.S.Eliot, F.D.R., e.e. cummings, Robert Benchley, Leonard Bernstein, Norman Mailer, *et al.* who were among the forty-nine anthologized.

Donald A. Hall, Harvard '51 and President, *Harvard Advocate* 1949-50, was editor of the volume, and it must have been his first book publication. The failure of what he called Twayne's "most handsome production" was as keen a disappointment to him as it was to us. In addition to serving as editor, Don also went into the bookstores in Cambridge and New Haven serving as a special salesman for the title. He persuaded the stores to stock the title but he couldn't get the customers to buy it. I like to think Twayne gave him a foot up on his later illustrious career.

Supplementing our promotion of the title was a mailing of 10,000 circulars to Harvard alumni. We were ready to mail more if this was successful, but the returns came in at less than 1%. And the response to our library mailing of 12,000 was equally dismal.

On July 4, 1951, on his way to Oxford University, Hall wrote to express his distress at the lack of response to our promotion. "Awfully sorry to hear that the book is definitely a flop! I hope I have done everything I could for you; I feel as though I had....the bookstores in the Square all made good window displays, especially Mandrake and Coop....The reaction of...customers was the same — pick up the book, get interested, look at the price [$5.00], gasp, lay it down..."

He pointed out that the reviews had been outstanding, including the *N.Y. Times* daily and Sunday; ditto the *Herald Tribune* plus *Saturday Review* etc. In a letter, responding to Twayne's decision to remainder the title, he asked for my analysis as to why the title didn't sell better than it had.

He had alluded to one factor — the price. Those were $2.95-$3.95 days but we opted for a quality production, thinking we could have the book out for Christmas. The manufacturer promised no later than mid-November delivery. The books arrived December 20th! Too late, too late by at least two months. But I think there was a more important lesson to be learned. It didn't dawn on me till long after the merger when I watched one trade editor's remarkable trail of costly error with books by famous people. They didn't sell either, because the contents of their books never came close to matching their authors' illustrious reputations. The contents of the *Advocate* anthology excited comment because of the subjects' subsequent careers but that didn't make for a good read. Drop the names and you couldn't sell it as a book property. Content *über alles!* One famous editor, Saxe Commins of Random House, with whom Joel Saltzman was taking a course then told him he didn't think the book would sell. Perhaps content was what he had in mind.

Another person connected with the anthology, not yet illustrious in 1951, comes to mind. Daniel Ellsberg, who succeeded Hall as President of the *Advocate*, read proofs of the anthology, and tried to be helpful with its promotion.

Another venture that Ciardi got for us was the reprint of a term-paper project entitled, *What Happened in Salem?* edited by David Levin. The letter from Twayne that John sent out to Freshman English teachers on behalf of the controlled materials project explains the idea of the approach.

Dear Sir:

I have always subscribed to the belief that the aim

of the Freshman English course should be to turn
out students able to prepare a good term paper, and
I have found in practice that the weakness of such
papers most frequently lies not so much in the handling of mechanics but in the methods of evaluating
conflicting evidence.

With this aim and with this basic observation as a
starting point, the English A course at Harvard
started a term paper project a few years ago, assign-
ing to Mr. David Levin the task of compiling a considerable body of evidence covering all the issues
involved in the Salem witchcraft trials. The idea
was to present the students with the documents a
professional researcher would cull from his sources
and to have that material equally available to the
student and to the instructor. In this way the instructor could criticize not only the handling of the
material actually included in the final paper, but the
relevance of material that should have been evaluated in the course of the student's particular inter-
pretation.

We did succeed in getting adoptions but not in
the quantity that Levin found satisfactory and we
eventually wound up selling the project to Har-
court Brace. However, as a consequence of the
initial book, we commissioned several other docu-
mentaries. Hans L. Trefousse, our history editor,
did a volume, *What Happened at Pearl Harbor?*
and Robert L. Smith did *What Happened in Cuba?*
Also on the drawing boards was the volume *What
Happened in Katyn Forest?* but this did not come
to fruition. The Smith and Trefousse volumes
were published after Ciardi left. The Trefousse
volume was pirated in the USSR, as I have previously mentioned.

There were a number of other Ciardi projects on
which we had differences. One of these concerned

a volume of bawdy or off-color limericks for which Ciardi proposed Gorey illustrations. My letter of March 25, 1952 contained news that I didn't think his project feasible, that I had checked my opinion with others and that only about half of his limericks, in our collective opinion, were publishable or funny. His blast of March 28, 1952 was understandable:

> Jack:
>
> Something's not functioning here. I've just started to check your reactions to the limericks and just don't understand. Will you explain to me in detail on what basis you decide #34 is not publishable? And by what cerebration #36 which is a damned good limerick is listed as Items out? I haven't checked more than the first ten, but we are completely at odds in this. Just as exhibit A double plus you list 43 as not publishable and 42 as good. What's the principle of selection? if there is one.
>
> Well, never mind. Except that after waiting all these months for your decision, I had hoped to be able to understand it But it's probably just as well. This book should not be published except with some unanimity about its possibilities. I mean to go ahead with it as Gorey produces his drawings, but it can't be done timidly and it can't be done by Twayne if this is the first approach. The selling attitude is wrong.

There was a further small exchange as indicated by this passage from his letter of April 6.

> Item: Limericks. Yes I was po'd. Our lines of communication are in bad repair and we can't function decently if they're not tended better. I sent you the batch for a judgement on obscenity. Could they or couldn't they get by the PO? That's not what you replied to. Whether the limericks are funny or not

is irrelevant at this point. Remember that I wrote these things for Gorey to illustrate. I'll take the responsibility for whether or not the final book works: you can't have two cooks on one sauce. What you were going to tell me was at what point the PO might object. That I still don't know. Well, never mind.

Those were the days of active private and public censorship, and Twayne was not equipped to tackle the financial problems posed by post office seizure and legal action. I said as much in my letter of March 25th.

> Most of us are in agreement that the book as presently constituted cannot be published except as a privately printed operation. But it's too dangerous to fool around with. It's one thing to take on a battle for Lady Chatterley; it's quite another to run the risk on this...

There were a number of other projects that Ciardi suggested, including some for which contracts were issued that didn't come to fruition for one reason or another. One of these was for the book of critical assessments of Faulkner by a number of critics. Permission fees torpedoed that one.

Another was for a mid-century view of America, its problems and prospects, by prominent Americans. He had thought of this as a possible volume for the University of Kansas City Press and had asked President Decker to participate. It was too ambitious a task for us I thought. After a few exchanges the matter was dropped.

We had no exclusive on Ciardi projects, however, and he was free to take them elsewhere if he so wished. That was our understanding but, of course, we did want him to regard Twayne as if he had a share in the enterprise. I think he too must have felt that way, for on November 3, 1952, he wrote concerning the Dante translations that were to make his name a familiar one on college campuses. It was item 9 of a long letter. At our meeting some time later in New York, we agreed that he was to continue trying to make a commercial placement but if not successful we would accommodate his plans. *The Inferno* was published in 1954, alas not by Twayne, and was a tremendous success.

While Ciardi was busy with the projects I have just described, I was trying with some success to get other titles for Twayne. *The Golden Age of Travel: Literary Impressions of the Grand Tour*, compiled by Helen B. Morrison, presented fascinating views of Europe's historic cities and picturesque by-ways by more than eighty famous travellers of the 18th and 19th centuries. It was a beautiful book, well reviewed, and nominated for inclusion in the Best Books of the Year compiled by the New York Public Library acquisitions staff.

Dictionary of American Underworld Lingo, edited by Hyman E. Goldin, Frank O'Leary, and Morris Lipsius was the subject of a most unusual multi-page article, "The Lexicographers in Stir"* in the *New Yorker*. The *Dictionary* was published in 1950 and hailed before publication by H.L.Mencken as "the best thing of its sort that I have seen." Mencken suggested to Rabbi Goldin, the chief editor of the book and chaplain at the

_____

*By John Lardner, December 1, 1951

prison, who had thought up the idea of the book as a useful project for the prisoners there, that he would be glad to recommend the title to Knopf, his publisher, and did so. Knopf decided against the book. I jumped at the chance to publish it. As indicated by the *New Yorker* piece, it attracted a lot of press attention but we were hard put to sell our edition bound in buckram for $5.00. There was one paperback edition published by Citadel which didn't do too well either. There was, however, plenty of excitement, not all of it literary. Take, for example, my letter of September 13, 1949 to Walter Winchell and the response thereto.

Dear Sir:

The reason for this letter is abundantly explained by the attached excerpts from our *Dictionary of American Underworld Lingo*. They are, I might add, unique in that no other individual apparently has been singled out for the honor of inclusion in the lingo of the American criminal.

In deference to your own well-known and colorful additions to the American vocabulary and to your activities on behalf of law and order, we are at this time making inquiry as to whether you would object to the inclusion of your name in both the Underworld-English and English-Underworld section of the publication as indicated.

In discussing the volume with Dr. Merrill Moore of Boston, who expressed an interest in it from the psychiatrist's point of view, the suggestion was made that we might try to enlist your interest in the volume to the extent of a brief Preface. May we inquire as to whether you would have the time or the inclination for such an undertaking?

I am enclosing a copy of the proposed press release that we are planning for the book....We shall be happy to provide a copy of the manuscript if you wish.

I might also add that H.L.Mencken has given us permission to quote him to the effect that the compilation is by far the best treatment of the subject that he has ever seen, a fine tribute to the thoroughness of the compilation.

Needless to say, we hope that the preceding is of interest to you and that you will be able to examine the volume in detail. We should appreciate the kindness of a response to this communication at your earliest convenience....

Mr. Winchell's answer to what I thought was a very polite letter came in the form of a short but emphatic response from his attorney:

> Sirs:
>
> In answer to your scurrilous letter, you will please take note that the proposed inclusion of Mr. Walter Winchell in your *Dictionary of American Underworld Lingo* is a violation of the laws of the State of New York, for which act, should it occur, you will be held most strictly responsible.
>
> Yours very truly,
> Ernest Cuneo

Despite Attorney Cuneo's warning, the *Dictionary* contains entries for Walter Winchell. No legal unpleasantness was forthcoming. This was my first but not my last experience with attempts at censorship as I detail elsewhere. I should have thought Mr. Winchell would have been pleased to be included in the *Dictionary*. Perhaps, secretly, he was.

There were other excitements as well connected with this project. One day, one of the inmate editors, recently released, turned up in my office with a tremendous roll of bills which he enjoyed flashing before me and invited me to lunch along with two companions, who I later learned were his bodyguards. I demurred...too much work, couldn't afford the time, etc. I heard later that the money he flashed was the reward he received from the FBI for having tipped off the authorities as to the whereabouts of the Number One fugitive they were seeking. Number One's friends, I was told by another editor, also recently released from the hoosegow, were looking for my would-be host and that it would be particularly dangerous for me to be in his company. "Amen," I said to that.

John Resko, a self-taught artist whose life sentence for murder was commuted by Governor Rockefeller, was commissioned to do the jacket for the *Dictionary*. His work so impressed us that we suggested he do the illustrations for *A Treasury of Jewish Holidays* which Rabbi Goldin also published with us. This book did very well, selling year after year as a backlist title. It was taken by the Jewish Book Guild, a popular bookclub at the time. The latter's full-page ads in the Sunday *N.Y. Times* and other prominent media provided a promotion we couldn't afford. The bookclub selection itself only provided a royalty of $.25 per copy but it really helped establish the book as a classic in the field. Two other books by Rabbi Goldin were published by Twayne, *Hebrew Criminal Law and Procedure* and *A Treasury of Bible Stories*, illustrated. Neither of them, however, sold nearly as well as the *Treasury*.

Another non-Ciardi title was Robert Elegant's first book, *China's Red Masters*. Both Ciardi and I were impressed with Elegant's work. In sending a copy of the dust jacket on the volume to Ciardi I wrote:

> Herewith the jacket of *China's Red Masters*. Pity the author is an unknown. We will, of course, buttress with experts but I, for one, am convinced that if a name had written the book we'd have a run-away best seller. But then I know you'll agree that part of our business is to make names for our authors. The book is well written.
>
> Please send me a package of the Ciardi energy. I could most certainly use it.
>
> Blessings on the house of Ciardi without which there would be no house of Twayne.
>
> Love to you-all.
>
> Jack
>
> P.S. That madman H.T. Moore suggests an edition of Lawrence on Sex. Mighty titillating!

Ciardi's response from Italy on April 26, 1951:

> Our friends (that were to take us to Sicily) haven't arrived, but the books have, including *China's Red Masters* and I have a good chance to read and be impressed. I certainly see nothing wrong with Elegant's literary treatment that a very little editing couldn't take care of — a matter of a questionable tag here and there and some structural suggestions.
>
> The primary structural suggestion — as far as keeping reader interest is concerned, is this: biography has a plot. These of course are sketches and leave little room for development of action, but the possibility is still there. A man with Elegant's information, intelligence and general skill, could become a best seller could he be taught to keep the opposing elements in such a story dramatically opposed. My impression on one quick reading: the Mao sketch is the most dramatically possible.
>
> A very minor suggestion: Chinese names are difficult for me, and (perhaps arrogantly) I assume they

are therefore difficult for many readers. I suggest one inflexible rule: refer to the man by the full name the first time he is mentioned; thereafter refer to him *always* by the same shortening of the name. Elegant does this as a rule, but sometimes refers back to Roll Hoop Far as Roll, sometimes as Hoop, and sometimes as Hoop-Far. (I won't defend my example, but the point, though minor, survives it I think.)

The other more important criticism is a matter of developing *pace*, i.e. the rate at which the writing reveals itself to the reader. This is the most difficult conquest any good writer must make. I certainly believe, however, that Elegant has all the potentialities for writing extremely well.

I personally should like to see him do a full dress history of the Red Rise to Power in China. There's lots of plot available: this impossibly small group opposed within and without, driven back and back and back, and still sweeping out at the end in an incredible way. And terrifically dramatic stuff to treat: the long march, for instance. I'd like to see it done with maps and analysis of the warfare and political cross currents....

Elegant didn't remain an unknown much longer. I never expected any of our authors to ignore their own self-interest and remain with Twayne. We couldn't possibly compete with the big firms, and I was glad that we could play the role we did in furthering a writer's career. I had occasion to remind his agent of this when an opportunity to reprint his book arose. Elegant or his agent wanted the rights after a number of years to revert to him so that he could make arrangements at will. I didn't feel this was right since we had invested considerable effort for what turned out to be a long haul and wrote on July 30, 1969 to his agent:

"Mr. Elegant will unquestionably remember that this publication originated with Twayne Publishers and that the contract for this volume was originally with Mr. Richard Howard. Mr. Elegant's Pulitzer fellowship was the initial step in his distinguished career, and he owes it to this book. He, therefore, should take a more generous view of Twayne's contribution to his career. If there is anyone who should feel abused, it is the publisher and not Mr. Elegant." Elegant must have been persuaded, for the hardback reprint was issued by Greenwood Press, under agreement with Twayne.

Another of the books I contracted was *The Refugee Centaur*. Written in Spanish by Antoniorrobles it had been translated by Elizabeth and Edward Huberman. The book was a commercial flop but its merits clamor for a second chance. Hopefully, some publisher will read this recommendation. Ciardi's appraisal dovetailed with my own:

MEMO ON THE REFUGEE CENTAUR

I understand why you had a split reaction on this book. Certainly the reviewers will also split. The literalists will be lost in it. But others will find it very nearly a great book. Perhaps more than very nearly, but that is not an appraisal to be tossed around after one reading.

Nevertheless, my one reading takes and carries me. This is a book in the great tradition — The Golden Ass, some of the Arabian Nights, the Decameron, of course Don Quixote, and the descendants of these. But I am of the minority that thinks Quixote is a silly book. To my taste, the Refugee Centaur is far richer. In Quixote, the incidents are so cheaply conceived, the conflicts are so surface and so dimmed by farce, that, for me, nothing happens.

But Auro is something. Kafka would take Auro to his heart at once. Vittorini would recognize him at a glance. There isn't a poet among the French Symbolists who wouldn't answer to his dilemmas.

For finally the central theme of the modern school in all arts — what marks it off from earlier schools — is the reinterpretation of man's experience with a critical sense of the author's own ambivalence. Auro is his own image of ambivalence. As Candide was of his philosophical doubts. In my mind the travels of Auro belong with the travels of Candide. It's a book to last. By all means go ahead with it. By all means give it every promotion possible within the budget. World as it is, I cannot answer for its present commercial success, because winning readers' attention today is too complex and competitive an operation. BUT IF YOU CAN GET THIS BOOK INTO PUBLIC ATTENTION it will succeed commercially....

After Ciardi joined the *Saturday Review* in 1955 our paths still crossed but not as frequently. He still had Twayne on his mind, however, as this letter written in January 29, 1957 from Rome indicated:

I have been turning a new anthology to succeed *Mid-Century American Poets* in my mind but I begin to think the timing is temporarily wrong. Donald Hall and Robert Pack are doing one — out this year, I believe — of poets under 40 and that one should grab some attention though briefly only. Let this one settle for another year or two and then we should be timed right for a poets of approximately 1960 that would work and stay reasonably solid.

I frankly don't expect much of Amy Lowell, but we

are covered for a break-even and the book will be worth doing as a document of something.

Actually, I'm about ready to reverse field on poetry. The Twayne Library taught me much. I was pushing harder for poetry publication than there was poetry to push for. In consequence we did a number of books I would not now touch. I am not pushing for any poetry publication now. I think poetry should push itself. Somehow the good books (a lot of crap as well) manage to get published.

Judith says "come and get it." Benn says "ee da-ee." That's Hawaiian for "eat, Daddy." Myra says "Eh Babe, a maggiare..." Myra and Jonnel are really talking fluent bad Italian these days. Hope you are the same.

I wrote again a month later.

February 21, 1957

Dear John:

The roof has just caved in on us. You will recall I mentioned Joel's not feeling well in my last letter. Last Saturday morning he was rushed to hospital with internal hemorrhaging. In the course of the bleeding he suffered two heart attacks. However, I am happy to report that the emergency operation that followed for the elimination of the ulcer was successful and that he is doing better than expected as of this writing. He will be in hospital at least six weeks, flat on his back in bed and very likely will require another month of convalescence. So much for gloom.

We have been following with tremendous interest your battle with the philistines and want you to know that we are in your camp as always. Business continues at a fairly high plane with money tighter than ever. I expect this to ease as soon as our *America's 10th Man* starts being sold in a large way. We must be just on the verge of this now.

x x x

Under separate cover I'm sending you a copy of the
Amy Lowell book just off the press and I want to
urge you to try to get more than the usual space
allotted to poetry in the SRL. If you don't want to
do the review yourself, I think very possibly Carl
Sandburg could be approached since Ruihley, [the
editor of the volume], has indicated that Sandburg
would be glad to help in restoring Amy Lowell's
position in the world of letters.

Please remember me to Judith and the little
Ciardis. We miss you very much.

Ciardi answered promptly.

Dear Jack:

I'm terribly sorry to hear about Joel. Please give
him our best along with the enclosed letter, but
damned if I can see that six weeks and four more are
enough time for a real recovery. Don't let him push
too hard. People kill themselves pushing.

Thanks for good words anent AMLindbergh. Actually the support turned out to overwhelm the
squawks. The first wave of letters did nothing but
call me dirty names. That seemed about it at the
time. Then about 10 days later a second and even
larger wave of letters began to roll in — over 100 a
day for a while — all in support. I conclude that the
outraged write letters faster than some other kinds
of people.

Good to hear that *America's 10th Man* is getting
set to move. And delighted again that the Sydney
Bechet ms. is due for revival. I certainly have no
objections to a re-write. Welcome it in fact. I'm just
glad to see the thing a-borning. Just make sure that
little gal is sealed up tight before anything rolls. I
wish I could think of working on it, but I'm so
swamped in Dante, a text I'm compiling and in SR
(with Bread Loaf going crazy at intervals in between), that I have trouble finding time just to read

never mind edit or re-write. I'm a fine one to be lecturing Joel. I've got to slow down or crack up.

If Sandburg is willing to do the review of the Amy Lowell book I can promise it considerably more than passing notice. Otherwise it may be hard to weigh it ahead of other books in sight. Please urge Ruihley to air-mail me his info on Sandburg's willingness in full necessary detail. As far as Sandburg's view of poetry and as far as a great deal of Amy Lowell's poetry is concerned, I am a shade less than enthusiastic, but a piece by Sandburg on Amy will be superb journalism and I should expect to get a lead article out of it, if Sandburg is willing. I'll alert SR on it and have Sandburg queried by somebody more important than one of the office girls. Meanwhile, if Ruihley has any special info it would certainly be a good thing to have on hand just in case.

Don't let the world get you down, Jack. And don't let it keep you up too much. See you in August.

Joel's illness was a serious problem. He recovered but heart attacks were to recur every year or so until he passed away in 1967. Toward the end, his involvement with publishing and Twayne became a central concern of his life.

He would struggle into the city, stay a few hours at his desk and then as his strength waned, reluctantly struggle back home. I spoke to his wife and to his uncle, a physician, pointing out that financially Joel didn't have to do this, that insurance would cover a good deal of his salary and that we would make up the balance. His uncle answered that he thought Twayne was keeping Joel alive. We did have a buy-and-sell agreement in force among the stockholders when Joel passed away but Joel had told his wife to "do whatever Jack did," and so we never exercised the agreement and his wife remained a stockholder until the merger.

The Amy Lowell reference in Ciardi's letter was to *A Shard of Silence: Selected Poems of Amy Lowell*, edited with an Introduction by G.R.Ruihley. The Sandburg review was not forthcoming. The volume was not a Ciardi project as his remarks indicate.

America's Tenth Man, also not a Ciardi project, mentioned in the correspondence, was a large, handsome volume, 8 1/2" by11". It was a pictorial review of the Negro contribution to American life today [as of 1957]. It was edited and compiled by Lucille Arcola Chambers and appeared with an appreciative Foreword by Henry Cabot Lodge, Jr., then the U.S. Ambassador to the United Nations. Mr. Lodge wrote in part: "In the United Nations it is my duty to represent the United States in relations with seventy-eight other nations. There are few aspects of American life that interest...those nations more than the way in which our country is moving toward real equality regardless of race. *America's Tenth Man* tells about that movement, showing in hard facts where the Negro citizens of America stand today in their steady march toward an equal share in the American heritage..." The book was well received, sold well to libraries and schools. The smell of success, however, attracted a number of entrepreneurs who approached the editor when a sequel or revised edition seemed probable. We finally dropped all future plans when the situation became too complicated. So far as I know, a successor volume was never issued by Miss Chambers. A contretemps of considerable proportions at the time — 1957 — emerged when a dignitary wrote to inform us that his picture had been included in error. He was not a Black! I discuss this situation in my chapter on *Tsurris*, pages 201 ff., q.v.

Over the years I had occasional notes and letters from John Ciardi but we drifted apart. Our last exchange came in April of 1984, when he wrote from the University of Kansas City, about two years before his death, acknowledging my plans for this book. The obituary in the *N.Y. Times* on that sad occasion in 1986 omitted his very important contribution to Twayne Publishers, and I am very happy indeed to be able to rectify that omission. He is remembered with affection and respect.

Two other authors who came aboard in the early years and became editors of different projects were Hans Louis Trefousse and Robert D. Leiter. Trefousse's field was history; Leiter's, economics and labor. Leiter taught at City College and Trefousse at Brooklyn College, my alma mater.

Leiter's first book, *The Musicians and Petrillo*, published in 1953 under the Bookman Associates imprint, was rescued from a bankrupt publishing company by the author and became our first bestseller when the American Federation of Musicians purchased 15,000 copies. On the strength of this showing we were eager for lightning to strike again when Leiter received a Rockefeller grant to do a study of the Teamsters. When *The Teamsters Union* was published in 1957, we contacted Dave Beck, the outgoing president of the union, and his successor, Jimmy Hoffa. They both recognized that the union came off very well in the study,

particularly at a time when Congressional inves-
tigations were turning out headlines about rack-
eteering. But the book was not a whitewash, and
we could not come to terms for large-scale union
purchase despite meetings in Washington and
elsewhere with the union leadership. Leiter did
another book for us on featherbedding practices
on the railroads which we released under the title
Featherbedding and Job Security. While we never
achieved any great prominence in Leiter's editorial area, the Twayne catalogue of 1971 lists fifteen titles ranging from books on the anti-trust
laws to a volume on the meaning of Keynes.

   Trefousse's first book for us was *Germany and
American Neutrality*, the subject of his doctorate
dissertation at Columbia University. He also
wrote two biographies for Twayne: one on Ben
Butler, the notorious Civil War general who
threatened to prosecute all women of New Orleans
found on the streets after curfew as prostitutes;
the other on Benjamin Franklin Wade, who, as
president of the Senate, would have become president of the United States had the impeachment of
Andrew Johnson been successful. Trefousse's
documentary, *What Happened at Pearl Harbor?* I
have already referred to. Trefousse also published a number of books with other firms.
   He also became chief editor of a historical series
we created to parallel the successful Twayne
authors series. Known as Twayne's Rulers and
Statesmen of the World Series (TROWS), the
books were relatively short biographies of mon-
archs and statesmen. Robert Remini's *Andrew
Jackson* in this series, paperbacked by Harper &

Row, epitomized our idea of what the books should achieve. Many were excellent volumes and critically well received but the series as a whole never reached the same level of reader or library support of the Twayne literary series. Robert Warth's biography of Stalin was hailed as the best short biography of that tyrant, and he followed up with equally compelling short books on Lenin and Trotsky.

As with the authors series, Trefousse selected sub-editors to deal with the ancient world and other areas that he did not want to handle personally. By the time the merger took place, about 20 volumes had appeared, all of them well received critically.

Two series that had originated with Washington Square Press as paperbacks were taken on as hardback series, reversing the usual sequence. We were able to utilize the typesetting of the paperbacks by enlarging the print for our offset editions.

The first of these, the Great Histories Series, was edited by H.R.Trevor-Roper and included the works of the most important historical writers from Herodotus to the present day. Each volume contained biographical and critical introductions by a noted modern scholar. For example, Gibbon: *The Decline and Fall of the Roman Empire and Other Selected Writings* was edited and abridged by Trevor-Roper; *Josephus: The Jewish War and Other Selected Writings* was edited by M.I.Finley; *Machiavelli: The History of Florence and Other Selected Writings*, edited and abridged by Myron

P. Gilmore — to list three of the twelve volumes issued.

The Great Thinkers series, devoted to the flow of American thought from colonial times to the present, was edited by Thomas S. Knight and Arthur W. Brown. The volumes were written by well-known scholars and tried to present the salient features of the subject's thought or philosophy rather than a critical appraisal of his writing, as was the emphasis in the authors series. Still, there was some overlapping both in coverage and subject. *George Bancroft* by Russel B. Nye; *Thorstein Veblen* by Douglas Dowd; *Thomas Jefferson* by Stuart Gerry Brown; *John Woolman* by Edwin H. Cady were four of the 17 volumes issued.

In 1964, Dr. Cecyle S. Neidle offered us a manuscript on a subject that was to become the focus of a new series for us, and of which she was to serve as editor. The volume was a revised study of her dissertation. Entitled *The New Americans*, it provided a view of America as presented by the autobiographical writings of immigrants to our shores, some of them famous and some unknown. This became the first volume in The Immigrant Heritage of America series. Other titles, which overall did quite well in sales, were *The Italian-Americans* by L.J.Iorizzo and S. Mondello; *The Black Experience in America* by Norman Coombs; *The Oriental Americans* by H.Brett Melendy; *Zion in America: The Jewish Experience* by Henry L. Feingold. A number of these were published in paper by Hippocrene Books. After the merger, the series was continued with additional titles documenting the history and contribution of various ethnic groups to the American experience. These included the Dutch in America, the German-Americans, the Irish, the Norwegian-Americans, the Puerto Ricans, the Pennsylvania Dutch, the Syrian-Lebanese, and other volumes dealing with the subject of immigration such as xenophobia and immigration, the radical immigrant, etc. It was my hope that this series would eventually cover every ethnic group in America with the same intensive coverage as the Twayne studies of American writers.

Being Jewish and a publisher, I found early opportunities to attract titles of Jewish interest to the Twayne list. At the time, the early 50's, the genre had not yet taken center stage on the publishing scene as it has today. An article written by Harold U. Ribalow describes the situation realistically. It appeared in the Philadelphia *Jewish Exponent* and a number of other Jewish media.

A PUBLISHING HOUSE DISCOVERS JEWS
by Harold U. Ribalow

Jewish Book Month will see the publication, in English-Jewish newspapers, of many articles on Jewish books and authors. This, however, is the unusual story of a general publishing house which discovered that Jewish books are as commercially successful as any books accepted by publishers. — Ed.

Jewish books — according to most of the publishers devoted to the publication of them — have a limited audience, an audience which seldom increases. Jewish books — the cynics assert — are a kiss of death in the book field, for only rabbis, Jewish lay leaders and a comparative handful of other Jews are steady purchasers of these volumes. Hence...the small number of Jewish publishing houses. Hence, the few Jewish writers who devote themselves to entirely Jewish themes. Hence, the feeling of pessimism in Jewish publishing.

Oddly enough, this attitude of defeatism, while prevalent among Jewish firms, is absent among larger and probably more imaginative general houses. Thus Crown Publishers have had much success with translations of Sholem Aleichem and with the books of Nathan Ausubel;...the Jewish Book Guild with monthly selections — mostly made of books issued by firms that do not specialize in Jewish titles.

Typical of this new and encouraging development is the story of Twayne Publishers and Bookman Associates, an organization which issues books under both imprints. Famous for a number of years as publishers of first-rate poetry and scholarly works, the men behind this concern thought that it might be interesting to see how they would do if they undertook to accept volumes of Jewish interest. Being a quality house, Twayne-Bookman first took on the unusual challenge of Jewish books by issuing *Biblical Hebrew Grammar*. The title certainly attests to the book's usefulness, and it received glowing reviews, including one in *Hadoar*, the only Hebrew weekly in the world outside of Israel. But what makes the book remarkable is that it was written by a Japanese scholar! His name? Toyozo W. Nakarai.

The critical reception given this attempt encouraged the men who run the firm to seek out other Jewish titles. Of course the Jewish titles were to have been a small proportion of the overall production of the outfit, but notice what happened. Twayne published Rabbi Hyman E. Goldin's *A Treasury of Jewish Holidays*. The response to it was great, the reviews many. The Jewish Book Guild selected it as a monthly choice. It filled a need, and the publishers found themselves with a steady seller. For a modest publishing house, it was in the nature of a "best seller."

The enterprising young men discovered that their few Jewish books were doing at least as well as their scholarly books, their volumes on contemporary history, their science fiction novels. "Jewish books," Jack Steinberg said, "appeared to open a new field for us. So we began to think of publishing some eight Jewish books a year, out of a total of about forty. We are, of course, a general house, but when we encountered this demand for good Jewish books, we decided it would be foolish not to cater to this demand."

Within a year or so, Twayne and Bookman accepted and published other interesting Jewish titles and what is equally significant, they do not echo the complaints voiced by the Jewish firms. They, on the contrary, are rather satisfied both with having entered the field and with their sales.

Their major book of this season is *Not By Power: The Story of Judaism* by Rabbi Allan Tarshish. "We felt," Jack Steinberg said to me, "that a history of Jewish ethical thought could be useful at this time because there already were a large number of one-volume histories devoted to the traditional history of the Jewish people."...Rabbi Goldin, a versatile and prolific writer, has given these publishers a number of other titles, including *Hebrew Criminal Law and Procedure*, a book which won its niche on specialized shelves and gave publishers and author unusual satisfaction. While it hasn't the popular appeal of the same author's work on Jewish holidays, its solidity has won for it glowing notices. When a publisher receives good reviews in outstanding periodicals it means more than potential sales: it means that this firm, within the book trade, is gaining a reputation; that its imprint has meaning. This leads to respectful reviews. It may also lead to new manuscripts by writers who are searching for

new, aggressive, imaginative publishing houses.
Thus, when Bookman issued rabbi Felix Mendel-
sohn's *The Merry Heart*, a volume of Jewish wit,
humor and folklore, not only did they expect sales,
but other manuscripts by Jewish writers who do
humor books, or, for that matter, books on any Jewish themes....

Twayne-Bookman is a comparatively new firm,
but it is alive and imaginative. It publishes many
good books: on D.H. Lawrence, John Donne, by
Thomas Hart Benton, by leading American poets, by
outstanding science-fiction writers. But Jews in
America will be grateful that here is a general publishing house which, in a few brief years, has made
available an excellent list of Judaica. More power to
the men behind it and to the books they publish.

Ribalow became a close personal friend as a
consequence of the Jewish books we published.
He had come to Twayne as the compiler and editor
of a very good anthology, *World's Greatest Boxing
Stories*. Harold was very knowledgeable about
sports, literary matters in general, and specifically about Jewish books and authors. We did a
number of titles by him in this area. *What's Your
Jewish I.Q.?* and *History of Israel's Postage
Stamps* are two examples. Harold became our
Jewish book editor and was always available and
an unfailing source of information about matters
literary and Jewish. He tried to make us rich and
famous by recommending that we reissue Henry
Roth's *Call It Sleep*, which was a tremendous
seller in reprint, and also asked me to invite Elie
Wiesel to become a Twayne author when the latter
was vainly seeking an American publisher. I took
Wiesel to lunch but that's as far as it went.

Harold also suggested that we publish his book, *The Jew in American Sports*, which replaced the fountain pen as the favorite Bar Mitzvah present for several generations of thirteen-year-olds. I was present recently at a Hadassah/Ribalow prize award for fiction set up in memory of Harold when the master of ceremonies acknowledged the republication of this title in new editions by Hippocrene Books. He remarked that he had received no fewer than six copies of the title as Bar Mitzvah presents!

Over the years we must have published well over 100 titles of Judaica and related areas, including the studies of Jewish writers in our authors series. Most of them sold better than our other trade groupings. Titles that stand out in my memory, in addition to those already mentioned, would include Chaim Grade's *Agunah, The Bas Mitzvah Treasury* by Azriel Eisenberg and Leah Ain Globe, *Jews in the Modern World*, 2 vols. edited by Jacob Freid, *Judaism for Today* by Abraham Cronbach, *The Laureates: Jewish Winners of the Nobel Prize* by Tina Levitan, *Zion Reconsidered* by Jakob J. Petuchowski, *Zion in America* by Henry L. Feingold, *The Flowering of Modern Hebrew Literature* by Menachem Ribalow, *The Samaritans — Heroes of the Holocaust* by Wladyslaw Bartoszewski and Zofia Lewin. We were broadly catholic in our selection of Judaica titles, including on our list books that appealed to orthodox groups and titles that sold well to readers of the more liberal persuasion, including anti- and pro-Zionist religious books as well. I somehow took it as an affirmation of our publishing policy when Rabbi Abraham Cronbach, one of our authors, stepped forward to officiate at the burial service for the Rosenbergs after their execution when other rabbis were reluctant to perform these traditional services. Books by Rabbis Cronbach and Petuchowski were among a number of excellent titles that originated with the American Council for Judaism under the editorial direction of Leonard R. Sussman, Executive Director. Mr. Sussman is now with Freedom House.

As a consequence of our involvement with Jewish books, we became members of the Association of Jewish Book Publishers (AJBP) shortly after its founding in 1962. As a non-profit group, it provides a forum for discussion of mutual problems by its membership, which includes publishing companies, and individuals (editors, authors, and librarians) interested in Jewish books. No religious affiliation is required. The organization has sponsored book exhibits at various conventions and issues a combined Jewish book catalog once or twice a year which it distributes free or at cost at book fairs and conventions. Joel Saltzman initially represented Twayne at the Association. After his death I became active in the organization and was its president from 1974 to 1981. One of the Association's most widely applauded activities was its efforts on behalf of Soviet Jewry from 1977 on, when it mounted Jewish book exhibits at each of the Moscow Book Fairs. I had the privilege as president to lead a four-person delegation in setting up the first such Jewish book exhibit in the Soviet Union in 1977 and to establish the procedures that enabled successive biennial exhibits to take place through 1989. See pages 192 ff. for a fuller description of the AJBP'S experience with Jewish books in the Soviet Union.

Later, after the merger, I became active in the Jewish Book Council (JBC) where I am a member of the Steering Committee and a vice president. The JBC, sponsored by the Jewish Community Centers Association of North America, formerly JWB, confers the annual National Jewish Book Awards and library citations; publishes *Jewish Book World* and the tri-lingual *Jewish Book Annual*; syndicates *Jewish Books in Review*; participates in international, national, and regional book fairs; conducts Jewish book conferences; issues a wide variety of annotated Jewish bibliographies, and provides consultation on setting up a Jewish book fair. It is generally regarded as the most prominent *pro bono* organization concerned with the encouragement and promotion of Jewish books.

III

Sylvia Bowman and the Authors Series

I INDICATE IN THE INTRODUCTION HOW DOUBTFUL we were of Sylvia Bowman's initial proposal concerning the publication of a series of pamphlets about American authors she proposed to edit. John Ciardi's negative response (page 16) summed it up for me as well. Fortunately for Twayne, other firms that Sylvia contacted, including her own university press, took an equally dim view of the project. Eventually, as I indicate, we took it on a couple of years later, but still well in advance of competitors who set up rival series to emulate our undertaking. These would include Barnes and Noble, Prentice Hall, Henry Holt, and other quite formidable organizations. Despite this competition, the authors series project was to become Twayne's greatest success.

Bowman had become acquainted with Twayne as a result of publishing a book on Edward Bellamy, *The Year 2000...*, under the Bookman imprint and seemed to be favorably impressed with our efforts on its behalf. Back then — 1959 — we had decided to undertake the publication of hardback reprints of American classics, which we called Twayne's United States Classics Series (TUSCS), for which an editor was needed. Would she be interested? She was indeed and became the editor of this series. We also agreed along the way to reconsider the series she had proposed. Thus it was that in her circularization of professors of American literature on behalf of TUSCS, she made mention of our intention to launch the authors series in the uniform format we suggested: hard-back books of approximately 160 pages each. The pamphlet idea had already been launched by the University of Minnesota Press and had been fortunate in getting USIA support. The Classics series published a number of titles, few of which did particularly well in sales, and eventually we sold our inventory of titles to College and University Press Services of New Haven, a small firm about which I shall have more to say later. We did retain title, however, to *The Variorum Walden* edited by Walter Harding and to Upton Sinclair's *Theirs Be the Guilt,* a revised edition of his epic novel of the Civil War, *Manassas.* Both of these we thought were good properties to hold on to.

On January 10, 1961, Twayne entered into an agreement with Sylvia Bowman to edit Twayne's United States Authors Series (TUSAS) consisting of critical studies of American writers. The uniform format was a very important element in keeping our costs down. And, I think it was an important marketing element as well. Bowman planned to include books about American writers who are relatively unknown to today's readers but who were important contributors to the mainstream of American letters in their own time. This meant that though we would have titles that might sell very well — books on Faulkner, Hemingway, and Steinbeck, for example — we would have others that would do well to sell initial printings of 2000 or less. In printing the newer titles, we were frequently able to add press runs at very reasonable rates on books such as those on Harold Frederic, Artemus Ward, Bill Arp, and the more than 100 titles of the 350 originally projected that were first studies of these relatively minor writers. While we had a number of distinguished American scholars writing books for the series, many of the books were by younger scholars, a point that Bowman was to make in an article she wrote under the title "One of Two Thousand," an early version of which appeared in the *Southern Humanities Review* in the Fall of 1968.

It became obvious a year or so after the first books appeared, both from the reviews and the reception, particularly from the libraries, that we had latched on to an extremely promising publishing property, especially for a small publisher. I wrote to Bowman to express our optimism and to suggest the extension of the series idea to cover the more important British writers, which we were to call Twayne's English Authors Series (TEAS), and some time later to the rest of the world's literature, which we proposed as Twayne's

World Authors Series (TWAS). Bowman responded that she wished to edit TEAS herself and
to serve as the general editor of TWAS. This last
meant that she would recruit sub-editors for the
various sections in what was to be a systematic
survey of the major writers of the world, and with
separate sections devoted to Yiddish, Hebrew, and
Classical Latin writers. It was a most ambitious
undertaking and when I wrote to Professor Bowman twenty-five years later in 1987 about my
progress on this book, I remarked: "Re-reading
our correspondence is a source of much pleasure
and considerable wonderment as to how we were
able to cope with all that befell us..."

Sylvia Bowman died on December 25, 1989 but
she knew that I planned to include the article she
wrote as a kind of editor's credo for TUSAS,
TEAS, and TWAS, which she had sent in response
to my letter. The article follows:

ONE OF TWO THOUSAND

If I use the word *I* too frequently, I do not do so
because I am here to "celebrate and sing myself"; I
use it because it is impossible to speak without
awkward circumlocutions of the different Twayne
series with which I was so intimately associated. I
write, in fact, *not* to recite what one — the editor —
is doing, but to relate what over two thousand pro-
fessor-writers around the world have been contributing to the study of the literature of the United
States, the British Isles, the British Commonwealth, and the major writers of the countries of the
world such as Russia, China, Poland, Germany,
France, Latin America, and Africa.

As *one* involved with these series, I often recall a
statement made some years ago by Norman Cousins
to the effect that the happiest moment in a person's

life was when he conceived an idea and was filled with enthusiasm about it: the fulfillment of the idea was sheer blood, sweat, and tears. This statement applies to the concept which I had in the late 1950's to propose to publishers a study in depth of the American literary heritage. We needed to become aware of the voices of the past that in their own day had spoken louder than the Melvilles, the Emily Dickinsons, and others, for the people and about the national problems of their era. Moreover, it seemed to me that our situation relative to the American literary heritage and ideology was comparable to the one that perturbed nineteenth-century Edward Bellamy and George Washington Cable. They were worried because recently arrived immigrants were ignorant of fundamental American principles, literature, and history — with its ever-present conflicts between liberals and conservatives. Bellamy advocated that these peoples of all nations attend night classes; Cable founded classes to Americanize them.

Today we wonder why Americans are intellectually, idealistically soft — why the public seems to be so uninterested in basic American principles, why fervor for American ideals is so easily lost in favor of bigger and better bathrooms, why anti-American practices are so easily accepted in the name of saving "life, liberty, and the pursuit of happiness." So, with no excess of patriotism — no desire, so to speak, to make "the eagle scream" — but with the intent of making the literary, ideological heritage of this country available for examination, I conceived the idea of Twayne's United States Authors Series (TUSAS), which I was fortunate in having accepted by a small publishing firm, Twayne Publishers of New York. For part of the irony of today lies in the fact that a too-big firm could not accept such a project — until it had proved successful! — because many big companies publish books only if they can initially run off thirty thousand copies at a time.

As an outgrowth of this idea and as a result of the success of TUSAS, we began the English Authors Series — and then the World Authors Series. The series about World Authors will be a systematic survey of the major writers of all continents from the beginning of literature and inclusive of the present.

The need for such a survey is apparent in at least one respect: As we seek to know ourselves, so should we seek to know others. As the Honorable Lucius D. Battle, former Assistant Secretary of State for Educational and Cultural Affairs, stated in an address given in June 1964 but equally true today: "We as a people stand now committed irrevocably and finally to a degree of participation in the world which would have been unthinkable when we were children. Forces of change challenge our knowledge of the world — particularly of Africa, Asia, and Latin America. Many fine books are written about these areas. But direct involvement with the thoughts and ideas of these nations is essential if we as a people are to understand better our own international commitment. The literature of these areas — and I use the word in its broad sense — can be an important aid to our insight into the stresses of change around the world."

As a result of our introductions to the literatures of Latin America, Africa, Asia, and other countries, we hope not only to call attention to the ideas expressed by sundry authors but also to open the door for the publication in translation of many of the original works discussed in individual volumes of the World Authors Series.

The aim of these three series is to fulfill this need for knowledge of ourselves and of others by presenting the material in clear, concise, jargon-free books so that they can be read by the intelligent high school and college student and by the interested layman; but the style of the book is not intended to dilute the scholarly value of the book for teachers or even for professor-specialists. Although the major intent is to produce critical-analytical studies, the biographical, historical, sociological, and philosophical material necessary to shed light upon the work of the author being discussed is included....We do plan in these books to profit from the skills of analysis of the so-called New Criticism — but not to divorce the writer's work from the context of his total output or from his life, time, and place. The value of the series depends, therefore, upon not presenting just a rehash of material already published but of providing, where possible, sound but new interpretations — such as may be found in Ed Cady's *Stephen Crane*, in Frederick Hoffman's *William Faulkner* or in Joe Lee Davis' *James Branch Cabell*.

Though I have cited books by some famous scholars, I might also add that many of the books in this series are first books by young scholars. Although some critics have made snobbish remarks about the authors as "unknowns" or about even the "unknown" institutions which they represent, I — as the editor — have firmly believed that young scholars of merit should be given the opportunity to be published and to be read. After all, if we look at the matter realistically, not one famous American scholar would be what he is if some editor and some publisher had not had the courage to publish him. And some of the "unknowns" who have written for Twayne's United States Authors Series have published books which are considered by the best authorities to be — like the Thornton Wilder book, for example — books that no future student of the subject will be able to ignore....And our major objectives in TUSAS have proved successful; we have reached a broad audience at home among high school and college stu-

dents, teachers and professors. Just as important,
the letters that have been written to me by professors from Israel, Germany, Poland, France, Russia,
and even Hungary express appreciation for having
made accessible books not only about the major but
about the minor writers of America.... as Professor
Frederick Shroyer, who is also book editor of the Los
Angeles *Herald-Examiner* pointed out in his review
of the series (May 20, 1962): "There is a refreshing
absence of 'deep thoughts,' 'symbol discovery,' and
other 'pretentious pipsqueakery' in these books; but
there is clarity, and precision." Perhaps we have
obtained clarity and precision because of our challenge to our authors to achieve these qualities. As
one French writer stated: "I received a long letter
because the writer did not have the time to write a
short one."

But, despite the success of the series from the
standpoint of sales and despite its favorable and
even laudatory critics, it has had its adverse critics.
We have the critics who — in defense of the Establishment or of the Monopoly — take pokes at the
"literary fledglings"; we have the Granville Hickses
who condemn a book because the school the author
is associated with is an institution which is to him
unknown or not an Ivy League one. And we have
also the critics or reviewers who — as Claude
Graves has pointed out (as did William Dean Howells before him) — use the book to be reviewed as a
springboard for the display of their own artistry or
cleverness. Instead of interpreting and objectively
evaluating a work, this critic writes a "hit-and-run
review calculated to amuse the reader at the artist's
or writer's expense."

And such a critic can be as clever and as devastat-
ing as Dorothy Parker was when she wrote of Lucius
Beebe's *Shoot If You Must*; "This *must* be a gift book.
That is to say, a book which you wouldn't take on any
other terms." She polished off one scientific volume

with this statement: "It was written without fear — and without research." Of a book by A.A. Milne, she wrote: "Tonstant weader fwowed up."

All in all, unfair reviews are to be expected; but sometimes as I read those written even by scholars who are specialized in the subject area which the book concerns, I wonder if the same book is actually being reviewed. But, as one European author wrote to me — he had read some hundred reviews across the States, "but only one — obviously the product of someone who not only read the book but brought to it a wide literary tolerance and literate intelligence — had put a finger on what the book is about." Much as such unfair reviewers hurt — or a fair one, for that matter, that is adverse — they are to be expected. But what hurts most was best expressed to me in a letter from a young writer who stated that perhaps when "I am more experienced, it will be no longer a surprise to observe from the comments made that the critic skipped about ten chapters." If an author is convinced that he knows what he is saying because he has done honest work, my advice to him is contained in this statement of Walt Whitman:

> Whether I come to my own today
> or in ten thousand or ten million years,
> I can cheerfully take it now,
> or with equal cheerfulness I can wait.

And I must admit that I often have to recite this statement to myself when I read the reviews — for I do read them to cull from them the valid criticisms in order to use them for the improvement of the series. Moreover, my attitude to all reviews, good or bad, was expressed by Edward Bellamy: "Bad publicity is better than none." But my ego is not so personally involved as that of the authors.

For authors, to have the courage to publish their ideas, must to a certain extent be egotists. Perhaps they need more ego than a musician — for a note played or sung is soon vanished and the mistake with it; but the printed error is immortal. In fact, we have the "Wicked Bible" as one excellent example. When this bible — now a collector's item — was published centuries ago, it was discovered that a NOT had been left out of one of the Ten Commandments. The commandment read: "Thou Shalt commit adultery." And the ego that authors can have was recorded in a story by Elizabeth Chevalier: A novelist met an old friend; after they had talked for two hours, the novelist said: "Now, we've talked about me long enough — let's talk about you. What did you think of my last book?"

And I might also add that the editor often is the most aware of the fact that he is editing the immortal prose of an egotist — even, sometimes, of a prima donna. And, since he is dealing with people who have egos, the editor must be diplomatic in his criticism; but, no matter how diplomatic he may be, he must also have limitless patience, a hide as hard as a turtle's shell, and a sense of humor. The editor must adopt and practice the following statement that a French writer used as an inscription for his library: "I do not understand; I pause; I examine." And for the books in these series, the editor must read each manuscript as a critic, a scholar, and a layman. After he has written his detailed criticisms and instructions and has returned the manuscript to the author he must then sit back and wait for the reaction — sometimes a volcanic explosion....

When I was corresponding with a descendant of the Washington Irving family about a project, I stated that I was not an authority on Irving but such an admirer of his that I had visited his room in the Alhambra in Spain. He wrote to me: "Since you made a pilgrimage to Wash's chamber (tut-tut!), you may appreciate a portrait of him that hangs on my wall. Two very poor snapshots of it are enclosed....

Perhaps you will tell me if the likeness is a good one — as *you* may remember him! Also, was he *really* wearing a wig?"

And sometimes one gets humorous views of lives — and tragic ones as well in these letters....from authors in the United States and from those in Vietnam, Africa, Sweden, Australia, Greece, and India who relate the news of their section of the world — and also the facts of life and death. Though the editor may be confined to a study with manuscripts, humanity walks through his door — and into his files.

As editor of these series, I accept the fact that I need not make the plea made by Sandburg: "Lay me on an anvil, O God./ Beat me and hammer me...." I know that I can be beaten, damned, refined, and blessed. But I take, for the most part, the long view and the impersonal one: I am grateful to the now over 2000 scholar-writers around the world who have had the faith in these projects and the courage to gamble upon this gigantic publishing venture which may — if it fulfills its objective — help us to know ourselves and also to know others as we move faster and faster toward the One World which modern man must for his own salvation create. To achieve this world, we need fewer and fewer "starved and stunted human souls" and we know that "vain is [our] Science.../To feed the hunger of...[men's] heart/ and the famine of their brain." Through literature — through the inspiring and provocative record of the ideas and experiences of the past and of the present — we may perhaps eventually become with these series what Sir William Watson called "The True Imperialist"; we may perhaps help to "build within the mind of Man/The Empire that abides."

In the selection of sub-editors for TWAS, Bowman secured a number of outstanding younger scholars, including a few to whom I refer elsewhere. But among others who performed capably, energetically, and well beyond the call of their duties and compensation, were two retired professors, seniors who were delighted to put their years of experience and scholarship to work on our behalf.

The first of these was Professor Maxwell A. Smith, University of Chattanooga, Emeritus, who became editor of the French section of TWAS. By the time of the merger, Twayne had published more than forty critical studies, ranging alphabetically from Jean Anouilh to Emile Zola.

The other was Professor Gerald E. Wade, Emeritus of Vanderbilt University. He was responsible for nearly one hundred contracts on Spanish authors, more than fifty of which had already appeared by the end of 1974, when he resigned because of failing eyesight.

Both Wade and Smith acknowledged their indebtedness a number of times to one of our copyeditors, Irving Benowitz, my cousin and also a retiree, for his careful work on their behalf.

Other capable and energetic TWAS editors that come to mind for special commendation and gratitude were Professors Adam Gillon and Ludwik Krzyzanowski of the Polish section, Professor Ulrich Weisstein of the German section, Professor Joseph Jones, editor of the New English Literatures (Australia, New Zealand, Canada, and Africa), Professor Egbert Krispyn, Netherlandic literature section, and Professor William R. Schultz, Chinese literature.

As Sylvia Bowman's article notes, the majority

of the series titles attracted good reviews and notices, but we had our detractors. They seemed to focus on these themes: the size of the undertaking, the younger scholars who were writing books for us, and the fact that we were threatening the elitist status of the scholarly book. The "Publish or perish" dictum which held sway in academic circles for so many years seemed threatened by the egalitarian thrust of the Twayne books.

A review article entitled "Publication Explosion" by Kermit Vanderbilt appeared on March 2, 1964 in *The Nation*. It sounded all of the notes I have just mentioned. The writer viewed with alarm "young professors enjoined by superiors to publish or perish...eager to serve in the publication explosion." The reviewer compared several series of critical studies issued by various firms and Twayne came off very badly. What was curious, however, was that Mr. Vanderbilt spent the greater portion of his space to bad-mouthing the Twayne performance than to the other series he thought well of, books written "by men of the establishment..." rather than by Twayne's "fledgling critics." I was struck by the oddity of the situation and called *The Nation's* book review department to complain, only to learn that the article had not been commissioned by that department.

Presumably, then, it was an editorial assignment. I wrote a letter fulminating against the cultural royalists who had orchestrated Mr. Vanderbilt's performance.

A better response than mine, however, had appeared in the form of a lengthy appraisal of TUSAS written by George Knox of the University of California which appeared in *The Western Humanities Review*, Spring, 1963 issue:

> It is evident to anyone who has read several of these books that this is a carefully planned and controlled enterprise....It is obvious that they are valuable for undergraduate and graduate bibliographical and research work. They may sometimes fall short of serving the specialist to any important degree, but the spectrum is great and the scholarship conscientious....So far, then, the series seems to have met the challenge to reach as wide an audience as possible with the desiderata of concise exposition and competent scholarship. *Only the finicky monopolists will be perky* [italics mine], and the "general" reader not put off....I feel that TUSAS is worthily carrying on the achievement of the American Men of Letters and the American Writers Series without imitating either predecessor.

Perhaps a greater affirmation of the value of what we were doing came from the marketplace. Our books were unquestionably being very well received. The National Council of Teachers of English, for example, had endorsed the series professionally by undertaking its sale.

Practically speaking, every permissions editor, unwittingly perhaps, exercises a censorship role. Since this is encountered everywhere in the publishing world, it may be viewed as a kind of "hidden" censorship of which the public is largely unaware. With the critical studies of the Twayne series, we occasionally encountered barriers to publication. These either took the form of prohibitive fees for use of copyright material, which effectively restricted the amount of an author's writing that could be commented on, hence adversely affecting the contents of our volume, or totally denied us access to any of the author's writings except for limited passages that were sanctioned by the "fair use" concept, a vague limitation that provided no objective way to determine how much material could be used.

We tried to point out in these instances that the Twayne series books were not big sellers and that the limited income would not permit payment of the large fees requested. Sometimes, this worked, but when best-selling authors were involved, permissions people, who were dependent on the income their department generated for their salaries, were often adamant. The result was that authors had frequently to limit their quotations, a most frustrating experience for them and their publisher and, in my opinion, very definitely not in the public interest.

On a couple of occasions we were totally refused permission because the author or his publisher did not think well of our study and we were threatened with legal repercussions if we published.

One of these actions involved the TUSAS book on Tennessee Williams by Signi L. Falk. Walton Rawls, then Twayne's executive editor, handled this difficulty with effective literary diplomacy. The upshot of the exchange which went on for a considerable time was that we were informed that permission to use the material would not be granted but that no legal action would be undertaken to restrict us either. That was fine with us. Seventeen years later, in 1978, however, the problem had been eliminated. The second edition of *Tennessee Williams* contains a full statement of permissions granted by New Directions on behalf of the playwright.

A different fate befell the Twayne title dealing with Edna Ferber. We received a letter from her lawyer informing us that we could not use Edna Ferber's name in connection with our book, either in the title or contents.* Since all of our series books carried the name of the author being critically evaluated as the title of the book and we had by this time (1967) published a few hundred titles, we were willing to go to litigation about this. Unfortunately, our author, who had been in touch with Ferber, decided to withdraw the book, though we assured her Twayne was willing to hold her blameless in the event of a suit and foot all the legal expenses involved. We felt sure that we would prevail had our attorney filed his action for a declaratory judgment under a number of options being considered. After Ferber's death, Twayne was given the green light by her literary executors but it was too late. One can speculate that Ferber's lawyer, the late Harriet Pilpel, may not have been in total agreement with her client's imperious and mistaken stand on the issue.

An author's proprietary rights under our copyright law should be protected, of course, but an author writes to be read and owes much to the reading public who has bought his books and should allow it access to criticism which quotes in reasonable measure from his works. But many times these rights are administered by agents or by the publisher to whom these rights are granted. The publisher or the permissions editor

---

*Shades of Haldeman-Julius! See pp. 208ff.

would do well to ponder the testimony presented before the Register of Copyrights on February 9, 1966 by Oscar Cargill as reprinted in The Round Table of *College English*, from which I quote in part. Professor Cargill was arguing for wide latitude in use of copyright material in teaching, but his cogent expression should apply to publishing practice as well, for a well crafted critical study is a teaching device intended to induce the student to go back to the original work being commented on.

It is my belief that teaching does more to promote the sales of authors' works than do all the publishers' promotional schemes. I offer two bits of evidence to this effect. Yvor Winters applied to the Macmillan Company some years ago for permission to quote from Edwin Arlington Robinson in a book he was doing on that writer and was refused. He published his book anyway without a single quotation but with a notation on the refusal. This created much indignation in the academic world and the teaching of Robinson fell off drastically. In an effort to counteract this slide, the Macmillan Company commissioned Professor Laurance Thompson, at Princeton, to issue a selection of Robinson's poetry under the title, *Tilbury Town* and this was done with much fanfare. But despite this, Robinson, who was a truly great poet, remains a dead poet.

Again, Edna St. Vincent Millay, who was one of the best lyricists this country has ever produced, had an agent who restricted the use of her poetry to five or six poems in anthologies on the theory that this would keep up the price of permission reprints. And so it did, but it choked off completely the use and the teaching of Millay in the colleges. The result is that today there is little general knowledge or market for Miss Millay's work. Contrast the fate of these two poets with that of Robert Frost, who was most generous with his reprint grants as were his publishers....

Sylvia Bowman's article referred to the fact that the World Authors Series had opened the door for the publication in English of many of the original works discussed in the individual volumes of the series. This was a goal devoutly to be wished for. If we stimulated an interest in a writer with our critical study, we ought to be able to back it up by making sure that some of his or her works were available.

To that end I began the series of Introductions — anthologies that would provide a reader with enough material in English translation to form a basic appreciation of national concerns and temperament of the foreign literature involved. Thus we published volumes on a number of little known literatures, and in this way managed to "show strikingly how a country's history can be made more plainly intelligible to an outsider through its literature..."* I do believe that the first comprehensive volumes of translations in English from Romanian, Bulgarian, and Yugoslav languages were made available in this way. Other volumes in the series included Introductions to Polish, Greek, Spanish, Pilipino and Classical Arabic literatures. These were supplemented by individual volume translations wherever possible and, as I have indicated elsewhere, we were particularly fortunate to have been able to develop on-going projects in depth with Scandinavian and Dutch books.

---

*Aileen Pippett in *Saturday Review*, August 4, 1962.

On the drawing boards when the merger took place was a project involving the works of new writers from the various areas of the world that we were covering. I thought it entirely possible that I could get enough standing orders from libraries already ordering the Twayne series titles to get this under way successfully. If it could be done, then I thought the next step would be to launch a similar series for new American writers.

Today I think I would modify the proposal so that the series for new writers might take the form of trial editions. Suppose we were to limit the edition to 1000 copies, carefully selected, sold only to subscribers, and send the books out for review to only a handful of prominent reviewers and critics. Suppose further we were to allow our writers to use these critical assessments to place these same books with the larger publishers if they could. We would continue, of course, to keep our trial edition available should placement fail. I think it is possible for a small publisher to break even at least on 1000-copy subscriptions to individuals or libraries. This kind of limited publication would not preempt the areas of promotion and sales of the larger house which could use the critical evaluations to launch the new writer commercially. I tried this proposal not too long ago on a few publishers who thought well of the idea.

New writers, I learned recently, are not the only ones who can use a helping hand. Artists are in a similar bind. Here, for example, is what happened to painter Ken Munowitz, who died in 1977 at a young age. A retrospective of his art held in the summer of that year at Cooper Union was reviewed glowingly by David Shirey for the N.Y. *Times.* Unfortunately, the article* was written when a prolonged strike occurred at the paper and was never published. Here are major excerpts from the review, attesting to the fact that Munowitz had achieved a status as an artist entitled to the appreciation of the art-loving public generally:

When painter Ken Munowitz died last year, he was only forty-two. Despite his brief career as an artist, he was able to produce a body of work of outstanding significance, especially the paintings he did in the few years before his untimely death. They deliver an extraordinary emotional and dramatic impact, filled with a powerfully spellbinding intensity. They give the startling sense that the artist had a presentiment of his impending death and felt the compelling need to pour the fullness of his soul into his last canvases.

A retrospective of Munowitz's art was held last summer at Cooper Union Gallery and it was one of the most rewarding shows in New York. It was curious that many of us were not aware of a painter of his achievement...

If there is a feeling of immediacy in the paintings it is because the artist kept his palette close to his own life. In his portraits, still-lifes and landscapes he depicted his mother, aunts, cousins and friends as well as himself.... He was a painter of interiors: interiors of places and of minds.

Munowitz's best endeavors are suffused with a quiet spirituality. There is a soft mystical presence in his people, and his objects — so important in all

*For permission to quote from this review, and for the illustrations contained in this book, I am indebted to Mr. Milton Mann, brother of the artist, who made the necessary arrangements with the N.Y. *Times* and the art critic David Shirey.

of his canvases — are moved by a kind of animistic energy. The low-key grays, greens, blues, and yellows glow with a quiet inner life. The artist's subjects unobtrusively impose their physical and metaphysical traits on us at once, baring their skins and their being. Action is not a central part of these canvases, only contemplation. There is no noise in them. Just a placid resonance.

The canvases have a surrealistic touch, but they are much too complex to reduce to a stylistic category. The precision of features and details reveals a strong understanding of realism. Yet the brooding quality of the works takes them beyond that. There is also a disarming freshness bordering on the naive. However, these canvases are too tutored, savvy and technically brilliant to be called naive. They have a medieval look, as if their bold contour lines and melancholic colors had a kinship with gothic stained glass windows.

The somberness notwithstanding, Munowitz's art is humorous. He had a fancifully diverting notion of distorted human characteristics. When he was poking fun at the body, he did not spare himself....

Much of the humor is heightened by a coy, perhaps wryly coquettish and witty preoccupation with sex. Cacti discreetly seduce one another or come close to encounters of an untoward kind. There is a muffled sexuality in some of the women who establish unabashed eye contact with the observer....

But the unequivocal splendors of Munowitz's paintings are the portraits....the paramount effort — a consummate tour de force — is a self portrait, last he did of himself. Wearing a Russian hat and a heavy coat, Munowitz captures our vision and holds it. He seems to be saying: "I am Ken Munowitz. I am an artist who expresses himself in paint. I have something to say to you about life before I leave it. Pay attention." We pay attention and learn that he did have much to say.

It seems to me that here too a much wider opportunity for artistic recognition could be attained by a series of short monographs or catalogues containing a brief biography of the artist and including enough of his work to provide an adequate assessment of achievement. Galleries and exhibitions are the traditional routes to recognition for artists but a well produced series with competent editorial overview could supplement these and provide a measure of redress for such artists as Ken Munowitz, who deserve to be rescued from oblivion. The costs of such an undertaking, however, because of the need for color, have been estimated at about four times the cost of the new writers series I have just described. Still, a subscription list of 1000 would be enough to handle it. Moreover, unlike the new writers project, there would be no need to limit sales, and bookstores could be solicited.

For a while we considered the possibility of selling Twayne to its authors. It wasn't that farfetched, and Sylvia Bowman was willing to sound out author sentiment. After all, we had more than 2000 authors under contract and most of them thought well of our enterprise and projects. Even if they were to use only their royalties for purchase of stock it would not have taken long to accumulate a sizable share of ownership. I would have stayed on to manage the company and at least long enough to permit acquisition of my shares, which I would have left for the last. But it seemed too cumbersome an idea for my fellow stockholders, and there were other eager suitors

KENNETH MUNOWITZ, Artist

PORTRAIT OF THE ARTIST AS A YOUNG MAN

The death of Kenneth Munowitz, artist, at an early age deprived him of the recognition that should have been his by virtue of his achievement. In this connection, readers are referred to the excerpts from the *N.Y. Times* review of his art on pages 126-128 of this book.

Born May 2, 1935, he was the youngest of three brothers born and raised in the Bronx of first generation parents who came from Krakow, Poland. He died December 20, 1977.

His love and gift for art was evident from his earliest childhood days. He attended public school in New York City graduating from Music and Art High School in Manhattan and, subsequently, from Cooper Union.

As Art Director of *Medical Economics* and subsequently Art Director of *Horizon* magazine, a highly regarded art publication, he received numerous awards for design which provided additional kudos for these publications. His free time until the late hours of the night was dedicated primarily to his oil paintings but included various other media.

Mr. Munowitz received additional recognition for his illustration of three children's books, *Happy Birthday, Baby Jesus, Moses Moses,* and *Noah* all written by Charles L. Mee, Jr. Each of these books was published by Harper & Row and received critical acclaim. His art work related to family, friends and his immediate environment and the mythical characters which he described as Beoples. He was unmarried with a *joie de vivre* and with strong ties to family, friends and co-workers. He had an extraordinary sense of humor and strong political feelings. When painting, however, he was oblivious to the rest of the world and would remain totally absorbed with the images on his canvas. His untimely death occurred during a very prolific period of his art activity, including the unfinished canvas on his easel.

Two Girls on Park Bench

CACTUS IN CLOUDS

BRONZE FIGURE

IN THE RED FOREST

FAMILY FROM CRACOW, I

FAMILY FROM CRACOW, II

MILTON IN SHORT PANTS

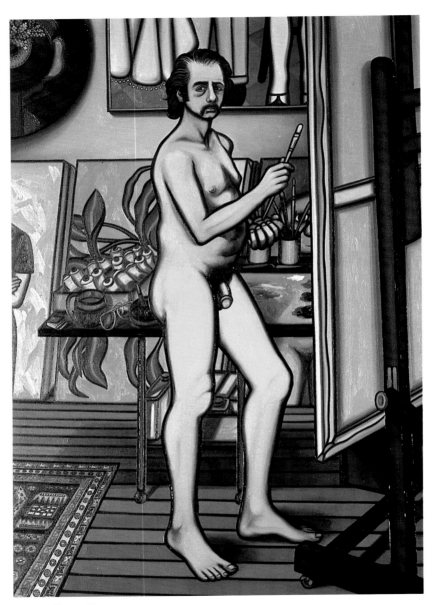

NUDE SELF PORTRAIT

THE BEDROOM

THE LIVING ROOM

CACTUS IN CIRCLE

MALE & FEMALE

TRIPLETS

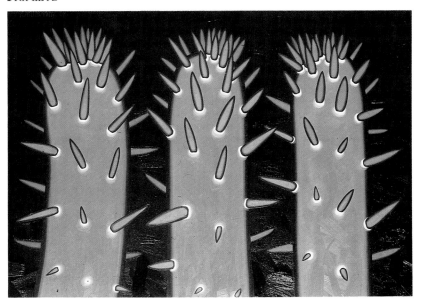

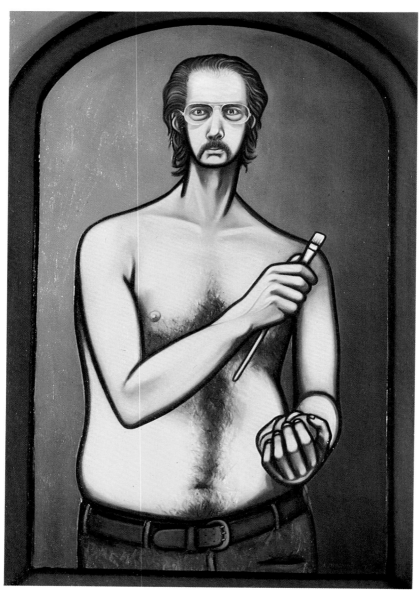

Self Portrait in Mirror

NINA

HERBERT

IRV-BAR MITZVAH

GARY

THE LAST SUPPER

THE THREE GRACES

JACOB ASLEEP

GARDEN OF EARTHLY DELIGHTS

ARTIST PAINTING MOTHER, BROTHER AND AUNT

Mom in Living Room

Museum Garden

SELF PORTRAIT IN SHEEPSKIN

in the wings. We had made a solid success with our authors series, despite the "finicky monopolists" who decried the numbers engaged in our literary "industrial complex."

One of the reasons for our success, I am convinced, was our consistent program of mailings to libraries. This I tried to do at least twice a year, frequently soliciting the participation of three other publishers to share the costs. In that way we could increase the reach and scope of such combined and usually third class mailings. For organizing these combined mailings, Twayne would receive a bonus by being allowed to utilize any underweight that might exist. In addition to the enclosures, a covering letter, usually written by me on behalf of all the mailers was included. Frequently the Twayne advantage or bonus took the form of an extra sheet or other insertion when the weight limitation would allow. We also tried to keep the mailings non-competitive in content. There never seemed to be any lack of publishers to participate, but Twayne was the only constant.

Occasionally, also, I would come across an unusual marketing or promotional opportunity. An example of this was the interest on the part of the National Council of Teachers of English (NCTE) in making available the Twayne series to its members. We prepared an attractive folder with returns to the NCTE. When the mailing resulted in a considerable quantity of orders (several hundred per title), I suggested that the organization consider supplementing the direct-mail offering with advertising in its periodicals, *College English* and the *English Journal*. I offered to pay for the advertising by increasing the discount on the sale of books to the NCTE. The result was that for a year or more a substantial amount of ads appeared in these two important journals, advertising that we probably would not have placed ordinarily.

I suppose that our success drew the attention and envy of some of our competitors who were considerably more affluent and could pay cash for their advertising. Eventually the NCTE informed us that because of the growing availability of other quality series titles by other publishers, they were withdrawing their participation in the sales area. It was wonderful while it lasted and the NCTE participation gave the series tremendous professional approbation, something no amount of money could buy. And it effectively countered the criticism of the *Nation's* reviewer and the others who followed his lead. I am also sure that the acceptance and recognition of Twayne at this professional level was of tremendous help later on when I launched the Twayne Lifetime of the Series (TLSS) promotion with the success I have described elsewhere.

I tried to duplicate the success of the NCTE venture by seeking to enlist state organizations such as the N.Y. State Council of English, but to no avail. Apparently, we had been dealing with a unique situation, both in terms of timing and product.*

---

*Still, the idea of placing book advertising on an inquiry basis (i.e., paying for the ad on the basis of customer response) has always intrigued me. There are thousands of publications of all sorts, not national in their coverage, but with many thousands of readers in the aggregate. In 1987, while acting as a

The authors series came at a time when Twayne had entered into a production agreement with a New Haven printer, United Printing Services. The latter agreed to finance the publication of selected titles from the Twayne list, including Bookman as well, through the medium of a new corporation, College and University Press Services (CUPS) jointly and equally owned by Twayne and United. Twayne was to be the owner of the literary property; College, and ultimately United, the owner of the physical properties, that is, the bound books and/or printed sheets. Twayne was to retain sole and exclusive marketing of all titles. A schedule of anticipated revenues was drawn up, and a percentage set up to pay for the expenses incurred in overhead, sales, promotion, and production. Ideally, the plan provided Twayne with an opportunity to expand its publishing operations dramatically and for its manufacturing partner to utilize its slack time, increasing its production efficiency to the maximum of plant capacity.

It was, I thought, a very good idea. But what started out as a cooperative, mutually rewarding venture, unfortunately turned into a clamorous and adversarial relationship. The contesting roles were chiefly played by I. Frederick Doduck

---

senior editorial consultant to Hippocrene, I tried such advertising on the title *The Christian Problem: A Jewish View* by Stuart Rosenberg in *Tikkun*, the new Jewish medium alternative to *Commentary* and *The Journal of Ecumenical Studies* at Temple University. The results were not overwhelming but enough plus sales were generated to indicate the approach had merit, at least sufficient for the small publisher to add the idea to his marketing strategy.

for the New Haven entity and Joel E. Saltzman for Twayne. Fred had two chief assistants — Michael Morgillo, who was in charge of graphics, and Sid Goldman, Fred's nephew, in charge of sales. Joel and Fred were evenly matched in stubbornness and recrimination. I can still hear their ringing assertiveness after nearly thirty years. One was always "Who, me? Who, me?ing" to the other's constant reiteration, "You see what I mean? You see what I mean?" If you repeat each of the rejoinders fast enough, you'll experience the unforgettable din of their exchanges.

Fred was a genius in keeping track of costs and the idea of CUPS originated with him. The project would have worked out very well if he had been content to stick to the original formula. But Fred wanted to be a publisher, and College eventually started on its own course, despite the agreement with Twayne. After Joel's death, I took over his role of contending with Fred, and we finally came to a parting of the ways about a half-year before the merger. Despite our differences, Fred offered to "give" me CUPS shortly before he went out of the printing business. I never investigated the full dimensions of his proffered gift and by the time I retired and might have been interested, he had made other arrangements.

The relationship with CUPS had its compensations, I freely admit. It unquestionably provided Twayne with a temporary respite from its always pressing obligations. The idea of a cooperative relationship between a publisher and his supplier, with each getting his proper share of proceeds, is mighty appealing. Perhaps we should have set up an arbitration procedure in advance to take care of the disagreements as soon as they arose.

The relationship also shaped the format of the authors series and led to the titles being issued in groups of five, making possible great economies in production and marketing, as I have already mentioned. Despite my disinclination to take on book production and manufacturing problems, after Joel's death I had no choice but to assume these chores. To my surprise I found that I had some hidden talents that resulted in considerable savings for the firm. Moreover, freed from dependence on one supplier, I encountered a widespread interest on the part of book manufacturers in the ready availability of series manuscripts scheduled for future release. My stipulation to potential suppliers was always to the effect that they could use these books as fillers for their composition needs if they were willing to defer billing to ninety days after the books became available from the bindery. I pointed out to them that these books were on standing order, that they were spoken for, and that my orders were on the average paid for in ninety days after billing. The argument must have been a compelling one, for we found no problem in getting fairly sizable operations to agree to our terms. We also had expressions of interest from suppliers abroad, but we limited this to a very efficient typesetter in Israel, to whom we sent mixed language manuscripts, thus avoiding the substantial penalties encountered in setting such material here.

I do not want to leave an inaccurate impression that my relationship with Sylvia Bowman was all peaches and cream. It was not, and there were a number of exchanges between us that enlivened our days. But these mainly concerned the fact that both Twayne and she had taken on this tremendously ambitious program of publication that was taking off and required more and more time and resources than we could give it. In addition to her editorial responsibilities — and despite the devoted assistance of Alberta "Taps" Hines and other part-time help — which would have normally eaten up the greater portion of her day, she was also a Chancellor of Indiana University and Professor of English as well. In an effort to keep up with the flood of manuscripts, she would devote the greater part of her summers to these chores. And I think she looked forward to retirement when she could devote full time to the series she had originated and in which she was so central a figure. Obviously, too, she concurred with Browning that our reach should exceed our grasp.

IV

Literary Diplomacy

GOVERNMENT INVOLVEMENT IN LETTERS HAS NOT always been a happy experience. I recall the scandals of the 1960's when it became known that the United States Information Agency (USIA) and the CIA had clandestinely subsidized American authors and publishers of reputation to issue hundreds of books reflecting the Administration's views on various aspects of foreign affairs. It would have been in keeping with governmental goals for these books to circulate abroad to influence foreign readers on behalf of the official American viewpoint. Some observers were even critical of this, pointing out that there was no way to keep such books from coming back home to unsuspecting readers here. But what became a matter of Congressional and popular domestic concern was the fact that both authors and publishers were feeding at the government's trough but releasing these books as presumably objective and independent conclusions. This secret literary handout came to much more than a million dollars according to a number of articles that appeared at the time.

Twayne was never approached with an offer for this kind of funding, but I must say that we were grateful for, and impressed with USIA purchases of our TUSAS titles for overseas placement in embassy and other American libraries. USIA also made possible foreign language editions of quite a number of these books. These editions, to be sure, were small, and the money never amounted to more than a couple of hundred dollars per title to be shared with our authors but it certainly was a morale booster for the author to know that his book was available in Brazil, India, Egypt, Korea, Italy, Romania, and even in Afghanistan where I had shipped a complete set of TUSAS to the Peace Corps for use by American teacher volunteers at Kabul University.

Poland, for a while, had an Information Media Guaranty program (IMG) sponsored by USIA, which, as I understood it, expedited payment in dollars for the purchase of approved American books by Ars Polona, the Polish government's export-import agency, in local currency, zlotys. These funds were blocked, that is, had to be spent in Poland, on projects which the United States and Poland could agree on. I had only one year's experience with this in 1966, when I went to Warsaw to set up a book exhibit of Twayne titles featuring our books of Polish interest, especially our newly released *Introduction to Modern Polish Literature*, but I could tell from our initial sale of

$5,000 worth of books that we could have had a significant and growing exchange of books had the program not been terminated shortly thereafter. I told the Polish literary authorities that I would use the proceeds from their purchases of Twayne books to finance the publication of Polish titles in English translation by producing them in Poland and shipping them to the United States free of duty. Back in the States, I transmitted the same proposition to the Polish embassy, pointing out in addition that there had to be many millions in blocked funds, both private and governmental, which in the best interest of both governments could be used to make available in English translation outstanding works of Polish culture, literature and history. The money was there needing only to be claimed and spent in Poland. Even Twayne had unclaimed zlotys in the bank. Why couldn't they see it! They didn't and wouldn't, alas! I also contacted two national Polish organizations in the U.S. that had blocked funds available in Poland but I was not persuasive enough, though neither gave me any reason for not trying the suggestion.

I even went so far as to forward the suggestion, at the insistance of one of our TWAS editors, to an international group of scholars, for, as I pointed out, blocked funds were available in many other countries — China, the USSR, the countries of Eastern Europe, and, I am sure, elsewhere. What a tremendous spur to international literary activity in the countries involved could be initiated with the released funds!

Our greatest success in Eastern Europe was, as

I have indicated elsewhere, in Romania, where we could build on the existence of a cultural exchange agreement with the United States which included books. We initiated our involvement by writing to the State Department, indicating our interest in the newly announced agreement of December 9, 1960. A letter in response came back from Mr. Frank G. Siscoe, Director, Soviet and Eastern European Exchanges Staff. He and his assistant, Mr. Ralph Jones, seemed genuinely interested in furthering our attempts. Mr. Siscoe wrote in June 21, 1961:

> ...both parties [Romania and the United States] agree to encourage and to support the publication in each country of literary works published in the other country...The Department of State's interest is motivated by a conviction that availability of American books and publications in Romania is one of the important means of achieving our policy objectives toward Romania....

I thought the opportunity too good to pass up. Romania might lead to similar projects in Eastern Europe and the USSR.

My curiosity concerning Romanian books was first stimulated by Edwin Smith, Manager of the Am-Rus Literary Agency in the late 1950's and early 60's. He and I had had some exchanges concerning the validity of remarks by Soviet and Eastern European writers which had appeared in the American press to the effect that only anti-Communist books dealing with their countries could be published in the United States. This had led to my reviewing some of the Russian titles being offered, a good number of which had already been translated into English and manufactured at

considerable expense in the USSR. In my opinion
the subject matter of most of them was not likely
to appeal to American readers. Moreover, since
many of the titles had been poorly edited and
translated, even a sympathetic reader would have
been put off by the frequent misspellings and
faulty English. I told Ed Smith, whose head had
been bloodied by the McCarthy hearings but not
bowed, that these books could scarcely be used to
test American publishers' commitments to the
principles of their profession; most of the books
were unpublishable under any circumstances.
There was no question in my mind as to the intrinsic right of writers everywhere to be read in other
lands. The sole criterion, it seemed to me, ought
to be the merit of the work being considered, not
the political complexion of the author. Smith
must have been impressed with my remarks —
Twayne had moreover published two titles offered
by his agency before this — for he rewarded me
with some books from the Romanian, among them
the works of Romania's then leading writer, Mihail Sadoveanu: *Evening Tales, Tales of War* and
The Mud-Hut Dwellers. The translations were
better than I had expected but I improved them
somewhat. These were published in 1962 and in
1964 and enjoyed excellent reviews and attention.
As befitted these literary first fruits of the recently effected Cultural Exchange Agreement between the United States and Romania, a gala
reception was held at the Romanian Permanent
Mission to the United Nations. It was well attended by notables from the academic, publishing,
and diplomatic worlds. In those early years, Ro-

manian books were a rarity in American publishing. They probably still are.

One very happy effect of the exchange agreement was increased attention given to the books by reviewers. Prominent media were all quite laudatory. These included *Time, Saturday Review, Booklist* of the American Library Association, *Slavic Review, Books Abroad*, and the like. The only conspicuous omission was the N.Y. *Times* which, sad to say, ignored the Sadoveanu books. Its front page review of Romanian expatriate Petru Dumitriu's *Incognito* at about the same time that it was ignoring our Romanian titles seemed to me to be making a political point, not quite in keeping with its masthead boast of "all the news that's fit to print."

In 1964, I was invited for the first time by the Romanian publishers to visit Romania, an invitation I eagerly accepted, for it enabled me to see at first hand the people and the land described in the pages of the writers I was reading. This trip was to be repeated a number of times and each time new literary experiences were to be enjoyed. On this first trip, I visited the Bucharest bookstores, inquiring as to the possibility of Twayne books being put on sale. We had in 1961 begun our tremendous series of books on writers. I got a hearing for this idea of putting Twayne books in the stores but it was not to be implemented for two or three years. I also dropped in on the American Legation in Bucharest (It was not an embassy then.) and met Minister William Crawford, who was kind enough to host a luncheon on the occasion of my visit and to call attention to the Romanian books we had published by putting up the jackets in the legation display cases facing the street, along with some information providing a framework of reference to the cultural exchange in which the titles had appeared. His First Secretary was kind enough to send me a letter from Bucharest which I quote briefly:

Dear Mr. Steinberg;

Enclosed are five Polaroid Land camera snapshots of the Embassy's window display of the three Rumanian titles published by you....I hope that the display itself pleased you and was of some effect in your negotiations with Rumanian publishers.

May I say again, personally, professionally and on behalf of Minister Crawford, how appreciative we are of your efforts to implement our exchange program....

Thank you once more for the list of important Rumanian contacts in the publishing field. It will be useful when the time comes to organize a reception honoring John Updike.

With kind regards,
Sincerely,

William A. Bell
First Secretary of the Embassy

I was given to understand that opportunities then for communication in the diplomatic area were severely restricted and that even getting together a list of publishing or literary dignitaries was a difficult task, as witness Secretary Bell's comment about the John Updike reception. I was glad to be useful to both sides. On my farewell visit, the American ambassador sent me back to my hotel in his official limousine with chauffeur and flags flying. I hope the Romanians were as impressed by my heightened visibility as I was!

My mention of Ambassador Crawford reminds me of the helpful role assumed by a number of people both inside and outside the diplomatic corps who recognized, I think, what Twayne Publishers was trying to do for Romanian-American literary relations. These people were in the main proceeding well beyond the call of duty and going to the length of some personal inconvenience to be helpful. Mindful that later visits to and from Romania (and Bulgaria, Poland, Yugoslavia, Hungary, and the Soviet Union) must have been the object of some unnecessary official attention, it is pleasurable to reflect that many in officialdom were determined to be helpful. The Voice of America interviewed me a number of times about our literary adventures.

Not in the helpful category was the interference with my mail that took place when President Nixon decided to visit Romania in 1969. I thought the occasion warranted an ad in the N.Y. *Times* with the heading, "Recommended Reading for All Travellers," describing all our Romanian titles and offering a vista for understanding the sights and sounds our President was experiencing at first hand. The ad was a fair-sized affair and scheduled for Sunday and the following or preceding Saturday (depending on space availability) on the occasion of Nixon's visit. It was sent special delivery to our advertising agency on July 7, destined for 655 Madison Avenue, less than two miles away from our offices at 31 Union Square in New York. It was not delivered until July 24, after Nixon's return. When I complained, the postal inspector had the nerve to ask me who had intercepted the letter. With this show of obtuseness on his part, I decided not to confide in him that I thought the President's men had something to do with it. Then I decided that I surely was entitled at least to the return of my special delivery fee. But no, said the postmaster, the mail was delivered...even if it was two weeks late. In thinking about it later, I was only slightly mollified by the thought that my Romanian activity had been noticed in the highest places of the land. There were other signs of official oversight. My business mail was frequently delayed, and I complained frequently that my phones were tapped during this period. A copy of the Twayne letter sent to the Complaints office of the Post Office on July 25, 1969 follows:

Gentlemen:

Enclosed is a copy of the special delivery envelope mailed on July 7 from Union Square West and received July 24 at 655 Madison Avenue.

We would like to have your explanation concerning this delay in delivery. May I also point out to you that other letters mailed that day have also been delayed in delivery. I am sure you will want to look into this matter as well.

I look forward to your response.

I was not deterred from going about my business but I did have some sleepless nights wondering what Big Brother was up to and why he wasn't in my corner.

One of the results of my 1964 visit was the first comprehensive anthology of Romanian prose ever to be published in the United States. This was entitled *Introduction to Romanian Literature* and was the first of a new series of Introductions providing representative anthologies of foreign literatures in translation for American readers. I was both the editor of the Romanian volume and of the series. It appeared in 1966. Perhaps the manner in which the anthology was compiled may be of interest to the professionals in this area. As I recall, a manuscript containing several times the number of stories that eventually appeared was sent in "rough" translation from Meridiane, the publishing house in Bucharest. All the stories were read by me, and I removed those that I regarded as unsuitable. A list of the removals was then sent to the Romanian editors to make sure that I had not removed a "diamond in the rough," for we were aware that a writer might be so mistreated in translation as to render his masterpiece unrecognizable. Thereafter, I graded the other stories in three categories, the last category providing the repository for additional deletions if necessary. Finally, the manuscript was ready for editing; the stage where all the ambiguities and infelicities had to be removed. It was this last stage that caused the most difficulty, largely because of the inordinate amount of time spent in getting answers to relatively simple queries. As I pointed out in the editor's preface to the anthology, I was grateful to two American professors in Bucharest on Fulbright exchange — Adrian Jaffe and Ralph M. Aderman — for heroic efforts to quicken the pace. The Twayne procedure was obviously trading time and home talent which we had in plentiful quantity, for dollars, which were then in meager supply. The ultimate result was good, however, though one discerning critic referred to the "creative" quality of the translation.

I think he was referring to the intuitive leaps I occasionally had to make when my queries went unanswered.

Professor Aderman helped Twayne again in 1968 when he edited Liviu Rebreanu's *Ion*. An English publisher's edition of this novel had been offered to us but was so largely the unedited Romanian manuscript put into print with all the "original warts and blemishes" that we had to decline the offer, though it would have saved us considerable expense. Aderman's work was, of course, thorough, scholarly, and professional in every detail.

Zaharia Stancu's *Barefoot* was the source of some publisher-author anguish. The problem related to the fact that we had accepted an early version of his Romanian classic that would have made a book of 250 pages. There were, however, no fewer than twelve editions in the Romanian, all varying to some degree and of differing lengths by the time our book was published in 1971. Imagine our consternation when Stancu's manuscript came into the office and it was obvious that what we had in hand was an epic that had to be published in two volumes, but for economic reasons not simultaneously. Stancu's reaction to our two-volume proposal was immediate and explosive, and the problem waxed and waned for a couple of years. Stancu, as the head of the Writers Union, had a lot of clout. Finally, however, when the book appeared, he was mollified. It was an exceptionally handsome book and experienced excellent reviews.

In 1972, we tried an experiment on which considerable thought had been expended in prior years. Essentially, this amounted to a barter arrangement; i.e., we would order titles from Romanian publishers and sell books from the Twayne list to the Romanians in equivalent dollar value.

In an earlier book exchange dating back to a visit in 1966, we had learned that we could not successfully distribute books that had been previously published in Romania without reference to our specific needs. Wholesalers here, as an example of an unanticipated difficulty, could not equate the titles which were in Romanian with the English equivalents by which they were being catalogued and ordered. There were other problems in connection with book exchanges but this difficulty alone cost us hundreds of copies in sales. Profiting from our experience, this time we commissioned specific titles to be produced for us in the book exchange area. The first of these, *Fairy Tales and Legends from Romania* was aptly titled both as to subject matter and source of origin for it was published in cooperation with the Eminescu Publishing House of Bucharest. It was a magnificent job of bookmaking, bound in silk, and with beautiful colored illustrations. The procedures involved selection and editing of the stories by Twayne. Thereafter, Twayne provided proofreading of galleys and pages. The books, however, were totally manufactured in Romania, as I have indicated, and free of duty and shipping charges.

The second volume in this unique arrangement was *History of the Romanian People*, compiled under the editorial direction of Andrei Otetea, and edited for Twayne by Professor Sherman D. Spector of Russell Sage. This was intended as the first volume of a projected series to be known as the "National Histories Series," which basically would provide views of history as the historians of a particular country interpreted events. Each book was to have an Introduction by an American specialist in the area which would provide a necessary framework of reference for the American reader. I thought the project might be helpful in airing disputes over ethnic and boundary disagreements and the like.

Another Twayne project relating to Romania was the inclusion of Romanian writers as a section in Twayne's World Authors Series.

In a number of Twayne catalogues I voiced my conviction that literature is preeminently a common ground on which all nations may stand, that writers, more than any other segment of a country's population, truly articulate national concerns, temperaments, and achievements or failures. In so doing, they provide a mirror of their times and provide a measure of comprehension that is indispensable to the attainment of international understanding. Perhaps I am inordinately proud of the fact that the company I headed was able to provide a modest bookshelf of foreign works in English translation which can be found in the more important libraries of America.

Regrettably, when Twayne became a part of a larger enterprise, the Romanian experiment was a casualty, as indeed were all of the East European bridge-building projects that had been so laboriously constructed. Ironically and paradoxically, little Twayne could successfully carry the ball but the project was deemed not feasible for

Twayne as a part of a unit of a then globe-encir-
cling giant communications company.*

Shortly before my trip to Romania in 1964, I
received a call from the Bulgarian cultural attaché in Washington. Mr. Peter Vassilev was an
energetic and concerned attaché and interested in
trying to find a publisher or distributor for books
of Bulgarian origin. I think he was attracted to
Twayne as a result of our activity on behalf of
Romanian books. But Bulgaria had no cultural
exchange agreement with the United States and
despite arduous endeavors we were not able to
achieve the same results. Still, even failure provides some lessons to ponder. We initiated our
interest by offering to publish a new edition of
Ivan Vazov's *Under the Yoke*. This was a highly
regarded classic of Bulgarian letters but badly out
of date for American readers, who had to rely on
either an old 1912 English edition or on the English translation that had been done in Bulgaria.
Neither seemed to be totally satisfactory to our
editor, Lilla Lyon Zabriskie. She did a superlative
job, so much so that the work was awarded a prize
in 1971, the year it was published, at the Sofia
Book Fair. Two years earlier, an anthology in my
Introductions series, edited for us by Frank Kirk,
for the American side, and Nikolai Kirilov, a Bulgarian, entitled *Introduction to Modern Bulgarian
Literature* had won the same award for 1969.

Despite these successes and my numerous visits, Sofia was a hard nut to crack. Things just did

---

*See Edwin McDowell's August 7, 1989 column in the N.Y.
Times, "As Book Companies Grow, They Seem to Become
Timid," a more comprehensive view of this phenomenon.

not work out. We had agreed to fund our publication program for Bulgarian books in the U.S. on the proceeds derived from a stock of titles published in Bulgaria in English translation. The books we received were badly scuffed. Far from the mint condition we expected, these books were obviously returned by dissatisfied customers to the Bulgarian warehouse. Moreover, they were supposed to be "on consignment." Apparently our definitions of the term differed radically. Still, we tried. I always had the uneasy feeling that I was the victim of contending forces representing different areas of power politics in Bulgaria. The edited manuscript of *Under the Yoke*, for example, was sent by air via diplomatic pouch to Sofia from the Bulgarian embassy in Washington. It disappeared for three months! With Romania I could deal with all elements of the cultural establishment through the embassy in Washington. Such was not the case with Bulgaria, though, as I have indicated, the cultural officer and even the Ambassador tried to be as helpful as they could be.

On my trips to Sofia I was usually greeted at the airport by someone from the American Embassy and someone from the Bulgarian side, frequently Ms. S. Stephanova of the Copyright Protection Agency. I recall on one such occasion the American Embassy representative insisted on VIP* treatment for me, carrying my luggage — heavy with reading copies of books from Romania which

---

*American Customs on my return were not so forthcoming when they learned where I had been. I was invariably given a thorough going-over.

I had visited first — and escorting me to my hotel. When we reached the desk for registration I could tell that his presence made a difference. Probably, I thought, this would make for surveillance. If there was, it was very discreet for I walked about Sofia quite freely on my own.

Much of the time I was taken on short trips to the surrounding countryside, visited various publishing firms to discuss projects, inevitably winding up sick from too much food and drink. I was no match for my hosts in re the latter. I recall an early morning business meeting following an evening of such debauchery that I had to hurriedly leave the room to deliver myself of the contents my stomach could no longer contain. I wanted to clean up the mess I left but my guide, a beautiful young lady, took it all in stride and said that I was not to be too greatly concerned. Perhaps she felt it was not all my fault.

America was not in favor on any of the occasions I visited. Regular denouncements took place when the Bulgarian legislature was in session. Out would walk the official American observer and his group and, invariably, that night the American Embassy's large store-sized display windows would be shattered. In the wintertime I could understand that this show of diplomatic displeasure had quite a drastic effect. I wondered what would have happened if an American diplomat had remained behind to listen to whatever complaint was being voiced. Had it spared the American Embassy windows in the wintertime I am sure embassy employees would have been grateful. I also could not help but reflect that at one time Americans were the Bulgarians' favorite people. Ivan Vazov, perhaps Bulgaria's most revered author, in a turn-of-the-century short story, had one of his characters in a card game voice this exhortation to a fellow cardplayer: "Play fair — be an American"!

Hungary was also a country in whose writings we were interested, and we projected an anthology of contemporary writing. Unfortunately, because of the illness of our editor, the volume was never published. However, some of the discussions concerning the make-up of the anthology are interesting because they reveal the intrusion of other than literary concerns, a perennial problem that I was to encounter again and again in dealing with the East European countries. I had visited Hungary to discuss the anthology with Dr. Gyorgy Botha of Artisjus, the Hungarian Authors Agency, and Dr. Eugene Simo, the director then of all publishing operations in Hungary. They had suggested that the anthology concentrate on the contemporary period because of the existence of an anthology along historical lines already published by Oxford University Press. As I wrote to our editor:

> There was some concern as to the inclusion of writers who are not resident in Hungary today, and some discussion was made of the fact that some of the emigre writers were politically motivated!...
>
> Our anthology, *Introduction to Modern Polish Literature*, ignores the status of the writer in terms of his geography and his politics and, consequently, is banned for private distribution in Poland. It may be ordered for institutional use. The Romanian anthology, however, which is billed as a literary introduc-

tion to Romania and its people, contains writings which are completely acceptable, with the result that a good deal of enthusiasm is being generated by the Romanians, naturally. I enclose a copy of the first review which has appeared, that of Radio Free Europe. As you can see, we fare rather well.

My own feeling is that if the anthology is to be regarded as representing the works of contemporary Hungarian writers, it might be possible to work closely with the Hungarians. If, on the other hand, the criteria you decide to employ are to be those of literary excellence only, then you may not get the same amount of cooperation or approval from them.

I impose no strictures on your editorial freedom, asking only that you be guided by professional considerations. It was for this reason that I decided to cut my visit short so that I would not compromise your situation. It would be a stroke of good luck if you could in conscience accept their suggestions but you will have to determine this for yourself...

As I indicated in the section on Romania, Twayne's interest in books from the Soviet Union originated with the Am-Rus Literary and Music Agency. I found the director, Edwin Smith, extremely helpful and professionally interested in furthering our efforts to find some common ground with the Soviets. Our first effort was a popularly written study of Russian medicine, translated and edited by William Horsley Gannt, M.D., then director of the Pavlovian Laboratory at Johns Hopkins. It was titled *The Achievement of Soviet Medicine*. It was followed by *Life in the Universe*, edited by Harvard astronomer Harlow Shapley and written by A.I.Oparin, a Moscow biochemist, and V. Fesenkov, an astronomer. It discussed the question of whether life can exist on other planets, particularly Mars and Venus. Neither of the books sold very well for us, but they did register our interest with Am-Rus and to the Soviets early on.

Later in the 1960's, when Soviet authors were again voicing their concern publicly about not being able to have their books published here, we tried to be helpful. Out of our meetings emerged a proposal called The Library of Contemporary Soviet Literature. It envisioned the selection by Twayne of titles nominated by the Soviet side. Translations were to be provided by the Soviets (Mezhkniga), passed on by Twayne editors, and published here. The Soviets were to agree to purchase copies for sale abroad, hopefully in the USSR. This provision became a standard feature of all my contracts with the European countries I dealt with — Bulgaria, Romania, etc. Aside from providing a built-in sale for the titles, it also provided an opportunity for the sale of other Twayne titles in Communist lands where the sale of foreign books was prohibited. Nothing came of the Library proposal, though it was the subject of many meetings and letters. The proposal was itself renewed a number of times over the years in one form or another, particularly when the participation of Soviet scholars in the Russian section of TWAS became a fact.

This interesting development came about as a consequence of Professor Nicholas P. Vaslef joining TWAS as Russian editor in 1966. He was with the USAF Academy as an associate professor of Russian at the time. He was also a colonel in the Air Force. In January of 1967, he wrote to me about his plans to enlist Soviet scholars to write books for his section. Both Bowman and I concurred. Eventually, we wound up with ten Soviet writers, but not all were those originally designated by Vaslef and therewith hangs an interesting tale.

Early on, Vaslef received a number of letters from the Russian scholars raising questions concerning royalties and translation fees and problems. I wrote to Vaslef concerning these matters:

> Regarding Professor P's question, I have to answer that we are limited in what we can do insofar as advancing money for the translations is concerned. The ideal procedure (for us) would be one in which the translator would be willing to receive his payment as the books are sold. As I have indicated to you earlier, the translation problem has never been satisfactorily settled. In some countries, Sweden, for example, the Swedish Academy has advanced varying sums for the translations of books written by Swedish scholars. This is an outright grant and does not require repayment, at least not by us. In a previous letter...I indicated that we would be willing to advance modest sums for the translations against authors' royalties if no other way could be found. Conceivably, some sources for this purpose could be found in the U.S. but I have not been successful in my approaches to the National Translation Center and I suspect that an effort would have to be made by a non-profit enterprise or individual to get any sort of help from foundation sources, ...we seem to be classified as a commercial or profit-making venture and, therefore, do not qualify. I think it wise to be completely frank in responding to Professor P's question, simply stating that, at the moment, no clear-cut source of revenue exists for the translations, outside of the limited advances which the publisher is willing to provide.

On the matter of royalties, I wrote: "Point out to Professor V. that he will for purposes of the contract be treated as an American author is treated with all the advantages this involves." I went on to describe the average sales achieved by the books at that time, that we hoped to see many of the books in paper editions, and that the average earnings ought to be better than was the case with critical studies then at most university presses. Professor V.'s work never arrived at the finishing gate.

The preceding will provide some basis for understanding my near jubilation when I received the following on April 2, 1968:

Dear Mr. Steinberg,

I am happy to inform you that the Novosti Press Agency Publishing House is ready to provide you with the manuscripts which we discussed with you...Novosti...also agreed to your financial terms to cover the expenses of writing and translation of the manuscripts into English. The material will be written by prominent Soviet authors and I hope to give you their names and the time of the manuscripts' arrival some time later...

The letter was signed George Isachenko, Information Department, Embassy of the Union of Soviet Socialist Republics.

I immediately answered Isachenko on April 4.

It may be that a slight misunderstanding exists which I should like to eliminate. Our editor has already contacted the Russian scholars whom he wishes to write books, and I believe that some have already informed him that they are willing to write the studies assigned to them. Of course, if the scholars who have been invited to write these books are unable or unwilling to accept our invitation, then we would ask you to suggest alternative writers to write the books we wish. I enclose a list of the scholars who have been invited to prepare the books we desire.

On May 17 Isachenko confirmed that Novosti had agreed with our choice of authors.

Vaslef thought his military affiliation might in some way prove detrimental to his good relationships with the Soviet professors. In a letter from Munich, he added: "Twayne has a very good reputation here...the Amerika Institut of Munich University has many of the TUSAS and TEAS volumes in their library...But they lack catalogues."

I sent him ten copies of our latest catalogue and wrote to allay his fears:

> I am hopeful that your military affiliation will not prove detrimental...Our catalogues and press releases identify you as being with the United States Air Force Academy and we have made no attempt to hide this affiliation ...On my several trips to Eastern Europe I have always tried to present the Twayne projects as a purely literary, cultural undertaking and I hope that they are so viewed by all parties concerned.

In the meantime, I decided to act on the Novosti Press connection that had been now established to revive some of the earlier proposals. Specifically, I asked Robert Milch, as a consulting editor, to visit Novosti on a trip he was making to the Soviet Union. He was unable to keep an appointment with Vladimir Bruskov, Editor-in-Chief of the Novosti House. He wrote to Bruskov on October 2,

1969, describing one of the perils of international publishing that he had encountered:

> I arrived in Moscow from Leningrad on Tuesday morning. While in Leningrad, however, I had the bad luck to fall ill. I was still ill when I got to Moscow, which is why I did not immediately get in touch with you, and, because my hotel room has neither heat nor hot water, and because the Intourist authorities have been unable to provide more adequate accommodations for me, my wife and I have thought it advisable to depart as soon as possible for the West and we are leaving early tomorrow morning for Switzerland. I am thus unable to visit you on behalf of Mr. Steinberg, as I originally intended...

He went on to inquire about the status of the ten manuscripts and to inquire about an exchange of books program similar to that which we had with Romania. Bruskov wrote back for more information and I answered on December 5, 1969. Bruskov's letter contained suggestions for additional subjects for the Russian section of TWAS. Many of these, however, were on writers of the 19th-20th centuries whom we had already assigned. Besides, we wanted to see how the ten studies we had already contracted for would turn out. I had some idea of the difficult terrain ahead as a result of my previous explorations. Ideally, I knew how translations should be handled, but we were not financially able to command ideal conditions. Bruskov wanted to change some of the terms of our authors series contract, and I had to explain that the contract was identical to all our other agreements on the authors series, and we could not deviate from it because we had pledged our authors that the terms would be identical for the scholar who wrote on a popular figure like Steinbeck or Faulkner and one who wrote on a comparative unknown. I think the argument that all authors would be treated equally was well received. The formula had its problems, but the Soviets finally agreed to our terms. Perhaps the fact that the Novosti contracts were to replace the individual contracts we had already signed with a number of the Russian scholars played a role. We could have published the manuscripts under these earlier agreements, without Novosti participation. Novosti, I was told some years later, when VAAP, the Soviet Copyright Agency was established, was not subject to the regulations that prevailed. It was beyond the law! (Where had I heard that before?) But in the USSR this was apparently the case. I assumed that Novosti was the Soviet counterpart of our USIA. That meant access to a lot of material not available to anyone else. It was a heady thought. Perhaps I had found the key to unlock the blocked funds or its equivalent.

My letter to Bruskov contained a good deal of information concerning Twayne's over-all publishing plans for foreign literature, and I quote therefrom:

> I am sorry too that Mr. Milch could not see you for he would have been able to describe at first hand what it is that we are trying to do. Perhaps, in the interest of mutual understanding, I should detail our program in greater length. In general, most of our books are sold to libraries and educational institutions, both at the secondary level and the college and graduate level. As a relatively small firm we

have a modest overhead and so we can make out with sales that the larger firms would regard as too limited. Too, we have made a virtue of necessity, and by confining our publishing efforts to the areas of specialization delineated by our catalog we have established a formidable library presence, so much so, that it is virtually impossible not to find the Twayne series books in any American library of any size. Many libraries have standing orders for our series titles and, of course, given an environment for growth, our literary children multiply.

A natural question arising from our series of critical studies is: If you have a book on a foreign author, why don't you provide some of his writing? To satisfy this need, we have started a translation program consisting of individual works and also of anthologies that can provide broader vistas of appreciation. The anthologies, of 300 to 500 pages, we call our Introductions series and thus far we have published five such volumes on Polish, Romanian, Spanish, Greek, and Bulgarian literature. We have others under way.

With the Romanians and with the Bulgarians we have been able to initiate publishing experiments, and I now feel that we can undertake, with some confidence, similar projects with other countries. We also think we have worked out a satisfactory formula for the Scandinavian countries, for the Netherlands, and certainly we would be very pleased to have your cooperation and your great writers.

In essence what we are offering is an exchange of books — our books for yours in the English language. However, because our experience has indicated that we cannot sell other publishers' books as well as we can our own, we ask that we be allowed to select the titles, edit the manuscripts which you provide in English translation, and have the manufacturing done in your country. (We would read proofs.) In some instances, it might be better to proceed with the manufacturing only to the point of reproduction proofs and have the books printed and bound here. We would pay for the books with our own books which we would supply at a discount of 50%. Each of us would pay our own transportation costs. And, of course, we could supplement the published books with imports of dictionaries, art books and the like.

Perhaps you will come up with other suggestions which we would be glad to entertain but since we are so very rich in books, I hope it can become a medium of exchange for us. Hopefully, if the approach is successful, more conventional methods can be used later on.

Professor Vaslef wrote on March 13, 1970, that he had received the first of the Soviet critiques.

At first glance, the monograph seems to be excellent. Of course there are strong ideological (Marxist) statements which overemphasize — I think — Marxist influence on Uspensky. My first thought is to leave all of these intact, lest the author is offended by the cutting, and, instead, write a disclaimer in a foreword, explaining to the reader that this book was written by a Soviet scholar from a Soviet point of view...

I thought his idea of a foreword a good one though the facts of Soviet identification with the studies was to be clearly indicated on the title page of our books. In a letter to I. Khokhlov of Novosti Publishing, dated June 12, 1970, I wrote concerning our agreement and this point:

With the exception of a phrase which we wish to add in paragraph 2, we are in complete agreement.

The phrase we wish to add are the words: "and edited by Twayne Publishers, Inc." which would follow "USSR."

Insofar as our future cooperation in relation to the book exchange idea is concerned, my letter to Mr. V. Bruskov of December 5, 1969, was an attempt to supply this information. I am enclosing a copy of this letter so you may consider it. My goal in this connection is to set up a continuing arrangement whereby works of fiction and belles-lettres generally can be provided for the English reading public in the form of a series to be called the Library of Soviet and Russian Literature. Prototypes for this project are already in existence for Scandinavian and Netherlandic literatures. A press release on the Library of Scandinavian Literature is enclosed for your information....We believe that if a way can be found, and I suggest the book exchange idea as such a way to get this program started, we shall have no difficulty in maintaining some success in our areas of sales, which are principally to libraries and educational institutions. I have discussed in some detail the plans for the Library with Mr. Isachenko of the Soviet Embassy, and I propose to send this letter and the signed contracts to him for transmittal.

On July 21, 1970, I received a letter from Mr. Isachenko:

While in Moscow I had the opportunity to discuss the implementation of the Library of Russian and Soviet Literature project. These ideas were met with enthusiasm. I will look forward to meeting with you in the near future in order to explain personally to you exactly what transpired.

Concerning your trip to Moscow from Frankfurt...our people at the APN Publishing House are anxious to meet with you. I think such a trip would be productive.

Despite the enthusiasm, I decided that the safer course of action was to wait, to test the quality of the manuscripts and the translations, and the cooperation we would receive. Colonel Vaslef was reporting difficulty with the first manuscript but nothing that he could not take care of. But the problems were time consuming and required correspondence with the author in Leningrad. A letter I wrote to Isachenko in Washington, dated November 3, 1971, was not reassuring:

> The volume of Uspensky has now reached the page proof stage. Many of the names provided in the draft index which accompanied the manuscript are not to be found in the text. Our Russian editor, and the in-house editor are of the opinion that the Uspensky volume, and possibly the following volumes, are translations of existing books which have been cut to meet our series requirements. If this is so, we think it would benefit the editors to receive either a copy of the entire Russian manuscript, or of the previously published book.

Vaslev's letter concerning the translations about a month later to our in-house editor, Ann Lindsay, was also discouraging. He wrote:

> ...Every one of the manuscripts sounds like a word-for-word translation from Russian, with no attempt to make smooth English constructions. I feel that Twayne's reputation would suffer if I were to overlook the stylistic atrocities perpetrated by the translators...

He went on in the same vein, indicating clearly how painful and laborious the problem was. I suffered with him because I had been through all of this before. Still, he persevered, and a letter to

Mrs. Lindsay a month or so later was more affirmative. Some excellent reviews of Professor Walter Vickery's *Pushkin* underscored Vaslef's prediction of a good year in 1972 for the Russian section.

But a problem other than literary soon made an appearance. Dr. Bowman's editorial assistant, Alberta Hines, wrote to Vaslef with a carbon to me that one of our Soviet scholars was in trouble. His manuscript had been turned down by APN (Novosti) as a "porochnaya kniga," ("vicious book"), the author had refused to alter it in accordance with the official directives, had appealed to no avail to the Board for the Protection of Authors' Rights, and had been told that "The APN is outside the law." Her letter of March 15, 1971 went on to say:

> Professor _____ is "forbidden" to correspond with us and sent the message through our correspondent who was visiting the USSR. He, having relatives in Russia, insists we must not only keep his name a secret but even the fact that we are aware of the true situation. Any attempt to smuggle the manuscript out of the country would, of course, be disastrous for the author.
>
> The gentleman writing the letter suggested that we could write to the APN and insist that the manuscript (and only his) be sent according to contract. It would seem to us that this would indicate we know what's going on and could make things more difficult for Professor _____. However, as the specialist in this area, Dr. Bowman suggested that you decide what course to follow.

I followed up with a letter on March 19, indicating that I thought it would be completely premature for us to attempt anything at the moment. I concluded with:

I think, in view of the nature of all the difficulties that may result and the fact that we are engaged in a project which has consequences well beyond the immediate confines of the Twayne program, that no course of action be taken by anyone without prior consultation among the Twayne membership, and that any official [Twayne] communication only be relayed through the Twayne office. I hope you agree with this.

Vaslef's letter of April 2, 1971 concurred with my views but is so illuminating as to what was going on in the USSR that I quote from it:

I feel very strongly that we have a moral obligation to protect our Soviet authors, as I am sure you will agree. Any attempt now to either communicate directly with Professor _____ or to smuggle his MS out of the Soviet Union, can only cause further difficulties for him.

A period of repression in literature (and other fields) has been going on in the USSR for some four years now. Part of it is due to the feeling of the post-Khrushchev leadership that writers were getting out of hand and that it was becoming increasingly difficult to determine what they could and could not write legally. A second, perhaps more important reason, but stemming directly from the first, is that underground literature — so-called *samizdat* — is flourishing now as it never had before. Finally, in preparation for the 24th Congress of the Communist Party of the Soviet Union, which is now in session, the party leaders called for stricter adherence to the ideological principles of Socialist Realism.

In an attempt to stop the dissident movement, Soviet authorities decided on a tough policy of censorship. This, however, has had the reverse of the intended effect: writers now know that the censorship is severe and do not even bother to submit possibly controversial manuscripts to the censors. They simply go underground from the very start. The authorities try to ferret out these writers and MSS, confiscate the MSS (which, in some cases, they later try to peddle in the West), and either imprison the authors or confine them to insane asylums (a fairly recent innovation).

I thought Vaslef had correctly analyzed the difficulty and so informed him. Since we had not received the manuscript and had had no direct word from the author we were really not in a position to determine the shortcomings, if any, of his manuscript.

I had had a similar sort of experience with a Polish writer, but not an author of a series book. In that case the author specifically requested us to do whatever we could to alleviate the situation. We were, therefore, able to proceed with his wishes, which, though transmitted indirectly to us, were unmistakably authentic, and to make representations on his behalf to the Authors Agency in Warsaw. I was clearly an interested party for fair treatment.

In June of 1972 I reported on a visit I had had with Isachenko's replacement at the Soviet Embassy, Anatoly A. Mkrtchian, who informed me that Professor _____ was sick but that a replacement of excellent academic standing was ready to do the book. I replied that since the contract had originally been signed by the author rather than the APN we would need word from him concerning his withdrawal. Mkrtchian also wanted to recruit other writers for us, particularly those of the Russian pre-Revolution era. I countered by presenting a frank report commenting on the deficiencies of the manuscripts we had received. Vaslef had written me:

> All of the Soviet authors we have are good scholars. The problem lies *not* in their knowledge of the subject, but first, the English translations which tend to be wordy, archaic, ponderous, and heavy-handed word-for-word translated from Russian. Secondly, the technical aspects of the manuscripts are poor, in that quotations are inaccurate — not only misspellings, but entire words are incorrect in all languages — Russian, English, and in the case of the Batyushkov ms., Italian and French. This is simply sloppy workmanship and is most time-consuming for the editor who must research various obscure works. Footnotes are either missing or numbered incorrectly, and the bibliography is a mess! But the scholarship is indisputably of a high order and makes all the work worth while.

On August 8, 1972, Mr. Mkrtchian confirmed that Professor____ had not fulfilled his contract and that the contract with him had been abrogated lawfully in 1969 by Novosti. He also indicated the other changes that had been made because authors had for one reason or another not fulfilled their agreements. All in all, four of the books were being written by other than the original scholars. But, as indicated earlier, it was not the competence of the scholars that was creating problems. It was the poor quality of the translations. Only a dedicated editor like Vaslef could make them whole, and he was spending an inordinate amount of time to do it, time for which we could not compensate him adequately. Mkrtchian also repeated that APN was still interested in the possibility of cooperating with Twayne on the suggested "Book for Book" project which I had broached several years before.

By then I had begun serious negotiations for the merger of Twayne with G.K.Hall and could no longer pursue the "Books for Books" initiative. And after the merger took place, it became apparent that bottom line considerations, and short term at that, were to be the guiding factors. A spring trip to the USSR had to be postponed to the fall but it finally took place at the end of September of 1974. I brought back a whole bag of projects but nothing was to come of them. Vaslef resigned as editor of the Russian section in December, 1974. I wrote, not as president of Twayne, which no longer existed as an independent entity, but with deep sincerity "to express my personal appreciation for your many professional contributions to the Twayne program. All of us have been aware of your insistence on the highest standards of scholarship and your positive approach to international understanding as exemplified by the presence of Soviet scholars in your section of Twayne's World Authors Series. With deep gratitude and best wishes..."

My bridge-building efforts continued after the merger, as I have said, but led nowhere. After my trip by invitation to the Soviet Union in September of 1974, I persisted with efforts to continue or revive Twayne's East European book publishing aspirations, including meetings with the various representatives of the countries involved and even went so far as to solicit a letter from the State Department as to the usefulness of the Twayne initiative in attaining our national objectives. I received such a letter on March 14, 1974, from

Ross P. Titus, Office of Soviet and Eastern European Exchanges, affirming the value of Twayne's endeavors, which I passed along to the head of G.K.Hall. It more or less repeated the sentiments of the letter I had received earlier, in August, 1965, from Frank G. Siscoe, Director Soviet and Eastern European Exchanges Staff of the State Department, on the occasion of his leaving on another assignment. Mr. Siscoe wrote:

> The exchanges programs touch nearly all areas of human activity and I have had, since February 1960, an unusual opportunity to associate with various sectors of American life. In this effort, I have worked with individuals, representatives of organizations and institutions, and government officials. All have reflected the diversity, accomplishments and strengths of American society. It has been a warming and rewarding experience.
> It would not be possible to leave without expressing my appreciation to you for your interest in these programs, your support for them, and your understanding of our national objectives.

Mr. Titus made the additional observation:

> ...We know that there is some concern among some officials in these countries over the difficulties they face in marketing their publications in the United States, including their essentially politically neutral classics. On the other hand, they are aware of the great desire among Eastern Europeans to read everything they can get from the United States. While there is little that U.S. Government agencies can do to help expand the market here for Eastern European authors in translation, I believe that your interest in giving Americans opportunities to read Eastern European authors in translation serves two important aims: providing wider access to signifi-

cant literature which otherwise may be available to only a small circle of specialists, and reassuring some concerned Eastern Europeans that the publications exchanges are mutually beneficial.

I hope you will be able to continue to give Eastern Europe an important place in your publishing plans...

This also had no discernible effect. In 1977, when I visited the Soviet Union again, on the occasion of the First Moscow Book Fair, where I headed a delegation of Jewish book publishers, and visited APN, it was apparent that all bridge building had ceased. My efforts on behalf of Jewish books in the USSR are detailed on pages 192 ff. below.

Yugoslavia was another country with which I tried to set up a publishing program. Unfortunately, my efforts took place relatively late, the first book, *An Introduction to Yugoslav Literature*, being released in 1973 after the merger but before the handwriting on the wall had become clear. After my trip to the USSR in 1974, I stopped off in Belgrade to see what could be done. Nothing, apparently, though I came back with a number of suggested projects which the Yugoslavs recommended. The bottom line wouldn't support them.

There were two other foreign areas in which Twayne launched significant book projects. Both of them were terminated shortly after the merger. The first of these involved the Scandinavian countries. We were fortunate here in learning through Mr. Erik J. Friis of the American Scandinavian Foundation's interest in a publishing program which would bring outstanding writers, past and present, of Denmark, Finland, Iceland, Norway, and Sweden to the attention of the English-reading world. As a consequence of this, in 1966, we began to issue these works under the rubric of The Library of Scandinavian Literature. As general editor, Erik was both knowledgeable and energetic. More than twenty titles were issued, ranging from translations of the old sagas to contemporary poetry, drama, and fiction.

Supplementing the Library was the Scandinavian section of Twayne's World Authors Series, edited by Leif Sjoberg. Professor Sjoberg was equally diligent and enlisted many Scandinavian scholars to write series books for Twayne. Frequently, these studies required translation into English and Leif was able to make the necessary arrangements with foundations abroad for this purpose. When Twayne was merged in 1973, ten titles had appeared, including studies of Ingmar Bergman, Halldor Laxness, Emanuel Swedenborg, and Nobel Laureate Par Lagerkvist. At least another thirty or so studies were projected. Sjoberg was himself a gifted translator, having collaborated with Muriel Rukeyser in translating *Selected Poems of Gunnar Ekelof*, issued by Twayne, and with W.H. Auden in *Markings*, a posthumous collection of Dag Hammarskjold's reflections and poetry. Both Sjoberg and Friis were honored by a number of the Scandinavian countries.

The second project was The Library of Netherlandic Literature and followed the example of the Scandinavian project. The cooperating parties were the Foundation for the Promotion of the Translation of Dutch Literary Works and Twayne Publishers, Inc. Representing the foundation was its director, Mr. D.J.J.D.de Wit and the editor for Twayne, Professor Egbert Krispyn of the University of Georgia, who also was the Netherlandic editor for Twayne's World Authors Series. My initial meeting with Mr. de Wit took place in early 1969 and by the end of the year we had evolved an agreement to publish two to three books a year by contemporary Dutch or Flemish authors, the sponsoring governments, Belgium and Holland, agreeing to a prepublication purchase for each title, enabling Twayne to advance $500.00 against royalties to the authors. I thought it a good deal for all concerned. Since we were dealing with contemporary writers, there was always the possibility of a breakthrough with some book of fiction that could command sales of commercial proportions. Moreover, I thought the Library would complement our critical studies. Incidentally, it was Professor Krispyn who initiated an inquiry on my behalf to the Modern Humanities Research Association concerning the possible use of royalty funds frozen in Eastern Europe. Louis Paul Boon's *Chapel Road* was the first title issued by the Library. It was followed by an anthology, *Modern Stories from Holland and Flanders*, *A Matter of Life and Death* by Anna Blaman, *Lament for Agnes* by Marnix Gijsen, *The Deeps of Deliverance* by Frederik van Eeden, *The Coming of Joachim Stiller* by Hubert Lampo, most of these published by Twayne after the merger. Professor Krispyn, like all of the Twayne series editors, was insistent on a high quality performance in the translations.

Another area of interest for me was China, but I was not to have the pleasure either professionally or personally of visiting that country until 1982 and 1983. I have already detailed my postwar interest in continuing with my Chinese studies and how this led to the founding of Twayne. While the *Dream of the Red Chamber*, was to have been our first book in the area, its long gestation period enabled several other books to precede it. The first of these was *Current Chinese Readings*, a Chinese language text, prepared by Chi-chen Wang, and intended primarily for his classes at Columbia University. It included excerpts from the writings of Mao, Hu Shih, Chiang Kai-shek, Kuo Mo-Jo, Chu Teh, Lusin, and attempted a balance between cultural and literary subjects and matters of political or topical interest. It appeared under the Bookman Associates imprint in 1950.

In 1951, Twayne released Robert A. Elegant's first book, *China's Red Masters*. The volume won for its author, then a graduate student at Columbia's School of Journalism, a Pulitzer Fellowship and launched Elegant on a distinguished career in journalism and writing as a novelist.

Over the years we published quite a number of titles dealing with Chinese philosophy and history. Among them were Carsun Chang's *Third Force in China, Development of Neo-Confucian Thought* (2 volumes), *Tibet: Today and Yesterday* by T.T. Li, *Within the Four Seas* by H.H. Chang, *Woodrow Wilson's China Policy* by T. Y. Li, and, of course, Wang's translation of the *Dream of the Red Chamber*, which was to run into a curious bedfellow, a rival translation by way of the German language issued by Pantheon. We didn't need the competition of another *Dream*, and one very well received critically, but still we did well enough, Doubleday finally accepting our version for its Anchor Books.

The next development in this area was the China section in Twayne's World Authors Series. Again we were fortunate in attracting an energetic and capable scholar to assume editorial control. This was Professor William Schultz, then Director of Oriental Studies at the University of Arizona. In an interesting exchange of letters with Sylvia Bowman, he suggested (July 15, 1970) that the "mix and organization of biographical, historical, and critical-analytical elements in books on nonwestern writers might be rather different than in those on western writers....Of the forty-two studies presently under contract in the China section, approximately thirty-six will represent the first such publication on the subject in English. In most cases, nothing is to be found on the subject in any major western language. Moreover, monographic length studies of a significant number of the subjects are not even to be found in Chinese or Japanese..." He thought that authors on non-western subjects ought to be allowed some latitude in following the prescribed format of the series books. His point was logical and well taken.

But so was Bowman's response (July 24, 1970):

...we have no intent in any of the series of fitting

any author-subject into a Procrustean bed...[but] the major part of these books should be devoted to critical-analytical discussion, the major reasons for writing the books in the first place.

She went on to point out that even in the U.S. Authors Series,

about forty percent is of first books about the subject authors...Moreover we have published over three hundred volumes...and I think it is now too late to change our intentions...I hope you will understand that, in summary, there is leeway in the series for what you want; there is not, however, any opportunity to change the stipulations for one section of the series....

I was not a hands-off head of house, but I had no inclination to get involved in this exchange. But, frequently, despite the best of intentions and the desire to be helpful, I did find myself in hot water. Such was the case with one of the TEAS books where I found Twayne on the verge of publishing a book that had not been approved for release and had eluded the safeguards we had set up against such occurrences. It only happened once, just short of printing, and my guard was up thereafter. But frequently I was called on for guidance as was the case with the TWAS volume on the ancient Chinese classic, *The Book of Songs*. The author of our study received a rather stiff bill for permissions, a perennial problem, and one to which I refer elsewhere as a form of hidden censorship. My letter (May 28, 1969) to Professor William McNaughton pointed out:

...whatever money is paid out for use of the materials would be chargeable against author's royalties...consequently, whether we advance the money or not, the fees ought to be as reasonable as possible.

From my previous experience...I would say the fees
are high...It would be entirely in order to get them
reduced...You might try the usual gambit of pointing
out that this is not an anthology but a critical work
which unquestionably would stimulate interest in
the authors quoted [Ezra Pound, e.e. cummings,
William Carlos Williams] and intimate that, while
you would prefer using all of the material...if the
financial conditions remain so onerous you would
have no choice but to cut drastically....I have had
many such letters from people who wish to use our
material and I frequently find myself reducing the
fee requested.

Another exchange with the author of *Tu Fu*,
Professor A.R.Davis of the University of Sydney,
calls attention to another frequently encountered
problem. It had been our practice, born of necessity* to send printed pages in advance of binding

---

*I prided myself on being the world's best proofreader and so I
was startled in the early days of Twayne to be taken to task
in an otherwise favorable review in the *N.Y. Times Book Review* for the transposition of lines in a scholarly book we had
published on the young Henry James. In those days of hot
metal, it was quite possible for linotype lines to be scrambled
in the handling. But I had personally slugged the lines on
this particular book before printing and knew that what had
happened couldn't possibly have occurred. It turned out that
in the page make-up before printing the worker had dropped
a galley of type and had not notified his superior but had relied on his own inadequate proofreading talents, with the results reported on in the *Times*. I got an apology and rectification
from the printer, but I felt the damage to our firm was incal-
culable even though we were not to blame. After that accident we tried to avoid a recurrence by providing the author
with a set of printed sheets before binding. Apparently, even
today in the era of computer typesetting it is still possible to
change the contents of a publication after it has been put to
press as the recent flap over the insertion of anti-Semitic material in *The Dartmouth Review* indicates.

to an author, who then had one final chance to reread his immortal words. We undertook to make any corrections involving transpositions of lines or faulty pagination — mishaps that might have occurred since the last handling of proofs — but we would not be willing to undertake the expense for any error of lesser magnitude. I wrote:

> ...I think you may not have understood that what we sent you were printed pages, not page proofs. This means that in order to make any of the changes you wish would require reprinting of the sections [involving 16 or 32 pages] and this would make for a considerably greater delay than the errors which you have pointed out would seem to warrant. Many of them are simply matters of preference rather than incorrect spellings. For example, "traveler" can be spelled with two "l's" as well as with one. The question of whether a unit modifier should be hyphenated or not is really not something to stop the presses for.... There are others which should be corrected, and I propose that we print an errata slip which could be inserted in the book. Then, after we have exhausted the first small printing...we can reprint with all of the corrections you have indicated, and perhaps with some more which usually turn up after a book has been around for some time...

The author was also concerned about the distribution of his book in Australia and in England. We had distribution in both areas but I was glad to have his concern, which I shared, and told him that I would write to the company handling Australian distribution and invited him to do so as well. I was always glad to avail myself of an author's offer to help and, more often than not, authors were helpful.

In this connection, I shall never forget Lady Dorothea Turner of New Zealand, author of the TWAS title, *Jane Mander.* This gallant lady deserves a special tribute from me; she and I engaged in an experiment to see if the Twayne New Zealand titles could be sold in satisfying quantities. She operated as a wholesaler for us in New Zealand, utilizing the premises of an existing business, and in a short span began to promote and sell the TWAS New Zealand titles we sent on consignment. She put on a most impressive performance, must have been well connected, and was obviously a friend of Twayne in particular and of books in general. I quote briefly from some of her letters but sufficient I think to show why I thought so highly of her, a lady I never met.

The books you sent are beginning to move. I put an ad in one of our two literary quarterlies; the other will run it in a few weeks, and there have been mentions in other places. Plenty more still to be done; but at least the cognoscenti have an address to apply to now and can follow through the interest aroused by some excellent reviews.

My bookseller consultant agrees with me that it would greatly help the NZ series to put with it the volume on *Katherine Mansfield* which is No. 23 in TEAS. Mansfield is still the leading NZ writer on every study list...I suggest 50 copies.

I'm just beginning on the libraries. The response there is slow because...[of] an Act granting authors royalties on library borrowings. The accountancy this involves has temporarily paralysed libraries.

Having grown up in a family of writers...I'm well used to hearing how little authors earn; but it's only these last few weeks, since entering the book trade, that I've realised how little publishers get out of

books. How do you do it at the price? The middle-
men's share — distribution, advertising, retail —
seems disproportionate.

Other letters indicate continuing activity on
Twayne's behalf: meetings with the permanent
secretary of the New Zealand Booksellers Association, librarians, reviewers who registered the
complaint in print about the unavailability of the
Twayne books, "and the methods of distribution
(or nondistribution) in the NZ book trade. The
book trade is somewhat chastened at last, as well
it should be." Unfortunately, the merger put a
stop to this activity. My view was that this was
excellent P.R. and could be justified for this reason alone but when the Twayne operation moved
to Boston, a more formal overseas distribution
procedure probably put an end to this promising
experiment to put Twayne in the forefront of New
Zealand literary consciousness.

I mention in my Introduction two wartime fellow students who crossed my publishing path.
One of them was Julian Schuman, who wrote a
book, *Assignment China.* The book is out of print
but should be revised, updated, and reissued.
Schuman had studied Chinese at Harvard while
in the army but had joined the Japanese cryptanalysts group in Virginia, where I met up with
him. He had tried to no avail to get to China
under U.S. Army auspices. After the war, he decided to pursue a journalism career in China. He
arrived in Shanghai at the end of 1947 and finally
landed a job as a rewrite man for the *China Press,*
an English-language publication. Two months
later, he was officially installed as city editor with

a salary of sixty million CNC (Chinese National Currency). Inflation was so rampant that this could not have amounted to more than $200.00 a month, about twice his starting salary as a re-write man. In the meantime, Schuman also became a stringer for the Chicago *Sun Times*. Feeling secure with his part-time activity with the *Sun Times* Schuman left the *China Press* to take on a temporary post with the *China Weekly Review*, an English-language journal which had been founded by J.B. Powell, an American journalist who had been decorated by the American government and applauded for his resistance to the Japanese invasion and occupation during WW II. Schuman's part-time post ended in 1948. In the meantime, starting in 1948, he wrote Sunday feature articles for the Denver *Post* and then became China correspondent for the American Broadcasting Company. In 1949, the People's Republic issued an order forbidding correspondents to work for publications of countries with which it had no diplomatic relations. In the early spring of 1950, Schuman became, as he put it, "...the dean — and sole member — of the American press corps in China." It was then that Schuman again joined the *Review* and remained as associate editor during the Korean war until the summer of 1953 when the magazine ceased publication. Schuman left for home in the United States by the end of 1953. He joined Twayne as a part-time editor and continued until he and Mrs. Powell, as associate editors of the *Review*, were indicted on a charge of sedition along with the son of J.B. Powell, John William Powell, who had taken over the *Review* on his father's death. Schuman left Twayne in order to raise money for his legal defense.

The government charged that Powell and his associates had published certain statements knowing them to be false "with the intent to interfere with the success of the armed forces" in Korea. Among the statements published was the charge, which first appeared in the Chinese press, that the U.S. used Korea as a testing ground for gas weapons and germ warfare. There also was some feeling that the *Review* in printing the names of American prisoners of war which it had also received from Chinese sources had thereby incurred the enmity of the State Department, which felt it should have had priority in the release of the names. Be that as it may, the case dragged on for a number of years before it was dismissed. The accused, apparently, were not permitted to bring a number of defense witnesses from China, including the military, to testify to the truth of the *Weekly Review* statements. Schuman, of course, had to abandon his journalistic career in the U.S. Today, however, he writes a column for the *China Daily*, an English-language publication in Beijing, which is widely read.

My other *tung shwe* (fellow student), Sidney Shapiro, studied Chinese with me at Cornell University. At the time, his interest in the subject seemed to take second place to the pulchritudinous attractions of the Ithaca co-eds. But once we left that beautiful scene for our barbed-wire installaton on Oahu, his love for the Chinese language — and I assume all other appurtenances thereto attached — became insatiable. He selected the midnight shift for his cryptanalyst duties, I am convinced, so that he could pursue his Chinese studies at every odd opportunity. And those moments were far more plentiful on the midnight shift than on any other. Both he and Schuman continued their studies at the University of Hawaii while on Oahu and were unceasing but unsuccessful in attempting to arrange a transfer, in which plans I was included, to China duty. After the war, Shapiro continued his Chinese studies, briefly at Columbia University but more fully at Yale. He wrote an autobiography, *An American in China*, which describes his years in China from 1947 on. It was published in paperback in the United States by New American Library in 1949. It recounts his life in China until 1979, a period of more than thirty years that was to witness the Korean War, the victory of the Communists over the forces of Chiang Kai-shek, the Cultural Revolution and the Gang of Four — truly a swirl of tumultuous events.

In 1948, Shapiro married Fengtze (Phoenix), a former Chinese actress and editor. Their daughter, Ya-mei (Ya for Asia;Mei for America) was born in January, 1950.

There was no need in China for an American trained lawyer, which Shapiro was by profession, and Shapiro gradually became a recognized translator of note. About twenty volumes of novels, poetry, and short stories are attributed to him. Two of these were published in the U.S., including the famous classic, *Outlaws of the Marsh*, published by Indiana University Press. He is also the compiler of *Jews in Old China: Studies by Chinese Scholars* issued recently in paperback by Hippocrene Books, the publishers also of the hardback edition.

Shapiro became a Chinese citizen in 1963, but continued to receive special privileges as a foreign expert. He writes in his autobiography: "I was somewhat troubled by the special privileges which the Chinese insisted that I retain. I drew the same relatively high pay as before, went on the annual free travel tours, still got a month's paid vacation, received complimentary tickets to the theater and sporting events, was invited to state banquets, had a place in the reviewing stands on national holidays..." In brief, he seems to have been accorded VIP status, which he enjoys even today. He is a member of the Chinese People's Political Consultative Council — China's highest national advisory body, which was set up by Teng Hsiao-ping. With the publication of *Jews in Old China* Shapiro seems to have become China's "maven" on Jewish affairs and delegate to a number of Jewish symposia and conferences, particularly in the Far East. A secular Jew, he is what the cognoscenti would call a "knapper Yid"* but he does seem to enjoy his newfound Jewish celebrity status which most recently has led to his being invited by the Jerusalem International Book Fair — "all expenses paid," he writes — where presumably the Hebrew-language edition of *Jews in Old China* will be on exhibit.

Over the years Shapiro and I have kept in

---

*"One who is 'short,' hence 'deficient' in Jewish learning and practice." He writes in his autobiography: "At thirteen, in 1928, I had my first and last encounter with the ancient religion of my ancestors. Under strong parental pressure I learned enough Hebrew to make a brief Bar Mitzvah speech... alleging that, 'Today I am a man.'"

touch. On his fairly frequent visits to the U.S., starting with 1971, I have been able to meet with him to discuss publishing or editorial problems and reminisce. In 1983, as senior editorial consultant to Hippocrene Books, I visited Beijing along with Hippocrene's publisher, George Blagowidow and his wife, Ludmilla. Hippocrene had just acquired Lee Publishing, a firm that had spent a lot of money in a largely unsuccessful effort to establish an on-going relationship with Chinese publishers. I had gone to China in 1982 to scout the situation for Hippocrene which seemed promising enough to warrant another visit the following year. George and his wife went on a tour of China to test the text of a new travel book, *The Official Guidebook to China.* I stayed on in Beijing to discuss new projects and to try to settle some of the problems Hippocrene had been saddled with as a result of the Lee acquisition. Shapiro was helpful in arranging some meetings and in passing along a suggestion that I thought would be useful to any American publisher who was interested in selling books of Chinese origin in English translation. It seemed to me that a ready market existed for those books among the growing numbers of tourists from English speaking countries. Whether in response to this suggestion or not, something of the sort is now going on in some of the hotels in China. Books are sent on consignment at substantial discount. I do not know how wide an opportunity there is at present but I do know that quite a number of copies of the hardbound edition of *Jews in Old China* were sold in this manner. The paperbound should probably sell considerably greater quantities in this fashion.

I have urged Shapiro to update and revise his autobiography. The result should be valuable and widely read, particularly if he is allowed to write freely about the exciting events that he has witnessed. He has also undertaken to write the biography of George Hatem, the American doctor who wiped out (for a time) venereal disease and greatly diminished leprosy in China. According to Shapiro the subject was one that interested Harrison Salisbury, Han Suyin, and Jackie Kennedy as an editor for Doubleday.

V

Tsurris[*]

IN ANY BUSINESS THERE ARE TIMES WHEN DISASTER strikes, when, seemingly there is no way out. My experience indicates that occasionally there are solutions, sometimes surprisingly successful ones. But, of course, at other times *tsurris* remains intractable and has to be endured.

I have been eternally grateful that my friends at Chase Manhattan turned me down for a loan in the late 1960's. President Johnson's Great Society program had created a multi-million dollar library market for books, and Twayne with its multi series was beautifully positioned in terms of product to take advantage of the situation. What we needed was money to reach every library in the United States with our direct-mail promotions. High school and college libraries, public and private libraries of every size and dimension were our goals. It did not matter that a library had a

---

*Troubles, usually big ones.

non-existent budget; I wanted it covered if it was functioning. To operate, it had to have access to funds, I reasoned. I felt that if I could cover them all, even in a cooperative mailing with other publishers sharing the cost, it would be a profitable promotion for our series books and would counter the efforts of our well-heeled competition — Prentice Hall, Holt, Barnes and Noble, to name a few — who had mounted similar series undertakings. Some of these competitors commented later on the success of our direct-mail activity in this area, and I quote from a note dated February 20, 1971:

> By the way your remarkable success with the Twayne Authors Series surprised me when I was at Barnes and Noble, where I had to turn over our similar series to Al Edwards of Holt, Rinehart and Winston. We did the wrong things just when you were doing the right ones.
>
> Cordially,
>
> Dr. Samuel Smith

But I have gotten somewhat ahead of the story of the encounter with my friends at Chase Manhattan. By 1968 or so, we had been a customer for eighteen years, including several small loans, had survived a disastrous series of notes signed in blank about which I write elsewhere, and enjoyed in general very cordial relations with the local branch manager. I thought the time might be ripe to try for a loan of $25,000, more than enough to cover my ambitious plans for circularizing the libraries. I described my plans to my banker friend, and waited for the response which he promised shortly. It came some days later in the form of an invitation to lunch in the bank's executive dining room with him and a vice president from headquarters. With that kind of cordial reception, I began to congratulate myself, prematurely as it turned out, on having reached the big time — a business loan without personal guarantees! Gently, very gently, his remarks cushioned by the excellent food and the alcoholic beverages I imbibed, my friend at Chase told me how much the bank appreciated the Twayne account, the obvious growth he had noted over the years...but how could I expect them to regard book inventory as collateral? I had a house,* an automobile, some bank accounts. Since I was so sure of success, why didn't I want to go along with the bank's need for personal guarantees?

I thanked them, promised to get back in a day or two, but this time I was determined to change the tune. I felt the business had reached the point where it ought to be able to borrow funds on its own.

About a year earlier I had been struck by a thought. Many of the libraries were ordering our series books on a standing-order basis. While they had the right to return these books for whatever reason, all of the books, practically speaking, were in effect purchased. What would happen, I wondered, if we offered a plan to let them buy and pay for these books in advance? I created a concept which I called the Twayne Lifetime of the Series Subscription (TLSS), and prepared a letter offering these books at "today's prices for tomorrow's delivery" when the price, I pointed out, inevitably would be much higher. In exchange for

---

* My wife's parents' home.

their prepayment, libraries could in effect control the inevitable inflation in book prices that was everywhere apparent. Since they were ordering our series books anyway, I suggested, why not take advantage of our offer? I also alluded to the fact that their prepayment would be helping us finance the unprecedented critical coverage of the world's literature we had undertaken. I made up an invoice for enclosure, guaranteeing future delivery of 350 titles each in TUSAS and TEAS, 800 in TWAS, and 200 in Twayne's Rulers and Statesmen of the World (TROW). Libraries were free to order in whole or in part any of the preinvoiced books. But not infrequently what I got back was an exact copy of my invoice as a purchase order, along with a check for the prepayment in the amount of $6230.00.

To the libraries who wrote that their standing orders had already yielded a hundred or more books, I pointed out that their order could be applied to multiple purchases of the more popular series books — the Faulkners, Hemingways, Chaucers, etc. — which would be needed eventually as replacements. I was determined not to forego a single order if I could help it and to permit libraries to use up any unspent dollars left in their annual budgets, an irresistible appeal for any budget conscious librarian aware of how unspent funds would impact next year's budget.

Our accountant's initial reaction to the plan had been negative, and I did not pursue it immediately, as I have said, but when the bank's response required personal guarantees for the loan, I decided to go ahead with the plan, at first limiting it to our library subscribers but advising the library wholesalers that they could place TLSS orders with us for their customers. In this way they too could participate in our success and help spread the word about our plan.

The results were electrifying. I had sought a loan of $25,000 with interest. What we eventually received by the time the plan was ended (against my advice) after the merger was almost five times that amount, interest free! And presumably our library jobbers had received an equal sum since half of our sales in those years were going to jobbers, who were participating in our plan. Moreover, what we had accomplished beyond dispute was the permanent placement of the Twayne series in libraries throughout the United States. When the budget crunch hit the libraries some years later and did not permit the choice of several critical studies on a subject author, it was frequently the prepaid Twayne series title that was given priority.

Why was the TLSS project discontinued by my successor? While I was not privy to the reasons, I would assume the objection to the plan was similar to that I had already heard. Principally the objectors pointed out that paying today's prices for books that might be published five years hence provided the purchaser with discounts that could not be accommodated by the usual pricing/cost structure of four to one, i.e. a book costing $1.00 had to be priced at $4.00.

My counter to this was to observe that adding 50 to 100 copies per title to the print runs to accommodate these orders (50 copies per title, meaning 50 advance subscriptions @ $6000.00 per TLSS) was not at all ruinous, adding little more than $1.00 per book. Moreover, the method was a dandy for sweeping up year-end surpluses in any library's budget. In addition, the terms of future TLSS orders could be modified to reflect the economic conditions that prevailed in any given year. What was very satisfying to me, in addition to the interest-free loan, was the fact that our publishing program had earned this solid endorsement from its patrons, the libraries of America. Maybe, after all, it was the recognition that at Twayne the emphasis was on "BOOKS not bucks" as an ad of ours in *Publishers' Weekly* headlined that made the whole thing work for this small publisher.

A smaller entry in the creative conversion of *Tsurris* department was made possible by a jacket printer, who created what I euphemistically called "lifetime jackets," i.e. jackets that were actually if inadvertently glued to the books so that they could not be removed. We had used a small firm over the years to print most of our book jackets. The firm was headed by two distinguished Austrian refugee printers who parted company after many years. Our relationship was cordial but not perfect. In the early years, as I have clearly indicated, we were not the first to pay their bills. On the other hand, there were many small infelicities that they perpetrated, which we overlooked. But we got along, and I think we respected one another. After the parting of the two principals we continued with the successor firm at the request of one of the principals, who told us that he would continue to look after our interests, though the firm was being run by others. One day we were rewarded with the new "invention," the non-removable jacket. About ten titles were involved, 10,000 bound books with permanent jackets and 20,000 plus jackets printed for the unbound books when they would be needed.

When we first encountered the problem, we thought the binder had to be at fault. But a subsequent investigation revealed the problem. The paper used for the jackets apparently was a job lot that had had some kind of paste or mucilage applied to the non-printing sides. When heat was applied in the binding process it caused the lifetime adhesion. The suppliers of the binding material, an imported vinyl with naturally adhering qualities, particularly in the summertime, offered to provide free material to rebind the books; the binder also cooperated, offering a special price for repairs — but the printer, the one actually responsible for the disaster, not only refused to reprint the jackets, but demanded payment for the additional faulty jackets he had supplied but for which we had not yet paid because of the difficulties already encountered. We had no choice but to sue. I was particularly upset when the printer confronted me in my office and obscenely threatened me so that it could be heard all over the place.

The court ruled against him for the financial damages we had incurred. The incident was a needless aggravation that could have been avoided by the printer had he recognized our common involvement. He also lost a customer.

I tried to convince our librarian customers that lifetime jackets supplied at no additional charge were actually a bargain — many libraries go to the expense of gluing jackets to the books — but to no avail. We had to rebind the lot. But the *English Journal* at the time was running a series about inexpensive materials with which to enhance the classroom, and I pointed out that our jackets, which carried a picture of the author discussed, were very suitable for display in the classroom. I offered them at cost and managed to get orders for quite a number. It didn't quite duplicate the TLSS success story but it does belong in the same genre.

My next entry in the *Tsurris* department concerns the Jews in the Soviet Union. Jews and *tsurris* are, of course, old friends. Well, maybe not friends, but certainly reluctant long-time companions. Where there is the one, there always is the other. My involvement took place some years after the merger so it was not exactly a Twayne affair. But there is a connection, as you will note.

In 1974 I became president of the Association of Jewish Book Publishers (AJBP) and remained in office until 1981. The Association had been founded in 1962 as a non-profit group to provide a forum for the discussion of mutual problems by publishers, authors, and other individuals and institutions concerned with Jewish books. In 1977, when the Soviet Union announced its First Moscow Book Fair, the Association decided to participate and to set up what was then a unique and unheard-of exhibit of Jewish books in the USSR. I headed the delegation and wrote an article describing the event. What I say about our experience — the censorship, the official harassment, the uncertainties, and the tumultuous welcome by

Soviet Jews — is fairly typical of what took place every two years from 1977 on, until the advent of Gorbachev's reforms. Mounting a Jewish book exhibit at each of the Moscow Book Fairs constitutes the AJBP's finest "hour" — a decade and more in which it was privileged to serve as the means by which American Jews were able to convey a sense of unity and pride through the instrumentality of thousands of books of Jewish interest to their Soviet co-religionists. The article appeared in the May-June 1978 number of *Freedom At Issue*, a Freedom House publication to which I am indebted for permission to reprint the material which follows:

THE MOSCOW BOOK FAIR — REVISITED

For the first time in three decades, a collection of books of Jewish culture and religion saw the light of public day at the 1977 Moscow Book Fair. Can Soviet Jews read hope for the future into this remarkable event — or is it to be a one-time-only phenomenon? After being permitted to display their wares at the recent Soviet book fair in Moscow, American Jewish book publishers find that an official Russian journal has made a vitriolic attack on them. Their spokesman here expresses bewilderment at the turnabout. Interestingly, the author was the founder of a U.S. publishing firm that pioneered in Soviet literature and minority views — including the earliest examples of black poetry, as well as anti- and pro-Zionist religious books in the Jewish field.

It is now almost six months since the Soviet Union's first International Book Fair took place in Moscow last September. Most of us hoped, despite contrary evidence of dissident imprisonment and harassment, that it might lead to greater détente between the United States and the USSR, and a strengthening of the Helsinki Accords. Some feared it was simply another futile exercise in cold-war strategy, a temporary thaw without major significance. As a participant, I was among the hopeful, and so, indeed, were most of the American exhibitors. Now I have to report that the "singular, perpetually mobbed exhibit" (*Publishers' Weekly*, October 3, 1977) that I manned as part of a four person delegation for the Association of Jewish Book Publishers (AJBP), has run into heavy flak in Moscow. Before discussing that, however, let me provide a proper framework for an understanding of the situation.

From September 6 through the morning of September 14, 1977, a public exhibition of books of Jewish interest, totaling almost 900 titles, attracted the attention of a startled, but appreciative, Moscow Jewish community. This public collection — in English, Hebrew, and Yiddish, and covering works of literature, history, and religion — was of a magnitude certainly without parallel in the recent history of Soviet Jewry, following Stalin's destruction of Jewish culture in 1948. (Prayer books were on the "forbidden" list as far back as 1929.) The books were to be found in two places, the booth of the AJBP, an American organization, and in the exhibition area of Israel, a state having no diplomatic relations with the USSR. Attendance at the fair was a phenomenal 165,000, with more than 65 nations participating, and the Jewish booths were filled wall to wall with people, especially in the afternoons and on Saturday and Sunday, when exhibits were open to the general public. The mornings were reserved for professionals, such as teachers, librarians, academicians, and graphic arts personnel. How the Jewish books got to the first Moscow International Book Fair, and what recommendations and conclusions can be drawn, should be matters of interest to Americans

concerned with the Helsinki Accords and their implementation in the USSR....

Late in 1976, Bob Garvey, executive secretary of
the AJBP from its inception, but now deceased, received a letter from Harry Lerner, a Minneapolis
publisher, suggesting that the Association sponsor
an exhibit of Jewish books for the Moscow fair. The
idea intrigued the membership and an application
for an exhibit was forwarded to Moscow. When the
application was accepted by the Soviets, there followed a period of hesitation which mirrored the differences of opinion on the subject in the American
publishing community. These differences were
largely voiced in a series of letters and editorials
that appeared in the New York *Times* in the weeks
preceding the fair. The Association, while it shared
the views of those who held that an American presence would strengthen the forces of liberalization
and would be in implementation of the Helsinki
Accords in the USSR, finally decided that it had
additional reasons to attend.

We thought if we could mount a large and impressive display of Jewish books, including prayer books,
we would in effect be expressing to our co-religionists our sympathy and support for their aspirations
(as well as making this support clear to our fellow
exhibitors and our host, the USSR). That the Soviet
Jews recognized this, could be found in the tears
that brimmed the eyes of exhibitors and spectators
alike at our booth. Moreover, the presence of a large
representative collection such as ours would testify
to the freedom experienced by Jews in America.
Additionally, being in Moscow meant that we could
witness for ourselves the condition of the Moscow
Jewish community and learn directly from its members how we could assist them. *We did not come,
however, with the idea of confrontation, but with the
hope of finding some common ground which would
be beneficial to all concerned.*

My own efforts, I thought, might best be directed toward the publishing connections that I had established with the firm I had founded in 1949....Twayne had shown its interest in Soviet literature in the early 1950s, and had published books by Soviet authors. It seemed to me that as a Jew I would be remiss in not utilizing whatever goodwill I had established with Soviet publishers on behalf of my fellow co-religionists. Accordingly, I had several meetings with publishing dignitaries in the USSR. Some of these I had known before, and they treated me most cordially, even to the point of meeting me at the Moscow airport and seeing me through customs. From these meetings there emerged the possibility of some cooperative efforts. For example, Aron Vergelis, editor-in-chief of the Yiddish magazine, *Sovietish Heimland*, suggested certain titles for which he indicated cooperation would be forthcoming. Among these were such as "Jewish Art in the Soviet Union," Jewish Music in the Soviet Union," and "Jewish Problems in the Soviet Union" (taken from books by Russian-Jewish authors....

There was some censorship of our materials, but not nearly as much as we feared....There was surveillance at our booth, but we were told this was to prevent the stealing of books. Our concern did not match that of the Soviets. They could not appreciate that we did not want to carry back, at considerable expense, books that had been read and fingered and were no longer in mint condition. Our choice was to leave them with the Moscow Jewish community. But we could not do this openly, for, we were told, the circulation of foreign literature was forbidden. And, indeed, some of our books did turn up in the hands of the authorities, but we refused to sign papers alleging that they had been stolen, although we were willing to accept them if returned. The Israelis also were under pressure because of inadvertent violation of this law. Their presence...can be attributed to the efforts on their behalf by the International Publishers Association and the Association of American Publishers. The latter was also helpful to us.

My colleagues were David Olivestone, editor-in-chief of the Hebrew Publishing Company; Myrna Shinbaum, who handled press relations, among other activities; and Dr. Joseph Drew, sociologist and journalist....We were also helped by a young woman — Natasha, who had a Jewish grandparent — whom we hired as a Russian interpreter. (We learned from others that translating for the AJBP at the fair was not a sought after assignment.) A request for reading options...was received, and a couple of books were sold through official channels, but most of the volumes found a home in Moscow, some by presentation.

We left the Soviet Union with the conviction that it had been worthwhile....Yet, now some five months after the event, the signals are becoming mixed. As I have written to some of my colleagues, the good news is that the AJBP has been invited by the Moscow fair authorities to exhibit at the Second Moscow International Book Fair in 1979. The bad news is that the Association has been the object of attack by an official journal, *Sovietskaya Kultura*, an organ of the Soviet Ministry of Culture. A rather lengthy article in this publication charges a world-wide anti-Soviet, anticommunist conspiracy. I quote a translation of two paragraphs of this article, "Ideological Saboteurs," by E. Evseyev, which appeared in the USSR on December 2, 1977:

After the campaign for a mass exodus of Jews from the USSR to Israel failed, the Zionist "defenders of the law" set their sights on the point of the Third Section of the Helsinki Agreement that concerns the questions of the free exchange of information, cinema and television material, and book production. A characteristic example is the attempt by the Zionist

propaganda *to exploit the First International Book
Exhibition and Fair in Moscow* [italics added].
Against the background of the considerable success
of that unique enterprise, the activities of the representatives of the American Association of Jewish
Book Publishers seemed quite ugly. This association was organized by the Zionists in the U.S.A. in
1961 as a "nonprofit" firm, engaged in the coordina-
tion of Zionist literature and its distribution. The
representatives of that group tried to exhibit at the
fair stands, with provocative aims, the publications
of the religious-Masonic Jewish "B'nai B'rith" order,
which is part of the World Zionist Organization...and the publications of the so-called "Anti-
Defamation League," which carries out the functions
of the punitive and the espionage-subversive organ
of "B'nai B'rith."

Hypocritically talking about "freedom of information," "freedom of exchange of ideas," the bourgeois
activists of the Zionist persuasion in reality have in
mind the "freedom" of spreading chauvinist racist
ideology under the guise of "Jewish cultural heritage," and it is for this purpose that the little-hon-
ored "book-traders" for the Association of Jewish
Book Publishers were sent to Moscow.

I wish Mr. Evseyev had checked his facts more
closely. As president of the Association, and presi-
dent-emeritus of a member firm that joined the Association a year or so after its founding, I could have
proved to him that the matter of adherence to Zionist principles plays no part in membership. Members of the AJBP may be Zionists; they may be
anti-Zionists. They don't have to be Jewish! And it
has never occurred to anyone passing on membership to inquire as to orientation on this matter. I
hope that Mr. Evseyev's incredible distortion of the
facts is his own "creative" contribution to imaginative literature, for it is difficult for me to believe that

he has been given official direction that will countenance no interference from the truth....

Compare the preceding with the seventh Moscow Book Fair, which took place in September, 1989. Charles D. Lieber, President of the AJBP, and head of the Hebrew Publishing Company, had this to say in part about the 3000 Jewish book exhibit he headed:

...all this took place in an atmosphere that differed considerably from that of the previous fairs, when "glasnost" had not yet made its impact: this time no books were confiscated, officials were friendly and helpful including the two or three policemen we had asked for to control the flow of the crowd at our instruction. Lastly, in contrast to previous years, we were given unsolicited help for the duration of the fair — two young men who acted as full-fledged members of our team when it came to lifting heavy cartons, guarding our personal property, guiding visitors to the desired segment of our display, distributing our catalogs to those waiting in line, and much else. Our job would have been far harder without them, and they stayed with us until after the fair closed and all the remaining books had been boxed and picked up by people from Jewish libraries in various parts of the USSR, most of them new and much in need of materials for information and instruction. These boxes went to Moscow, Kharkov, Minsk, Kiev, Riga, Sverdlovsk, and other places with aspiring Jewish populations. In this context we should mention one of the recipients, an old friend of the AJBP, Yuri Sokol, a retired Soviet army colonel who has been struggling to establish a Jewish library in his four-room apartment. His work has only recently come to partial fruition: the location was recently given official Soviet sanction by its recognition as the "Moscow City Jewish Library" of the "Moscow Society for Jewish Culture and Education."

While the AJBP has been the leading organization in setting up Jewish book exhibits at the various Moscow Book Fairs, it had recognized from the outset that this outreach to the Jews of the Soviet Union is a proper concern of American Jews everywhere. As a consequence, the AJBP has solicited the participation of Jewish communal organizations and has voiced its gratitude to many who have given of their time and support in assuring Jewish book exhibits at the fair. Among the many individuals and organizations deserving special commendation: Charles D. Lieber, past president of the AJBP and head of the 1989 delegation; Martin Levin, attorney and publisher, an unfailing source of help and advice; Robert I. Goldman, an early participant and supporter; Bernard Levinson, head of the 1985 and 1987 delegations; Sol Scharfstein, head of the delegations in 1983 and 1981; Bernard Scharfstein, head of the 1979 delegation; the founding delegation of 1977, which has already been described; the American Jewish Committee provided early support (David Harris, its current executive director, was a member of one of the early delegations.); B'nai Brith's Anti-Defamation League has provided at considerable expense magnificent Russian language catalogs for distribution at the fair; the National Conference for Soviet Jewry was always helpful; generous financial assistance has also been forthcoming from the Littauer Foundation, the Jewish Book Council, the Meyerhoff Fund; Workmen's Circle for Yiddishists and Yiddish material and books; and the individual delegates, too many to mention here, who paid their own way to support their co-religionists in the USSR, also deserve special approbation.

America's Tenth Man, a pictorial presentation of Afro-American achievement in the U.S., with a Foreword by Henry Cabot Lodge, was, as I have already indicated, welcome news everywhere except to one honoree, who wrote that his picture and biography in the educators' section, had been included in error. He did not deserve the honor: he was not a Black! This was in 1957 and a similar situation in a Southern state only a few years earlier had had serious legal consequences. Our error involved a distinguished educator at a large urban university in the North. He was not certain, he wrote, of what if anything he should do, and requested a meeting with me to discuss the matter.

At our meeting, he confessed that he had been puzzled of late when, as a participant in a number of educational conferences, he noted the number of Blacks who had come by to shake his hand. Now, he knew why. While he was with me, I was able to show the sequence of error that had led to his being included. The original sin was really attributable to the public relations person at his university, who, when approached by the editor of *America's Tenth Man*, for photographs of outstanding African-American scholars, provided his photo and the biographical information included in our volume. In going over the pictures for the book prior to publication, I had noticed this particular inclusion because the subject seemed by name to be Jewish and, despite a somewhat dusky countenance, white. As a consequence I had queried the editor concerning this. Alas, instead of verifying the data by contacting the subject, she simply confirmed the fact of the university's submission of the material, with the results I have reported. It never occurred to me that she had not gone back to the subject for verification! While our contract with the editor-compiler specified that she was legally liable for her error I had no doubt as to who would be held ultimately responsible.

I told the perplexed educator that we were willing to correct the error by sending notices to all purchasers of the books we could identify and by providing stickers containing the information that our noted educator had been included in error, requesting that the recipient paste in the correction sticker below the subject's photo on the designated page. He finally accepted this solution, after, I am sure, consulting his colleagues and attorney.

Other brushes with disaster involved a number of plagiarism problems. The earliest one was personally very painful. It involved one of our editors, whose dissertation, published by a distinguished university press, turned out to have so liberally borrowed from other sources, without attribution, as to result in the university rescinding the scholar's Ph. D. degree. The ramifications affected an on-going series of works in philosophy, in which the offending scholar was involved with two other colleagues. The latter insisted on disassociating their names from the plagiarist before proceeding with the books which were well under way and had been announced. I had become friendly with all the editors and had even profited from promotional material prepared by the errant scholar for release by Twayne which I sent out under my signature after his departure. It turned out that even that was not his but had been written by a graduate student, now a distinguished scholar, who also worked briefly at Twayne.

Another embarrassment of a similar nature occurred when a University of Chicago Press author provided indisputable proof that a Chinese scholar in Taiwan had written a Twayne book on a Chinese poet in which she had borrowed liberally, if not flagrantly, without attribution. The initial suggestion of the Press, probably at the instigation of the author, was that we withdraw the book from circulation and retrieve all copies.

This seemed to us a particularly onerous measure since just a year before, Professor Walter Harding, the distinguished Thoreau scholar, had documented unauthorized and uncredited borrowings from his Twayne title, *The Variorum Walden*, by a scholar of standing, who had written a text on Thoreau published by a leading firm. The offending scholar had sent a long letter of explanation to Professor Harding, and I felt his explanation and apology to Professor Harding quite sincere and his transgression inadvertent. Accordingly, I wrote as follows to Professor Harding, who had asked my advice:

Dear Professor Harding:

The initial reaction that I have from our attorney in an unofficial recommendation is that unless you were prepared to pursue the matter with zeal, there is not much that can be gotten in the way of legal redress. Financially, it would be necessary to prove a deprivation of income, which would be quite difficult to do. As for the remuneration that Professor_____ hints at, I do not think that the monetary returns could possibly be of interest. Rather than to accept a token fee...I would suggest you indicate to him that in any revision of his work an explicit statement of indebtedness to your prior work be acknowledged. You would be giving him the benefit of the doubt that he transgressed without conscious knowledge of the violation of accepted procedures. I think you would agree that a scholar of good standing ought to be permitted this opportunity to redress the wrong he has committed.

My advice then is to admonish graciously, to indicate that you expect a more explicit acknowledgment of his indebtedness in any new editions or reprinting, and to let it go at that. While we would have normally requested a fee for his use of copyright materials, I think the request coming now would be regarded as vindication of his words concerning the publisher's zeal to make a mint. We will, of course, do whatever you wish in the matter and if you decide that our suggestion is not to your liking please let me know.

Professor Harding accepted my recommendation, writing: "I am still disturbed at his wholesale lifting, but I agree with you that this is probably the best way to bring the whole unhappy situation to an end. Many thanks for your thoughtful advice on the matter..."*

---

*On January 12, 1973, Harding wrote again about an Indian edition that had cribbed from his volume: "If you recall, this is the second time that someone has helped himself to portions of *The Variorum Walden*. I should consider myself honored, I suppose."

To return to the University of Chicago Press plagiarism charge...Walton Rawls of our office informed the Press of Twayne's action in *The Variorum Walden* matter, suggesting that the Press recommend a similar procedure to its author. This, plus a letter of explanation from our errant author to the Press's Chinese scholar coupled with our willingness to pay a portion of the royalties on our book to the Press and to include an acknowledgment of literary indebtedness to the Press's title in any new printings or editions settled the matter. Interestingly, our author's explanation referred to the fact that ancient Chinese scholarship and custom permitted a considerably greater latitude in literary borrowings than is permitted by our copyright laws.

An unnecessary and self-inflicted piece of craziness almost put us out of business early on. One of our suppliers, a binder, was referred to as Rabbi _____ (probably an honorific; he held no pulpit.) but he was far from a holy man as events proved. He had befriended us when we first began. When we couldn't pay our bills, he would take our promissory notes. When we couldn't pay our notes, he would ask for replacements, and in that manner helped keep us afloat. Of course the interest we paid was higher than what the bank would have charged but it was not extortionate. He was our friend, we thought. The one-sided generosity went on for a year or two. Then, it was our turn to repay his generosity. One day the binder's assistant, a young matron, perhaps a relative, turned up with a request from our benefactor. Would we help him out by signing some notes for future work? If we couldn't meet the notes, not to worry, the binder would work his usual magic, which we had witnessed many times before, so much so that Twayne notes on New York's East Side (where the binder's bankers were located — small merchants, bookstore owners, *et al.*) were regarded very highly; "as good as gold," I heard one of them say before the disaster struck.

What do you do when a friend asks for help? We helped him. But what I did not know was that my associate, Joel, had been lulled — gulled, hypnotized...he never could explain it! — into signing blank notes! This was equivalent to issuing a signed blank check... forgive me, not "a" but "many" blank checks. How many and how much we were to find out later. We had not long to wait.

Some weeks later while Joel was on vacation, I was startled to receive a call from the bank to the effect that the Twayne account was overdrawn, that some of the notes presented could not be paid. I had expected a relatively carefree week while Joel was away, for we were supposed to have what was for us then a very comfortable balance of more than $2000.

There was little sleep for me until I reached Joel but we still didn't realize what we were in for. Surely by Monday when we reached the binder, he would wave his magic wand and eliminate our problems. But Monday came and our friend had disappeared! By then, it dawned on all of us that we were in for real trouble, maybe more than we could handle. The binder's assistant didn't know where her boss was, didn't remember the amount or number of notes, couldn't help us at all... so she said.

Joel went down to the bank, verified that it was his signature, and immediately got in touch with his attorney. Of course, as a corporate officer he had also involved Twayne. Joel transferred his assets to his wife, probably a futile step I was told, but we never considered any action against him. I felt that as the head of the organization I was as culpable as he. And, of course, I can only hope that I would have been more prudent were I the person involved. We were, of course, sued by the holder of the notes no longer signed in blank. The judge, in recognition of our naivete, perhaps, and our victimization, instructed the holder to stipulate payments in interval and amounts that would not wreck Twayne. The amounts, while not large in today's economy, would have been impossible to pay in those early days if demanded at one time. The binder eventually reappeared months later, went back into business, and made some restitution by deducting small amounts from bills for binding he did for us. He will forgive me for the thought I had that whatever he deducted had already been incorporated into his price! Thereafter, all Twayne checks, notes, and orders had to bear two signatures. But after Joel's demise, we gradually reverted to a single signature. The incident truly emphasizes the miracle of our survival. It also abundantly illustrates that just as the road to hell is paved with good intentions, the road to wisdom, as I have abundantly proved, is truly paved with "blocks of ignorance"! We were fortunate to have survived our mistakes, and that, I have been told, makes us wise today.

Albert Mordell, a Philadelphia lawyer by profession, but an anthologist *extraordinaire* who had been attracted to our firm as a member of the board of the Jewish Publication Society of that city, provided a number of books which he edited. These included *Literary Reviews and Essays* by Henry James, *The Autocrat's Miscellanies* by Oliver Wendell Holmes, two volumes of essays by Gideon Welles, and a volume on William Dean Howells and Henry James entitled *Discovery of a Genius*. But the most memorable volume he compiled for us was *The World of Haldeman-Julius*. That one provided Twayne with a new dimension of *tsurris*. It started out propitiously enough. Harry Golden, who was then riding the crest of fame as a result of his best-sellers — *Only in America, For 2¢ Plain* and the then-pending publication of *Enjoy, Enjoy* — had agreed to write an appreciative Foreword, "in affection and gratitude to the late Haldeman-Julius," his friend.

Emanuel Haldeman-Julius sold over 300 million copies of "The Little Blue Books," a forerunner of the modern paperbacks, for five and ten cents each. Millions of them were reprints of classics — the Bible, Shakespeare, Goethe, Aesop, etc. Will Durant's *Story of Philosophy* got its initial push to immortality through publication in the little Blue Books. Other writers he published were Bertrand Russell, Upton Sinclair, Frank Harris, H.G. Wells.

Our first indication of trouble came when Golden returned the proofs of our book which he read in order to provide the foreword, claiming that some of the material we were using had originated with him, was in fact correspondence which had been "embellished upon and changed in some minor degree...which I 'loaned' Haldeman-Julius."

Mordell wanted to argue the issue, pointing out that the articles allegedly based on Golden's letters had been printed and reprinted under Haldeman-Julius's name and copyrighted by him without objection by Golden. I saw no point, however, in fighting this. There were many other articles to choose from, and I proposed that we accede to Golden's wishes. We wanted his foreword and his good will. On December 22, 1959, I received the following from Golden:

> Dear Mr. Steinberg:
>
> I am enclosing the foreword to Haldeman-Julius' book.
>
> I want to confirm the letter you sent to Mr. Greenbaum, [his lawyer], regarding the deletion...from the book...the pages you enumerated in your letter of November 5, and that it would be satisfactory to use the material... which I had written originally for Haldeman-Julius but to which he had added enough to make this his own work.
>
> With kindest regards,

But this was not to be the end of our problems with Mr. Golden, as the copy of the press release we sent out makes clear.

HARRY GOLDEN IS AMAZED. . .

...and so am I. Twayne's forthcoming *The World of Haldeman-Julius* isn't even out yet and already we have fireworks. I thought July 18th was big enough for both *The World of Haldeman-Julius* and *Enjoy, Enjoy* but apparently this is a matter of opinion. Harry Golden, who contributed the Foreword to *The*

World of Haldeman-Julius, indicated his thoughts on the matter of pub. dates in the following telegram:

=AMAZED THAT JULIUS BOOK RELEASED ON SAME DAY WITH MINE STOP IF THIS HAPPENS WILL BLAST THE ENTIRE THING IN MY PAPER STOP HAVE UNCOVERED VAST CORRESPONDENCE CONCERNING MY CONTRIBUTION TO MOST OF HIS HUMAN INTEREST WRITINGS STOP I WENT ALONG WITH GENEROSITY AND WILL HELP A GOOD DEAL BUT BECOME OUTRAGED WITH CHUTZPAH=
HARRY GOLDEN=
=CHUTZPAH= TWAYNE=

Now the choice of July 18th as a pub. date for *The World of Haldeman-Julius* was purely a matter of happenstance — we are also publishing *The Laureates*; *Dimensions of Faith*; *Lincoln's Administration*; *Feminine Superiority*; and several other books on this date. However, in deference to Mr. Golden's wishes, and swallowing my "chutzpah," we are postponing the pub. date of *The World of Haldeman-Julius* to July 25th.

Despite the press release and a conciliatory letter from Douglas Thompson, of our office, who had written the release, to Golden apologizing for the coincidence of publication dates and emphasizing that he had notified all reviewers of the publication date postponement, we received a letter from Golden's attorneys, which requested copies of our book and the dust jacket, adding:

"We must advise you...that Mr. Golden does not intend to permit any advertising or promotion of your work using his name or picture or in any way based upon the foreword which he wrote for your work...Similarly, there should be nothing in the appearance of the book itself or its wrapper that gives undue prominence to the name of the author of the foreword..."

We sent the material requested and, sure enough, Mr. Greenbaum replied, advising me that the dust-jacket was "in derogation of the rights of our client, Harry Golden," and assuring me further that "the distribution by you...with the jacket as it now stands would give rise to a variety of legal actions. We...repeat again our demand that the jacket be changed prior to the publication of the work and that any new jacket... be submitted to our client for his approval."

I answered this a week later on July 15, informing Attorney Greenbaum that we were reviewing the correspondence concerning the foreword. I also pointed out "that we have already acceded to Mr. Golden's wishes in two previous requests. The first of these concerned the deletion of articles from the book, and the second led to a postponement of publication."

In the meantime, Golden had written to Douglas Thompson with a carbon to Mordell about the brouhaha. Apparently what had upset Golden was a letter from Mordell.

Golden wrote in part: "The whole thing was fantastic...Mordell wrote me this amazing letter, 'We have decided to publish on the day your book comes out and believe it will not *harm* you! Harm? Why should this word have been considered — when a man did a generous, decent and kind thing. Why?...You and Mordell should be ashamed of yourselves — is this not so?..." He added a postscript, "Please make sure that you confer with Mr. Greenbaum, my lawyer, if his inquiries are in good taste and legal as I am sure they are and always will be." Since Thompson was away on vacation, I thought it wise to answer Golden. It seemed to me that he was trying to explain or justify his actions. So I wrote in a most conciliatory fashion:

Dear Mr. Golden:

Mr. Thompson is away on vacation, and I am sure that he will write to you immediately upon his return on July 18th.

However, we do want to assure you that no one here has anything other than a genuine feeling of gratitude toward you and that your reaction to Mr. Mordell's letter is understandable, if he had written what you attribute to him. Mr. Mordell insists he is being misquoted.

Actually, despite your initial reaction, we feel that your tribute to Haldeman-Julius will be understood for what it is: a generous praise of the man's many accomplishments and not an endorsement of his social or political views. Seen in this light it will be understood as a courageous gesture of good will and redound to your benefit, as it should.

Finally, since the book is scheduled for prominent reviews, I am sure the reviewers will mention your Foreword, thus giving your contribution additional attention.

Time will prove that far from interfering with the sales of your latest volume, *The World of Haldeman-Julius* will stimulate the sales of your volumes and add to your reputation as a generous and courageous human being.

I hope that you will not permit your attorneys to mar this reputation.

With all good wishes,

Again, I wrote on July 13:

Dear Mr. Golden:

Events are confirming the contents of my letter to you of 8 July, as witness the enclosed clipping.

There will be many more of these, I am sure — all attesting to the fact that we are getting you favorable publicity. Now, how can all of this harm you?

Finally, on July 22, I wrote the following to Mr. Golden's attorneys:

Gentlemen:

We have completed our examination of the correspondence relating to the use of the Foreword by Mr. Harry Golden in our book, *The World of Haldeman-Julius*. We have not found any expression limiting our use of the Foreword in any way. On the contrary, Mr. Golden's letters abound with expressions indicating a keen interest in the success of the volume. He says, for example, that he has written the Foreword "to bespeak my affection and gratitude to the late Haldeman-Julius..." and later in the same letter, "I want this book to be a success."

We hope Mr. Golden has not changed his mind in this respect. If he has, however, then I would be willing to recommend that we change our jacket for any future printing or edition that our book may have.

I hope that this settles the matter to every one's satisfaction.

That seems to have been the final exchange. I heard nothing further from Mr. Golden or his lawyer. I wish I could report that the book was a smashing success but it wasn't, never even earning the moderate advance we had paid Haldeman-Julius' widow and son. In October of 1960, Mordell sent me a postcard.

It read: (From *The American Freeman*, July 1951. Harry L. Golden, Charlotte, N.C. to Haldeman-Julius):

> "Your output is a wonderful sight to behold, with column after column producing the same reaction — I wish to hell I had written that. Great work. If I were a praying man, I'd say, 'God bless you.'"

So, dear reader? You figure it out.

In my account of the Benton lithos (see page 69) I referred to the disappearance of nearly 10% of the edition, for which Benton's lawyers held us responsible. Actually, our experience with book shrinkage in the warehouse would indicate that this was a rather small percentage for the ten years or so of storage during which the material was moved from one warehouse to another location. Still, the problem, complicated by wrong deliveries made by personnel who could not read, apparently, became a deep and intractable problem. My letters and memos following phone calls that were mostly ignored clearly showed my desperation. Take, for example, the letter which I sent the shipper as a result of a phone call from Campbell and Hall in Boston, then one of our leading library wholesalers, who reported receiving 250 of our books which the firm had neither ordered nor been billed for. Why the gift, they wanted to know!

Dear _____:

> This generosity with Twayne's books is unquestionably one of the elements in the shortages which we are taking exception to. Furthermore, because these things have been taking place so frequently,

we urge you to investigate the possibility that this is a deliberate attempt on the part of someone to make it appear as though the shortages were inadvertent or accidental. Sooner or later, you will have to face the possibility that someone on your premises may be selling books as a sideline, a suspicion that, incidentally, has been voiced by more than one of your publishers...

Here is another sampling of what we were up against:

This was a week that should never have been! Here are some of the highlights of what you did to us this week: Your receipt, copy enclosed, initialled M.B., could not possibly correspond to the contents of the returns from Baker and Taylor. The customer mistakenly duplicated two pages of one return. Your checker, without paying attention to what he was doing, simply copied the return without, obviously, opening the package. I have nothing against M.B. except that I wish you would let him work on some of your other favorite customers' returns. Let them share in the pleasure of his creative activities!

I am also enclosing another testimonial to the generosity of your employees with your customers' books...Please note that there is no indication on the invoice that the Stephen Vincent Benet book had been sent and if the customer had not been honest about the matter we would be out one book, which could easily have been a hundred. I say "easily a hundred" because of the shortage that I am about to discuss again in connection with the H.G.Wells title.

But before I get to that happy situation, let me notify you about the exchange with Educational Reading Services, who reports receiving a carton of books, the invoice for which indicates should have been sent to Davidson College. Again, an honest customer not only called us long distance to inform us of the fact, but also pointed out that he had not received the shipment of books which had been ordered. Presumably, and hopefully, these are at Davidson College!....

You are now shipping short *H.G.Wells*. The original shortage on this book was 165 copies. We sent you more than 700 *less than two months ago*. Our sales show that you should have more than 200 copies left. Surely, these books must be on your premises somewhere. It's impossible for a shortage of more than 200 copies on the shipment of 700 to exist!

Would you please pay attention to your business? Obviously, no one else in your organization is doing so.

Sadly but truthfully,

But, of course, our shipper was always very prompt with his bill for services, never mind when actually rendered. Take, for example, the fact that while we were being dunned by him for past-due shipping services that presumably had taken place, actual shipment via truck or motor freight was frequently delayed for weeks or months. My letter on this matter follows:

...When you called last week about the past-due Twayne account, I started to call some of the customers who, seemingly, were long past-due with us. For example, I called the Bro-Dart people [another large wholesaler] and had a long conversation with their president concerning the $6,000.00 and more that according to our records was more than 90 days past due. He responded that this could not be and that there must be something wrong with our figures. Yesterday he called me back and really pinpointed our common problem. Books on a May invoice had been delivered in July, a June 24th invoice had been delivered in August, and a July invoice had not yet been received. Of $6,000.00 in billing, only

$1,000.00, less than 30 days old had been received. How could this happen?

In checking through the greens [a copy of the invoice presumably showing shipping date by the shipper which we entered on our books as proving shipment and therefore billable], we noticed that these had been returned to us promptly — within one week from the receipt of the order generally — but, quite obviously the freight deliveries either did not leave your premises for more than a month or were kept by the trucker for more than a month with the result that nearly two months passed between the time of the receipt of the green and the receipt of the merchandise by the customer. *In other words, you billed us two months in advance of shipment or receipt of goods by our customer!*

To prove that this was not an isolated instance, I went to the Baker and Taylor file, where a similar situation exists....A May 31st invoice was received on June 26; a June 13th invoice was received in the first week of August....In view of this...I have issued instructions that we are not to enter any greens for payment to you or to bill our customers until we have had proof of shipment in the form of a bill of lading. This will enable us and you to really know when the Twayne account is past-due, and in what amount...

I hope you recognize in all of this a sincere attempt on my part to improve the functioning of your operation for the mutual benefit of all concerned...

Why did we tolerate this? We had very early on been involved in the transfer of books from one location to another. That one move had disrupted our business for months. To move 10,000 square feet of books piled ten feet high on open shelving was not to be regarded lightly. Moreover, the cost of moving would involve thousands of dollars, and I really could not see any satisfactory solution except to set up our own operation, perhaps in concert with others. We were slowly moving to a reluctant decision to do this. We had no choice, for, ironically, all of our promotional and editorial efforts also had to channel through this inefficient shipping operation. That we were not alone in our dilemma didn't make it any easier. The merger, of course, eliminated the problem for me but newspapers continued to report on the market for thousands of books stolen from other warehouses, so I am sure this is a continuing problem that has to be monitored constantly.

VI

Author-Publisher Relations

A SYNDICATED COLUMN BY LESLIE HANSCOM, DATED March 15, 1987, led off with this sentence: "Among writers, one perennially favorite theme of discussion is the villainy of publishers, who in the eyes of those they publish are typically seen as double-dealing parasites, growing fat from the talent of others."

Why this long-standing attitude should be so prevalent when each of the parties is so dependent on the other probably can be attributed in part to mutual myopia. The business of publishing and its myriad details remain a mystery to most authors, who feel that their function is to write the books, period. And, of course, many publishers do not welcome input from their authors as to how to increase sales of their titles. After all, aren't the trade publishers the holders of a unique record that features losses on 70 to 80% of their

offerings!* Why should they attempt to ameliorate this splendid achievement? Excuses abound,
of course, and any seasoned publisher can trot
them out at command: the competition for space
in the bookstores; the number of books being published (now more than 55,000 annually, though
not all trade); the incompetent reviewers; TV; etc.
But not one will attribute it to poor editorial judgment.

I have by and large found author suggestions
helpful and tried to keep my authors informed as
to what was happening with their books. Most
publishers will expend a certain amount for promotion and advertising of their titles. If a firm
has been in business a number of years it will
have evolved through trial and error the procedures that work for that particular firm. What
worked for Twayne, essentially, were continuous
mailings to libraries and to academics, as I have
already indicated. And to supplement, we backed
this direct-mail activity with advertising in the
pertinent scholarly journals for the particular
subject matter covered. A full-page Twayne ad on
our authors series and related titles could be
found in many issues of *PMLA*; one on our Rulers
and Statesmen series in the *American Historical
Review*; occasional ads for our economics titles
in the *American Economic Review*; etc.

Activities of this kind kept our authors aware of
what we were doing on a consistent and large-
scale level. And we also resorted to annual round-
up letters such as those Sylvia Bowman sent

---

*Income from subsidiary rights does ameliorate the situation
somewhat but revenues from sales alone are as I have stated.

touching on the highlights of the year's activities at home and abroad. We tried to make all our authors* well aware that they were participants in an important international publishing program. We really believed this, and I think a fair amount of this came across. It was excellent PR overall. But, of course, our books had a finite market as our authors understood and we were obviously effectively reaching that market most of our authors agreed.

But I got my lumps occasionally. I recall with amusement the letter I received from an irate professor whose series book in the French section had been delayed well beyond the provenance promised by our agreement and who had grown weary of our explanations and excuses. He wrote that he was coming down to the MLA annual meeting to "knock your block off." My attempt to mollify him included a postscript to the effect that I had been successful in my bout with a Golden Gloves quarter-finalist! Of course I omitted the essential information that this had happened some thirty years before, while I was still in college. His book was eventually published to good reviews so I think he forgave me...at least he never showed up to carry out his threat.

And then there was the gentleman in Washington, D.C., an early riser as the postscript to my letter indicated, and undoubtedly an author but not one of ours, who took me to task for not having the book on his father — the subject of a TUSAS title — in the D.C. bookstores. His letter read:

---

*Regrettably, the relationship changed after the merger. See pp. 262 ff.

Monday, November 15, 1971
5:20 A.M. — an early riser — my Truman training
you know.
Dear Mr. Steinberg:

Since you are collecting items for your forthcoming
book "How to be a Publisher for Fun and Maybe Even
Profit in Your Spare Time," here is another sample.

I have just received a letter of November 10th from
my sister, who lives in St. Thomas, Virgin Islands.
She writes me: "You are luckier than the rest of us.
So far little luck in getting Father's book but we are
still trying & so is Mother..."

We are a mighty Clan with connections from here
to Alpha Centuri. This first biography (more are
coming) of our progenitor is an event of unusual
interest to all of us. If you could merely fill our
orders with reasonable celerity you might be able to
retire with a considerable fortune and turn over the
helm at Twayne to a younger and possibly less ide-
alistic but more efficient man — thus benefitting
both yourself and mankind.

I admire your competitive spirit in trying (I guess
you're trying) to meet the challenge of being a publisher without selling your books through the book
stores — a concept that I admit would never have
occurred to me. But it seems to me that this sporting modus operandi (a bit like fighting with one arm
tied behind your back because it matters not
whether you win or lose, it's how you played the
game) would strongly suggest the very great need of
developing a fast and efficient sales and delivery
operation of your own.

This advice is for free and well worth it....

I now bid you a welcome Adoo (Artemus Ward).

My response follows:

I am truly sorry to have annoyed you with our
"inefficiencies." The fact of the matter is that our
distribution system does work. It evolved as a re-

sult of our experience with the bookstores when it became apparent that the Series books, which contained many relatively unknown figures, would not sell as bookstore items. I hope you will derive some comfort in realizing that when the paperback editions are published — approximately two years after the appearance of the hardback items — the stores will be more apt to carry the title.

I hope you will not think me ungenerous in refusing to accept your advice, which unquestionably is free and well worth it, but the fact is that we could not have continued in business if we followed your inclinations to consign us where you apparently are determined to send us.

Be that as it may, I am enclosing as a gesture of regard a letter from a distinguished editor of another company, in which he pays reluctant tribute to our method of selling the Series books.

Insofar as the _____order is concerned, you will note that in our eagerness to please, a duplicate of the order was sent. Quite obviously you will recognize from all of this that monetary considerations are not the determining factor. However, in all fairness as a rather objective but concerned viewer of these matters, you should recognize that perhaps some of the inefficiency is attributable to the postal system since both orders were sent out on November 4th.

Thanks for your generous hand-outs, which I enjoy reading.

P.S. Apparently I was the first of your epistolary concerns since it was dated 5 a.m. Would it be slightly better for me if you were to push me back in your correspondence schedule, say to 2 or 3 p.m.?

But as gratifying as the results may have been with the promotion for our series titles, I cannot report the same success for the trade titles, comparatively few in number, that Twayne issued over the years. We tried ads in the N.Y. *Times Book Review* on a number of occasions and struck out each time. Moreover, when I was president of the Association of Jewish Book Publishers, the member firms placed cooperative full-page ads twice in the *Times* on members' books and could do no more than break even, even though coupons were attached to the ads. Since then I have had occasion to check publishers' views of the subject, and they agree: Advertising does not sell books.

Fon W. Boardman, Jr., a veteran of the publishing wars for thirty-eight years with Columbia and Oxford University Press, underscores all of the preceding in an article he wrote for the N.Y. *Times Book Review*, some years ago.

"...books do not sell because they are displayed in stores; books are displayed in stores because they are selling....Books don't sell because they are advertised; books are worth advertising if they are already selling for some other reason. Authors and editors don't like to believe these axioms..." His recommendations? Direct to the consumer sales, either by mail order or through coupon ads. And he points to the growth of book clubs as confirmation of this: "...A book club is simply a generic term for a business that builds up mailing lists of people who will buy books on given subjects."

What about reviews? Do they sell books? My experience indicates that overall there is little direct connection. At least that's the way it turned out with the twenty-six pages and more the *New Yorker* devoted to our *Dictionary of American Underworld Lingo** and the twelve pages in the same peri-

---

*The review appeared on November 11, 1950 but was followed

odical devoted to Max Nomad's *Aspects of Revolt.* The same result attended the two-page syndicated feature by Lowell Limpus on one of our first books, Robert S. Elegant's *China's Red Masters,* which appeared locally in the N.Y. Sunday *News.* But that was nearly forty years ago and the *News* reader doesn't buy books. Right? Well, what about the lead review in the N.Y. *Times Book Review* by Gore Vidal, headed "The Subject Doesn't Object."* He was reviewing Ray Lewis White's *Gore Vidal,* one of the TUSAS titles. And nothing happened! If the publisher who has seen this happen again and again can still have great expectations when the big reviews break, what about the author? Can you blame him for harboring bad thoughts about the publisher when the latter reports the actual number of copies sold even after a blockbuster review?

Of course, reviews do make first-rate selling material when they are culled and disseminated in the form of an eye-catching direct-mail piece to an interested audience, and that is what we did with great success to the libraries, our chief customers, as already detailed. There's no gainsaying that prominent reviews are great ego builders for publishers and authors. But with the occasional exceptions aside, they don't necessarily sell books, at least not for someone who *never had a best-seller.*

What sells books? I don't think anyone can provide a satisfactory answer. Certainly the trade

---

by John Lardner's article, "The Lexicographers in Stir" on pp. 101-25 of the December 1, 1951 issue.

* The N.Y. *Times Book Review,* September 1, 1968.

publishers can't if all they can do is turn out two or three winners out of every ten. That's why very early on Twayne turned away from the crap-shoot called trade publishing. We didn't have the money and we couldn't compete with the big firms. Making a virtue of necessity, we concentrated on areas where we could compete, and the libraries became our best friends. But we didn't turn any bookstore business away and maintained trade discounts which enabled the stores to order and stock our books if they wished. After the merger, the discounts were changed and the trade titles dropped. But I had nothing to do with that.

There are other flashpoints of irritation between author and publisher. One of these is remainders, a practice I discuss elsewhere. Suffice it to say here that the example of a few firms paying royalties on such sales deserves to be emulated. Paying royalties on such sales might serve as a useful corrective in reminding publishers of the fact that they are responsible for the success or failure of the books they publish. Let them take measures to improve their abysmal batting average by more careful selection and more vigorous promotion of the books they publish.

Authors need also to be aware of the provisions of their contract that affect their royalties in regard to direct-mail sales, sales through special channels and sales at discounts greater than 50%. The reduced royalties that usually apply in this area are generally rationalized by publishers as resulting in increased bookstore sales where full royalties apply. This is probably true for direct-mail sales, but I would question the practice as fair today. At the very least, before reduced-royalty sales take place, the author ought to be queried as to his view of the proposed transaction.

Despite the best of intentions, publishers confronted with cash-flow problems find authors' royalty accounts a convenient interest-free and legal source for funding their operation. Since royalties are usually paid twice a year, the sums to be dipped into can be sizable, even for small publishers. Most publishers will argue that with return privileges there is no other configuration possible in this area. I would agree that it makes bookkeeping more costly and onerous. Perhaps, however, a *quid pro quo* for this free borrowing privilege ought to be a kind of affirmative action toward the author wherever possible. I would also recommend the elimination of the provision in most contracts which defers payment of royalties until the sum reaches $25 or so. I would recommend payment of what is due regardless of the amount and enclose a friendly note from the publisher voicing hope for better days ahead.

All in all, had I to do it over again, I would tend to take the course of recognizing the central role of the author in the publishing configuration. Certainly a prevailing attitude of this nature on the part of publishers should work to change the adversarial nature of the relationship which is apparently still the case today.

VII

The Subsidized Book

I HAVE EARLIER REFERRED TO THE ESTABLISHMENT of Bookman Associates as an imprint for books of scholarly or specialized studies, many of which required subsidization in part. After the firm was merged with Twayne, however, what had been conceived as a way to keep us afloat, gradually took on the dimensions of a coherent and effective publishing program for books that seemed to have only a limited and non-commercial market but deserved publication. Our promotions and advertising for such books in the scholarly media featuring the excellent reviews these books received started to pay off. And some of the subsidized titles became book club selections, doing better than the titles we had published solely with our own funds. There were many many reprints of these books, some of which are still in print nearly forty years after publication.

Finally, however, as our series and related programs took hold, I found the demands on my time so onerous as to require all my attention and could not consider taking on anything that did not fit in with our on-going series titles that were doing so well. I must confess that finally it was a great relief to be able to finance our books totally with our own resources. My experience has been that even accepting a partial subsidy makes demands that impact on the freedom and initiative of the publisher's normal operations and procedures. Still, I must record a twinge of regret when I received the following letter from one of our authors, who had offered us another book he wanted us to publish with the help of a subsidy.

Dec. 14, 1972

Dear Mr. Steinberg,

I have your nice note and the check. I was not half as interested in the Regency as I am in the Free Negro Study. I know it is not a money maker because it is extremely controversial and somewhat narrow in range. I am not ashamed to confess to an old friend that the manuscript has been the rounds. I am in the position where I need another book — my professional standing demands it...There was a time when anything with "Black" on it sold at the drop of a hat. But I don't sell big — I am used to it. I want to leave it with you because I don't have the courage to attempt the role of literary agent for myself right now. If there is any chance that things might change favorably for it I am willing to take that chance....*The Regency paid for itself in the professional prestige it brought. You got me into every journal and every research library in the nation and abroad.* (italics mine) I have always been grateful for that. But the Regency brought very little in

financial returns. Do what you can. Have the best
of the blessed season.

As a consequence of my "expertise" with such
books, I was invited by the National Association of
Book Editors (NABE) in the middle 60's to be a
panelist* in the discussion of the question: Where
Might a Good Manuscript with Little Commercial
Value Find Publication? Twenty-five years later
the question still remains of concern to publishers
and scholars. Excerpts from my remarks to NABE
follow:

> At the outset let me point out that most publishers
> would, I think, regard the books issued by Twayne
> and its affiliate, Bookman Associates, as non-com-
> mercial. I think also that one could with consider-
> able justification say that the manuscript we are
> talking about, at least in one respect, might find
> publication with practically any publishing house
> you can name. If we assume that half of the titles
> published today lose money — and this estimate is
> certainly a conservative one — then at least twelve
> thousand titles of the 24,000 published last year can
> be called of little commercial value. If publishers
> were to face up to the fact that this overwhelming
> percentage of their output is going to be unprofitable

---

*My fellow panelists were Margaret Mahoney, then of the
Carnegie Corporation and William Sloane, director of Rut-
gers University Press, and the founder some years before of
William Sloane Associates and its president to 1952. Sloane
had the misfortune [*sic!*] to publish a best-seller the first
time out. It was *Thunder Out of China* by Annalee Jacoby
and Theodore White and Sloane thought he could duplicate
this success with every subsequent publication, a procedure
that led to predictable results. He was, however, a knowledgeable and experienced publisher, well respected in the
field. I had this disaster in mind when I wrote about the haz-
ards of best-sellers in my Introduction.

anyway, they might then begin to consider the possibility of revising their annual lists to assure representation of the book of poetry, the occasional scholarly study — books of quality in general, even if of limited appeal. It is with the kinds of non-commercial books just mentioned that the small publisher can make an important contribution to the total publishing situation. Paradoxically, he, far more than his big-business associate, can afford to be centrally concerned with the primary function of publishing and only peripherally concerned with its necessary by-product, profits. As a result he can experiment with the traditional patterns, and, perhaps, effect some modification of stale attitudes and procedures.

One of the possibilities that needs to be discussed here is the consideration that the manuscript we are talking about might see the light of day by means of a subsidy. I have had a good deal of experience in this area... If subsidy is to be regarded as one of the possible answers for the non-commercial manuscript, certain safeguards ought to be instituted, not only for the subsidizer, but for the publisher as well.

1. The subsidy ought not to be paid directly to the publisher. [Since presumably it would be required for manufacturing.]
2. It ought not to come from an individual.
3. The royalty rate can be no higher than the usual royalty paid on commercial ventures. It can be argued cogently that it should be lower.
4. The underwriter ought to ascertain whether the firm that issues the book commands sufficient respect to get the book reviewed and sold.
5. As it is being done at present, the underwriting of fiction and poetry is a very dubious procedure at best. Some kind of procedure involving an authoritative certification of the value of the manuscript ought to be established.

You will note that I am somewhat sensitive in regard to the publisher's position in the subsidy arrangement. "Subsidy" is a dirty word in publishing circles, and damage to the publisher's reputation — if he is frank and open about his participation in such ventures — is assured. Frequently, I think this deters a well-meaning and capable firm from taking on such a manuscript because of what the consequences might be in terms of public relations. And yet, if appropriate safeguards are taken, the subsidy arrangement can make a meaningful contribution to the total publishing situation.

Partially responsible for the negative view of subsidy are the out-and-out vanity presses, firms that offer immortality in the guise of a printing service they call publishing at a price to the author of several times the cost. The practice is reprehensible because the firms with very few exceptions dangle prospects that are by and large unattainable. Their prospectuses abound with the names of famous authors whose books would not have seen the light of day if they or their friends had not had the courage to underwrite publication. "Martyrdom's long list," says Edward Uhlan in his readable but self-serving *Rogue of Publishers' Row*, "included James Joyce....Finally Sylvia Beach, urged by Joyce's friend, Ezra Pound, printed a thousand copies at her own expense in Paris." Uhlan mentions Dreiser, E.A. Robinson, Upton Sinclair, Walt Whitman, Edward Fitzgerald, and Zane Grey among those who paid cash to publish. What Uhlan of Exposition Press does not mention are any of his authors of even remotely comparable stature or note.

I worked for Uhlan when I was still in college in the 1930's. My job was to edit at $.40 an hour "masterpieces" of poetry that had been "selected" to appear in his vanity anthologies. Most of the illiteracies had to be transmuted into acceptable English. Not once did any poet object to the transformation, some of which bore very little resemblance to the original gibberish. Surprisingly, occasionally I would encounter a polished poem worth reading. Since I was also hired to do the proofreading after the type was set I was given another whack at the Muse. But with author alterations at $.08 [*sic*] a line, I was cautioned against too many liberties. I learned at first hand the incredible lure of immortality that these anthologies held. The approach worked, and the authors were generally happy with their copies of the anthology containing their work, purchased at the rate of one book for each half-page of poetry. As I have indicated earlier, I worked for Uhlan again just before the founding of Twayne. Some of the manuscripts that were offered Exposition Press seemed to me to be publishable in at least small editions, and I tried to persuade my boss that he could strengthen his imprint and his standing as a publisher by taking some of these on at his own risk. I was not successful.

The author who is contemplating signing with a vanity press ought to know that bookstores and reviewers are disinclined to handle books issued by the known vanity firms, despite the occasional exceptions that these firms would like to have you believe is the rule. As a matter of fact the royalty that the firms offer — usually 40% of the list price — would preclude any bookstore sales, where the discount would average at least 40%. Forty percent to the author and 40% to the bookstore leaves only 20% of the sales dollar for the publisher's overhead which I would estimate at least at 31 to 35%. My query, therefore, were I offered such a royalty would be: Mr. Publisher, how do you derive the money necessary to keep your operation going? The honest answer, of course, is "It can't be done." The vanity operator knows it cannot be done, but he doesn't expect to sell many books and he probably has made a handsome profit on the production of the book, and the chances are he hasn't bound all the books. Authors involved in any subsidy deal ought to make sure that all the books in the edition contracted for are bound. Should they eventually be faced with the fact that the publisher cannot sell any more copies of the title and want to take over his inventory they will find unbound books an additional expense. It is also a good idea that any promotion or advertising the publisher agrees to, be so specified in the contract for publication.

Today it is still possible for a small house to publish profitably scholarly specialized titles in editions of 1000 copies. Reprinters, such as Octagon Books, for whom I acted as consultant and president when it became a part of Hippocrene Books, reprint profitably as few as 400 to 500 copies of an existing work. What makes such a limited edition profitable is the elimination of the cost of typesetting, for what is being reprinted is an already existing text. Today's electronic typewriters are able to provide manuscripts in acceptable book fonts, edited and properly aligned, and ready for printing. The ratio of price to cost of such editions would range from eight or ten to one and ought to be sufficiently profitable without subsidy, my experience indicates. In fact the publisher probably could accommodate a small advance to the author against royalties in order to provide copy ready for camera after the editorial processing. Overhead, however, would require that such an undertaking involve a publishing program, not a single or occasional title.

VIII

The End of Twayne, Inc. and Thereafter

WHY DID WE SELL TWAYNE? I HAVE OFTEN ASKED OR been asked the question over the years. The answer varies over time but essentially it had relatively little to do with greed. Twenty-three years after its founding, thanks to the success of our Lifetime Series subscriptions, Twayne had a very comfortable sum in the bank, and our production line was humming. As I have indicated earlier, in 1972, the last year of Twayne's independent existence, we had published more than 100 titles, most of them series books that had already been spoken for. So, money wasn't the problem it had been for most of our years.

But the question of succession was beginning to bother me. Joel Saltzman had died in 1967, and no one in my family was in a position to carry on.

My son seemed well on his way to a promising medical career, and I had been unsuccessful in attracting the necessary talent from the outside. Joe Jones, editor of the New English Literature section of TWAS, dealing with the British Commonwealth areas, put it to me quite bluntly over luncheon one day. What happens to my authors, he wanted to know, if something happens to you? His intimation of my mortality, while flattering in the context of his remarks, brought me face to face with an awareness of my responsibility. Twayne had agreed to shoulder this very large publishing program and had made commitments to the authors who had agreed to write books for us, hundreds of which were nearing completion. And, of course, I owed a good deal to my family as well. But a catastrophe could wipe out everything, and so it was that when a then ITT unit, the G.K.Hall & Company of Boston — now a part of Macmillan — a well regarded publishing house that catered to a library clientele, came knocking at our door, we were inclined to open it.

All the necessary credentials seemed in order. ITT was then a world communications company, so our growing aspirations in foreign fields would seem to be with the right headquarters company. And, of course, since libraries were our best friends, the marriage with Hall seemed to have been made in heaven! But there were sacrifices of which I was aware. I knew Twayne's poetry list was to be a thing of the past and so was the occasional fiction we had published. I should have suspected that my Judaica list would follow shortly. Gradually, over time, there were other casualties, in areas which I thought originally were safe, including many series titles in TWAS.

Perhaps all this was unavoidable, given the nature of the constraints under which the public corporation operates. The bottom line dictates the course of empire. Whereas I was free as the head of Twayne, Inc. — or little Twayne as I like to call it — to undertake publication of titles that I knew would lose some money but gain the firm some benefit in prestige or principle, my successor could only do so at his peril. The irony of the situation has been noted more than once. The big firm cannot knowingly undertake publication of the sure losers. Only the small firms with their limited overhead can undertake these books.

I remained president of Twayne until the end of 1974 when the corporation was phased out. Actually, however, my input was severely limited after August of 1973 when Twayne was moved to Boston as part of the G.K.Hall operation. I could not move with the firm, as I had made clear at the outset, because of personal obligations. There was initially some talk of maintaining the operation in New York; I was producing the books at a lower cost than they could be manufactured elsewhere. But the move to Boston eventually took place without me and after the move I was effectively out of control, though I remained available for advice, if not for consent, on a number of matters.

Quite a few changes I wholeheartedly approved. The format of Twayne series books has been improved considerably. G.K.Hall has been a pioneer in the use of permanent/durable acid-free paper now used in printing all Twayne books, which are today bound in long-lasting buckram. Editorially, also, there have been changes. Since Sylvia Bowman's retirement, each title seems to have been edited by a recognized specialist on the subject or area written about. The result is, I think, a better book, both as to content and format. But the literary bridge-building to other lands that Sylvia Bowman called attention to in her article is largely gone, and that I deplore. For me that concept had provided the link that united our enterprise and I was convinced that any money lost on an occasional book in this area would be more than reversed in the future. But, obviously, I was a poor salesman, perhaps because of my absence from the scene.

About one of my strengths, however, there seemed to be no question. And that was my ability to get rid of excess inventory. In a way it was an agonizing experience for me. My books had assumed a persona of their own, and I was being asked to preside at the slaughter of "my innocents." But I had to provide a proper burial and, perhaps, a new lease on life for some of the titles. The process is called remaindering.

When a book stops selling or slows down to the point where storage costs exceed sales revenue, the publisher is faced with an insoluble situation. He is damned no matter what he does. When I ran Twayne, I tried to be creative about it. Since our printings were small, I never faced wholesale dumping. What I tried to do periodically was to gather up the returns from bookstores or other customers and try to sell them to libraries at a reduced price, offering them as "with scuffed jackets but otherwise perfect" and try to get as close to cost as possible. This and similar stratagems ameliorated the situation somewhat. But there were non-series titles that did not move at all, and we were glad to get whatever we could for them or give them away to save the cost of storage. Prior to remaindering, of course, the title had to be offered to the author at a reduced price, in keeping with the terms of contract. Recently, some well-known authors — William Buckley, for one — have tried to keep their titles in print by buying up their books scheduled for remainder and, presumably, selling them on demand.

My success with Twayne overstock had made me a marked man, and when I was no longer president of Twayne I took on the chore of disposing of overstock for a number of ITT Publishing companies. I was appointed "Director of Special Sales," a euphemism for "Remainder Maven." I think I got rid of more than a million books.

Stanley Sills, brother of Beverly, was then the head of ITT Publishing. He and I got along quite well despite our continuing disagreement as to what I should be paid. But compensation was not a major factor. Having been an employer myself for nearly twenty-five years, I knew where he was coming from. Besides he thought well of me and my achievements and pro bono extra-curricular activities, not docking me for the time I spent at the first Moscow Book Fair in 1977 when I had the privilege of leading the delegation that set up what was probably the first public Jewish book exhibit in Soviet history. He had tried to get Twayne attached to Bobbs-Merrill, also an ITT operation, prior to the merger with Hall. Had that happened, I would have continued to run Twayne in New York.

Many of the remainders were the "indigestibles," the results of mergers where the editors who had conceived the projects were no longer there to implement them. In the hands of those who had no idea of their provenance, the promotions failed or never took place. The acquiring company then could argue that the title was not selling, or that the title did not fit the new line or the new marketing plan. There were some beautiful books that went down the drain.

One of my last efforts to continue bridge-building even as a part of my remainder activity is contained in the proposal to establish a "World Literature Book Club" which I reprint below:

To: Stanley S. Sills
From: Jacob Steinberg
Re: In-House Remainders

The usual approach to remainders involves dumping to the highest bidder. Possibly this is the *most expedient* way of handling unwanted inventories. It may not be the most *profitable* way. My experience indicates that there may be as much as $1.00 (or more) difference between a "dumped" book and the same book where a special effort is expended.

I am suggesting setting up a special unit to deal with remaindered books for the ITT Publishing companies. It would develop direct-mail skills in attempting to find a market for our books other than the ones we normally seek out. For example, the Twayne line does not now attempt circularization of individual buyers though the line should appeal to scholars, particularly in the humanities or in selected ethnic areas. I do not believe that Bobbs-Merrill does any kind of individual circularization either.

I therefore suggest as a "special effort" attempt in the areas we are talking about, the establishment on a trial basis of a "World Literature Book Club" with selections of low-inventory value from Twayne and the various Bobbs-Merrill lines.

Estimates indicate that a 25,000 circularization of the Modern Language Association membership would involve a cost of $6,000-$6,500 for preparation and mailing at bulk rate of a 4-page 8 1/2 x 11 circular in two-color effect including a promotional letter (and envelopes) extolling the exciting dimensions of our new book club.

Since existing stocks and warehousing would be utilized, the plan could be put into operation in relatively short order once the "go-ahead" decision is made.

My effort, alas, was in vain.

Once my attempt to sell a remainder involving a series of books led to a reappraisal of the project and a reinstatement of it in the publisher's plans. Such was the case with the Bobbs-Merrill series for younger readers, "Childhood of Famous Americans." The prospective buyer wanted to buy all stock, sheets, and the rights to the series. He was much taken with my sales pitch and paid me an unusual compliment. He wrote: "...If it were possible for you to work with me as an advisor, this would be important to me. In the conversations we have had, I have known you to be fair and honest, with an insight to this business to which I would like to have access." I wanted to help the potential purchaser but decided that the conflict of interest required at least a clearance from my employer, which I secured. I thought the idea of the series an excellent one, perhaps in need of updating, but here it was perilously close to disposal. Bobbs decided finally to give it another lease on life, and I think that my remainder efforts helped to revive it.

Remaindering a title is one of the activities that embitters author-publisher relationships, as I have noted elsewhere. Usually, if the book is sold below cost, no royalties are paid to the author. Recently, Farrar-Straus — incidentally one of the firms interested in acquiring Twayne early on — announced that it would pay royalty on remaindered items. This is a step in the right direction, but I am waiting for the Messiah. With the coming of the Millennium, the publisher will declare: "I will pay royalties on all books that I print [Please note that I did not say "sold."] excepting only books given away for review and promotion." And, of course, the percentage of failed books, i.e., titles that do not return a profit to the publisher, will no longer be pegged at 70 to 80%, an astounding percentage that I have been assured is correct. The figure owes much I am sure to the crazy practice of return privileges which permits booksellers to return for full credit within a time frame set by the publisher all unsold copies of a title purchased. As I have indicated in the opening pages of this book, the practice of full returns makes it most hazardous for a small publisher to encounter a best-seller.

With certitude, of course, will come the end of days for remaindering. At least remaindering still puts books into the hands of readers. But shredding — a practice that some big publishers contemplated as a result of a misguided view by

IRS as to the value of books in inventory that held books to be no different from nuts and bolts — seemed to me perilously close to book-burning, and I wrote the following letter which appeared in *Publishers' Weekly*:

RESPONDING TO "THOR"

What's the difference between book burners and book shredders? Surely, publishers who are resorting to the latter method to get rid of surplus inventories as a result of the Thor decision ought to reflect on what they are doing. Aren't they in essence lending credibility to the IRS assertion that there really isn't any difference between nuts and bolts and books?

I should think a professional approach would require that these books wind up with readers, whether by way of remainder or donation to libraries and schools, or even with authors who don't want their work destroyed and can arrange for their books' distribution themselves. For those slow-selling books that can still sell a hundred or so copies a year, which the larger firms can't or won't handle in-house because of overhead, etc., there are smaller houses who would be glad to cooperate in the sale and distribution of quality titles.

The Thor decision is an abomination but our response to it can be handled responsibly and maybe even creatively.

Jacob Steinberg, President
Assn. of Jewish Book Publishers

I was still with ITT Publishing when the letter was written but Stanley Sills was no longer with the company. His replacement had decided to get rid of a massive number of books and had not requested my input. So, I thought I might get my

view across by putting on one of my other hats. I
made sure he got a copy of the letter, but I don't
know if he got the message.

With the departure of Sills, it became quite evident to me that ITT had become disillusioned with
its publishing properties and would be seeking an
early opportunity to get rid of them. Eventually
the publishing companies, including Hall and
Twayne became part of Macmillan. The move I
think was in the best interests of all the parties
involved at the time.

But before that happened, I decided to retire.
This was in September of 1981. While life was
pleasant, it was quite obvious that I wasn't being
given any responsible activities. A consulting
agreement was offered me, but I finally turned it
down. I remained idle for the balance of the year.

In early 1982, however, I joined Hippocrene
Books, as senior consulting editor. George
Blagowidow, the publisher, had been a friend
since the late 60's when he left Funk and Wagnalls
to set up his own marketing group, which represented Twayne for a few years before the merger.
Hippocrene had an active list of travel books, dictionaries, and quality paperbacks. I was able to
assist in a couple of acquisitions Hippocrene
made: Octagon Books, a hard-back reprint house,
and Lee Publishing, a firm interested in China.
As a consequence of the latter acquisition, I was
able to make a couple of trips to China and improve my Chinese language proficiency. Hippocrene published quite a number of books
dealing with China, including Sidney Shapiro's
Jews in Old China which I have already mentioned. I also established a good list of Judaica

titles for the firm, including Stuart Rosenberg's *The New Jewish Identity in America, The Jew in American Sports* by Harold and Meir Ribalow, *Choosing Judaism* by Lydia Kukoff, Alex Goldman's path breaking novel, *The Rabbi Was a Lady* and half a dozen other titles. I left Hippocrene to write this book.

What of the future? One of my associates thought I would never retire. I would hope that he was right. It does not make much sense to spend more than a half-century in a field surviving most of the errors that can be committed and learning therefrom, and then sit back and do nothing. I think it is much better to use out rather than rust out and hopefully an updated version of this title will reveal where I went from here.

AFTERWORD

Twayne Since 1972

JACK STEINBERG HAS ASKED ME TO BRING THE Twayne story up to date, from the time his company was acquired by ITT for G.K. Hall & Co. to the present. I was appointed Senior Editor of Twayne at the time of the acquisition in January 1973 and served as Senior Editor and then as Executive Editor until August 1978, when I became President of G.K. Hall & Co. While my involvement with Twayne became less direct at that point, because of my own background and interests as well as its importance to G.K. Hall's results, Twayne received a great deal of my attention over the following 13 years, until I left G.K. Hall in May 1991.

I first met Jack at the 1972 Modern Language Association Convention in New York. I had been at G.K. Hall & Co. only six months, having been hired as Editor of the Gregg Press reprint division in June 1972. I came looking for Jack at the MLA because I had been told that Twayne Publishers, Inc. was to be acquired shortly, that I would be working with Jack and would be responsible for Twayne at G.K. Hall. Although I was familiar with Twayne through my Master's and Doctoral work in American literature, I had not been involved in any of the acquisitions discussions, didn't know Jacob Steinberg and didn't know how I would be received.

I should not have worried. Jack was warm and welcoming, pleased to learn of my background in American literature and our common experience as graduate students at Columbia. He was also very positive about what could be done to develop Twayne in the future through new series and programs and better marketing. I came to find that Jack's positivism was truly limitless, that he could face any change, any difficulty or unpleasantness, and always imagine reasonable outcomes. Indeed, as he relates in this volume, one of his greatest talents was "the creative conversion of *tsurris*," i.e, the ability to convert trouble into advantage. Ours was a very easy and affirmative collaboration.

I don't want to give the impression that Jack was prepared to walk away from Twayne and hand it over to a perfect stranger. What he was prepared to do was to satisfy himself that I could be trusted with Twayne, that my values were in line with his on what should be done for and with Twayne. Once that trust was established (and it did not happen right away, though Jack's marvelous affability may have given others that impression), Jack did allow himself some distance from what was happening at Twayne.

To me Twayne's history since 1972 falls into four periods: Transition (1973-77); Consolidation (1977-82); Growth (1982-91) and Maturity (1991-).

Transition (1973-77)

This was the period of my most active personal involvement with Twayne. By way of background, I feel I should say a few words about why Twayne was acquired by G.K. Hall, since the rationale for that merger certainly guided my decisions about how to grow and develop Twayne over the full 18 years I was involved. It also casts light on what happens to a small, specialized publisher when it is merged with a larger entity.

ITT's main interest in Twayne was in the Twayne series, primarily the three Authors Series: Twayne's United States Authors Series (TUSAS), English Authors Series (TEAS), and World Authors Series (TWAS). To ITT the Twayne name was synonymous with these series and represented a "franchise" that could be developed and extended by creating other series, not only in literature but in other subject areas.

It is depressing to make these comparisons, but, in a small way Twayne had become like McDonald's: it had won a place in the minds of consumers (in this case, librarians and teachers), who recognized the name and associated it with certain positive, consistent qualities that they value. The values in the Twayne series were: 1) consistency of format (all titles featured common elements, such as a chronology, a brief literary biography, a comprehensive critical analysis of the author's works, a notes and references section, an annotated bibliography, and an index); 2) conciseness (most books were 176 to 192 pages in length, and not lengthy, intimidating tomes); 3) accessibility (the jargon-free prose that Sylvia Bowman referred to earlier, which meant that Twayne books could be read by readers ranging from high school students through graduate students to the general reader); 4) comprehensiveness of coverage (Twayne proposed to include in its series every writer of literary merit); and 5) reference value (the series maintained a scholarly standard and could be relied on as sources of information).

In evaluating a "franchise," a potential buyer is very interested in what is known as market share, which is a portion of total spending on products or services of the same type that is "owned" by a given franchise. In the case of McDonald's, market share is based on the number of locations it occupies. Twayne's market share was based on the standing orders Jack referred to earlier — not only the Lifetime Standing Orders he mentioned (which were prepaid orders), but also what are known as regular standing orders. A regular standing order is a commitment by the library to acquire all titles published in a given program or series until the program is completed or the library cancels the order. Standing orders offer many advantages to a library: they are a predictable form of acquisitions; insure that no titles will be overlooked; guarantee earlier delivery (because they are always shipped first); and usually offer savings in the form of discounts and/or other considerations, such as free shipping or free catalog card kits. For the publisher they are also highly desirable, since they represent firm advance orders for all titles to be published in the program. The Twayne series, particularly the Authors Series, had high standing order levels.

ITT was also attracted by Twayne's potential "synergy" with G.K. Hall. "Synergy" was a corporate concept favored in the 1970s and 1980s by conglomerates to justify their acquisitions. In brief it is the idea that the whole is greater than the sum of its parts. In the case of Twayne, it was argued that the Twayne franchise in literature would help G.K. Hall develop reference programs in that area, and G.K. Hall's contacts and expertise would help Twayne develop new series in nonliterary areas. Oddly enough, synergy actually worked with Twayne, though G.K. Hall was by far the greater beneficiary initially, as will be seen.

The decision had been made by ITT to move Twayne to Boston and consolidate its operations with G.K. Hall as soon as possible. Under New York state law, Twayne Publishers, Inc., the corporation, had to remain in place for a period of a year to allow any creditors to come forward. During that period Jack remained as President, I was Executive Editor and G.K. Hall acted as Agent for Twayne Publishers, Inc. Shipping and warehousing stayed at Twayne's contracted service on Long Island. Because G.K. Hall still had manual order processing systems, Twayne continued to be invoiced by the PCS data processing service in New York (PCS continued to invoice Twayne until 1978 when G.K. Hall finally installed its own computer system).

Only two people moved up to Boston from the staff at 31 Union Square West: a bookkeeper who only came for a few months to make certain that Twayne's accounting was handled properly at Hall; and Twayne's Managing Editor, Harvey Graveline, who stayed for two years and played a critical role in the transition. Harvey assembled a Boston-based group of freelance copyeditors and proofreaders, established links with Twayne's field editor network and helped set up a new group of production vendors (typesetters and book manufacturers) while managing a heavy workload (124 new titles with half again as many reprints in 1974).

The Editorial staff at that time consisted of myself, Harvey, an editorial assistant and a part-time production assistant. Marketing was handled by a separate Marketing department, which added one person to manage Twayne promotions and another to handle book reviews and conventions.

The first three years (1973-76) were spent organizing and evaluating editorial programs in order to focus development on programs and areas with the greatest potential beyond the Authors Series. With limited staff we could not provide editorial support for non-series titles, and the relatively few titles of this kind (including those in Judaica that Jack refers to) began to go out of print.

The translations area was one I tried to preserve through expansion, and with Jack's help I was able to increase activity in the Library of

Netherlandic Literature (edited by Egbert Krispyn, who was also editor of the TWAS Netherlandic Literature section) and the Library of Scandinavian Literature (edited by Erik Friis) and launch the Library of Classical Arabic Literature with Ilse Lichtenstadter, Professor of Arabic at Harvard. We also kept the Introduction Series going by adding Introduction volumes on Classical Arabic (by Professor Lichtenstadter) and Filipino literature. The exchange programs Jack had started with the Romanians and Bulgarians (and had tried to get going with the Poles), simply could not be sustained. To provide a marketing context for the translations we created Twayne's International Studies and Translations Program (TISAT), and this allowed us to keep the translation program active well into the 1980s.

The main problem with TISAT and many of the other Twayne series we tried to launch or develop outside of the area of literary criticism was what can be called a lack of critical mass. The Authors Series had critical mass because the flow of manuscripts from Sylvia Bowman and the TWAS Field Editors allowed us to publish 60 to 100 titles per year (a minimum of 20 titles in each subseries). TISAT titles, for example, were few and far between. The lack of a reasonable level of title output makes the marketing of a Twayne series very difficult and expensive. The best Twayne programs provided enough manuscript flow to allow us to publish a consistent number of titles per year and thus be able to offer and market Standing Order plans.

All of the four other Twayne series that had been started when Twayne was acquired were in

non-literary areas and had relatively low rates of
title output. Of the four the Immigrant Heritage
of America Series (IHAS), edited by Cecyle S.
Neidle, was a program that we were able to sustain in its own right. Even though we were lucky
to publish three or four titles per year in the
series, the new titles (and each title in the backlist) sold very well. In those days in the 1970s the
interest in ethnic and multicultural studies was
high and we could sell up to 3,000 copies of each
title.

The three other series were: Twayne's Rulers
and Statesmen of the World (TROW), edited by
Hans Louis Trefousse of Brooklyn College; the
Great Thinkers Series (GTS); a series Jack had
acquired from Washington Square Press that was
edited by Arthur W. Brown of CUNY and Thomas
S. Knight of Adelphi; and the Great Educators
Series (GES), a new series edited by Samuel
Smith, a distinguished editor from Barnes & Noble. Each of these programs published a small
number of titles per year, ranging from one or two
in GES to as many as 10 in TROW.

The President of G.K. Hall, Phillips A. Treleaven, was not very fond of these programs. It
was his view that we should concentrate on developing more series in literary and related areas
where Twayne was stronger and it was easier to
develop high-output programs. I was able to convince him that we could improve the results by
consolidating the three little series into one larger
one, to be called Twayne's World Leaders Series
(TWLS). This series would correspond to TWAS
and make it clear that the series was doing for

biography what the Authors Series had done for literary criticism.

So TWLS was formed and did reasonably well, with some titles like Donald Koster's *Transcendentalism in America* outselling most Authors Series titles. The relative success of the series and my argument that Twayne needed an Authors Series in the Social Sciences did not change Treleaven's mind. In 1976 the decision was made to terminate TWLS. I did not agree with this decision. I was able to get authorization to offer publication to any author who had begun substantive work on his or her manuscript and who could deliver the manuscript within a reasonable time. It turned out as we went through the process of contacting the authors of each of the 125 contracts outstanding that more than 80 (almost all in the former TROW series) had not done any work of consequence and had no objection to cancellation of their contracts. Some 10 to 20 did not want to have their works published in a terminal program and withdrew. The rest did have their works published. TWLS carried on publishing committed titles until about 1980. I still maintain it was a good and needed series. The proof of this is that not many years later we replaced that program with another, Twayne's Biography Series.

While we were making negative progress, so to speak, in the Social Sciences, we were undertaking major projects in the Humanities. My first real contribution to Twayne was the Twayne Critical Editions Program (TCEP), a thoroughly scholarly venture dedicated to publishing definitive editions of the works of American writers. This program was born at the 1974 Modern Language

Association convention. There I was approached by Lewis Leary, my mentor at Columbia, to see if I could help move *The Complete Works of Washington Irving* away from the University of Wisconsin Press. Wisconsin had published the first three volumes in 1969 and 1970 and then lost interest in the project. Leary was the Chairman of the Edition's Editorial Board. To cut a long story short, I committed Twayne to the project and made an arrangement with Thompson Webb of Wisconsin to sell their inventory so that the edition could remain intact.

The Irving edition was the only one of some 20 editions of American Authors accredited by the Modern Language Association's Center for Editions of American Authors (later Center for Scholarly Editions) that was published by a commercial publisher. All of the rest were published by university presses. Twayne was also one of the few to complete an edition: it took 14 years (until 1988) to publish the remaining 27 volumes, and all that happened in the course of finishing the project is a story in itself!

TCEP was designed to enhance Twayne's image in the scholarly community by making clear our commitment to authoritativeness and quality. Twayne did gain some of that authority and many many friends through TCEP, but it was largely a labor of love. Most of the Irving volumes sold fewer than 800 copies. The other projects we undertook in this program did little better, but I am still proud that Twayne was able to publish *The Complete Works of Anne Bradstreet, Selected Letters of W.D. Howells* and two volumes of the *Collected Writings of Edgar Allan Poe*, in addition to the Irving Edition. As part of this program we also published five volumes of a scholarly annual, *Studies in the American Renaissance,* edited by Joel Myerson of the University of South Carolina, from 1977 to 1981.

My other early contribution to Twayne was Twayne's Theatrical Arts Series (TTAS). I originally conceived of it as a section in TWLS dealing with achievements of individuals in the performing arts. However, I thought it wiser to start another series, and was fortunate enough to persuade Warren French to edit the heart of the program, the section on film directors. Warren was then in the English department at Indiana University and was easily Twayne's best author in terms of style and approach: we had just published in TUSAS his revised editions of *J.D. Salinger* (1974) and *John Steinbeck* (1975). Warren launched into the idea with characteristic vigor and in less than two years we published the first three volumes, all on film directors, in 1977.

This series had a fairly successful run. We tried to add a dance section but this amounted to a total of three titles. What remains of the original TTAS is now called Twayne's Filmmakers Series. A separate Twayne's Music Series was started at the same time, but like the dance program it resulted in very few titles in proportion to our editorial efforts. There are very few who can or will write about musicians and dancers, and we were unable to find enough authors to sustain either program. Most of the authors in film were literature professors and many, like Warren, had written critical studies of authors for Twayne.

Consolidation (1977-82)

While these other developments were taking place, Sylvia Bowman, the founding editor of the Authors Series, had a stroke in 1975 and was hospitalized for some time. Although she recovered remarkably well and took a year off, she was no longer able to keep up the incredible workload she had sustained since the series had begun. This workload consisted of personally editing 15-25 titles per year each in the U.S. and English Authors Series (most of the editing was done during summer vacations) and directing 23 specialist Field Editors in the World Authors Series. Sylvia also issued all contracts in all three series (though we kept the signed contract files in Boston) and kept track of due dates and work in progress. All this while she was a Chancellor of Indiana University! During 1976 and into 1977 a backlog of manuscripts developed and even contracts began to back up. It reached the point where we were no longer sure what manuscripts were with Sylvia being edited.

It was an impossible situation that was only solved by nothing less than a complete restructuring of the Authors Series editorial process. Sylvia agreed to step down as General Editor of TWAS and as Editor of TUSAS and TEAS. (She then went to work on her own study of Edward Bellamy which was published as TUSAS 300 in 1988.) All editorial responsibility for the series was shifted to Boston in the summer of 1977. I had to come up with not only a new way of relating to the 23 TWAS editors but create two editorial boards — one each for TUSAS and TEAS. In the end we needed 11 Field Editors to take Sylvia's place in just those two series, and we still had to administer TWAS!

The 11 new Field Editors helped us catch up in TUSAS and TEAS by the end of 1978 and, I must say, brought more scholarly authority to the series, since each was responsible for a specific period that he was a specialist in.

The TWAS situation was harder to gain control of because the record of contract deadlines and extensions we inherited was unclear and we had to work through the 23 TWAS Editors to find out what was due, what was coming in and what was complete in manuscript. By the middle of 1979 more TWAS manuscripts had showed up than anyone expected and, even though we were publishing 60 TWAS titles a year at that point, a backlog developed and began to build steadily. By the end of 1980 we had more than 100 TWAS manuscripts in house waiting to be put into production (in addition to the 30 or so in production at any one time).

To make matters worse, a recession began in 1979 that had an unprecedented negative effect on library spending. Sales weakened in many Twayne series but they plunged in TWAS to a point where we were lucky if we could sell 500 copies of some titles. Inventory mounted to horrifying levels. Standing Orders were canceled as customers complained that many of the titles in TWAS were too obscure or on very minor authors. All this led to a crisis that, sadly, led to a tragedy.

It is a fact of corporate life that when things are going well you get very little attention but when things go bad you have more help than you can manage. In 1981-82, we were flooded with assistance from ITT, and not just because of sales problems. (There was also an unsuccessful UAW organizing drive at G.K. Hall in the first six months of 1981.) It was clear that if we priced TWAS titles at the level we would have to in order to print 500 copies or less, the price for TWAS titles would probably have to be doubled. At the time it seemed likely that that kind of increase could lose us enough of the remaining Standing Orders to kill TWAS. I am now fairly certain that the price increase would have worked, but then I was very uncertain.

The advice we received from ITT in 1982 was simple and direct: don't publish the titles that won't sell. The lawyers argued that "market conditions" had changed so drastically since we signed the contracts for these books that we were no longer obligated to publish them and incur losses, even though the authors had kept their part of the agreement by completing the manuscripts. Both Liz Kubik, Hall's Editor in Chief and my successor as Twayne Executive Editor, and I objected to this opinion and argued against it. In the end the lawyers prevailed, and 78 TWAS contracts were canceled.

It was an action I deeply regret. To be perfectly honest, I simply did not realize at the time what I was agreeing to do. My experience with TWLS had shown how a flexible approach can lead to a fair outcome. I did not understand that legal opinions in large corporations are by their nature inflexible and thought we could take steps to ameliorate the bad effects on our authors. I found out how wrong I was after the contract cancellations were done: even though many authors approached us with ameliorative proposals, the legal response was to stick to the argument and tough it out. As a result many good people suffered. ITT and G.K. Hall were sued by 17 of the authors in a very nasty class action for fraud and deception as well as breach of contract. The process of the suit took more than five years to resolve. When Macmillan acquired G.K. Hall in 1985 the legal climate changed, the wrong was admitted and an offer was made to publish, with compensation, but it was too late because positions had hardened on the other side by then. In December 1987 the authors lost the class action for fraud and deception in U.S. District Court and a subsequent appeal was denied in June 1988. We renewed the offer to publish and some of the books finally appeared in TWAS.

This is clearly a case where if Twayne had still been a small publisher, the cancellations would not have happened. Instead, a practical solution — Jack's "creative conversion of *tsurris*" — would have been found. (I suspect Jack would have tried raising the price and would have discussed the backlog problem with the authors to reach a compromise. As it was, Jack had no part in the decision, having retired from ITT by then.)

The sad effects of this action extended beyond the injury to the authors and the toll it took on Liz, the Twayne staff and myself. It also cast a shadow in many quarters on the achievement of TWAS and even the Authors Series, and many scholars, in foreign languages particularly, no longer wanted to have anything to do with Twayne, to their detriment and ours.

This mistake should not take away from the achievement of the Authors Series. In the past 30 years Twayne has published more than 1,900 studies of individual authors or literary movements in the Series. Many of the titles were the first published studies on their subjects and nearly all have been both well researched and well written. The Authors Series is the largest single project in the history of publishing: no other program has produced so many volumes of such quality over such a long period of time.

Growth (1982-91)

Twayne over time has become much more than the Authors Series at G.K. Hall. In addition to the filmmakers and critical edition programs I developed with Harvey Graveline and his successor, Alice D. Phalen, Twayne under Liz Kubik and her Editors (Caroline Birdsall, Anita McClellan, Meghan Wander and Anne Jones) produced a virtual explosion of new series between 1982 and 1991. By May 1991 there were 30 Series with published titles (and five or six more in process of development, if I recall correctly). Sixteen of the series were in Literature, four were in The Arts (all developed in the 1970s) and ten were in History, Social Science and Political Science (all but one developed in the 1980s).

In Literature we launched the first of a series of what we called closed-end series (because they included only a specific number of volumes and were not open to additions like the Authors Series) in 1983 with *The American Short Story, 1945-1980: A Critical History*, the first volume in a planned 10-volume Twayne's Critical History of the Short Story Series. This Critical History idea was further developed in 1987-89 with Critical Histories of the Novel, British Drama, and Poetry.

The major additions to Twayne's literature offerings, however, were three open-ended series, developed in-house, that substantially added to the Twayne idea. They were: Twayne's Young Adult Authors Series (begun in 1984), a separate program of studies of authors for young adults that are written for young adults/high school students; Twayne Masterwork Studies (1986), a program offering short, classroom-centered critical studies of individual works of literature; and Twayne's Studies in Short Fiction Series (1988), collections of essays, interviews and other material on individual short story writers.

G.K. Hall's Library Reference group also contributed to Twayne in literature by developing with OCLC, the cooperative library network, a CD-ROM program called DiscLit, published in June 1991. The first volume, *DiscLit: American Authors*, features the full texts of 143 Twayne U.S. Authors Series titles together with 127,000 bibliographic citations on these same authors drawn from the OCLC Online Catalog.

As much as I was at heart a Literature publisher, Liz Kubik's strongest interest was in History and the Social Sciences, and in these areas she and her editors broke ground and developed a number of important programs for Twayne, all edited by distinguished scholars. Liz began in 1982 with a closed-end series, American Women in the Twentieth Century: this is a decade-by-decade review of the status and progress of women in the

United States; it is designed to be used as a definitive history when completed. This was followed by the Social Movements Series (1984), a program of critical studies examining the goals and histories of major American social movements, from the Civil Rights to Temperance to Gay Rights to Conservatism, all in a comprehensive yet concise format.

TWLS itself was partially resurrected with Twayne's American Biography Series (1986), a program of longer but still concise biographies of American leaders, from Henry Luce to Lyndon B. Johnson. If development is continued on this program by Macmillan, it will evolve into an international program and be a very worthy successor indeed for the World Leaders Series.

The Immigrant Heritage of America Series was revived and strengthened and a Business History Series (1984) was launched as well. Two series were started in Social and Cultural History: American Thought and Culture (1989) and Studies in Intellectual and Cultural History (1991).

The program I most admired, however, was Twayne's Oral History Series (1987), developed by Anne Jones. These are priceless collections of eyewitness accounts of historical developments, from the wartime work of women in armament factories (*Rosie the Riveter Revisited: Women, the War and Social Change*) to the Nazi death camps (*Witnesses to the Holocaust: An Oral History*).

Overall, this was a period of great creative growth at Twayne. Whether it was the horror/stimulus of the TWAS cancellations at the beginning or simply the fact that a whole new group of editors came to Twayne in those years, the results were nothing less than phenomenal.

Maturity (1991 to now)

I call this final period "Maturity" because that is my hope for Twayne now. In July 1991 the editorial and marketing activities of Twayne Publishers were moved to New York from Boston as part of a radical restructuring of G.K. Hall by Macmillan. Of the 11 acquisition and production editors involved with Twayne only one moved to New York. I was not there at the end, having left shortly after the plan was announced in May. Twayne is now an operating unit of Macmillan Publishing Company in New York, part of its Reference Division.

Conclusion

I am proud of my part in the history of Twayne. Save for the regrettable episode with the TWAS cancellations, a great deal was achieved in Twayne's name for the benefit of scholarship and understanding during the 18 years Twayne was in Boston.

Having said that I must also add that I do not think that book publishing benefits from large corporate ownership. Large corporations tend to think of publishing as a manufacturing process and continually look for ways to increase the profitability of the business, such as creating economies of scale through consolidation and ramping up production. ITT was certainly like that and in the end so was Macmillan (though until Maxwell acquired Macmillan in November 1988 that company was run as a publisher and not as a corporate holding company).

As you have realized in reading Jack's book, publishing is too intimate and personal a business to thrive in a corporate environment. I would like to believe that Twayne was able to grow as it did because it was part of a small appendage of the corporate body (G.K. Hall) far away up in Boston. At G.K. Hall the scale was right for Twayne.

The truly impressive thing about Twayne is how, over 18 years, it retained the sense of hope and enterprise that Jack had brought to it. Jack Steinberg may never have had a best seller but he did create one of the greatest enterprises in the history of scholarly publishing — and in my book that is achievement enough.

THOMAS T. BEELER
Hampton Falls, New Hampshire
March 1992

Index

Achievement of Soviet Medicine, The (Gannt, ed.), 152

Aderman, Ralph, M., 144, 145

Advertising, on an inquiry basis, 130*n*.; does it sell books? 223f.

Afrocentrics, 53

Ainsley, Claude, 28

Albany, N.Y., 21, 23-26

Anti-Semitism, 23f., 25

American Academy of Arts and Letters, 52

American Council for Judaism, book program, 104

American Federation of Musicians, 95

American in China, An (Shapiro), 181

American Jewish Committee, the Moscow Book Fairs, 200

American Scandinavian Foundation, publishing program, 169

American Sexual Tragedy (Ellis), 77

America's Tenth Man (Chambers, ed.), 94f., 201f.

Am-Rus Literary and Music Agency, 138, 152

Anti-Defamation League, at the Moscow Book Fairs, 198, 200

Army Specialized Training Program (ASTP), 34

Ars Polona, 136

Artist in America, An (Benton), Twayne edition of, 57ff., 66, 69

Artisjus, Hungarian Authors' Agency, 151

Artists, a subscription plan for, 125 ff.

Aspects of Revolt (Nomad), 225

Assignment China (Schuman), 178

Associated American Artists Galleries, 57, 59

Attica uprising, 51

Association of Jewish Book Publishers, at the Moscow Book Fairs, 104f., 192-201; advertising experiment for members' books, 224

Authors, ego involvement, 115f.; proprietary rights but not censorship, 120ff.; trial editions for new, 125; clandestine government subsidies, 135; intrinsic right to be read in other lands, 139; royalties on library borrowings, 177; author-publisher relations, 219-27, 244; who paid to publish, 233

269

Authors Series, a solid success, 129; *see also under* Twayne Publishers, Inc., Twayne's U.S. Authors Series, Twayne's English Authors Series, Twayne's World Authors Series

Bagby, George, *nom de plume* of Aaron Marc Stein, 35
Barefoot (Stancu), 145
Barter arrangement for books, 146, 159, 166, 167
Battle, Lucius D., 112
Bechet, Sidney, *Treat It Gentle*, 55f., 92
Beck, Dave, 95
Beebe, Lucius, 114
Beeler, Thomas T., 9*n*., 18; Twayne after 1972, 249-68
Belgium, aid to Dutch or Flemish authors, 171
Bell, William A., 141
Bellamy, Edward, 108, 111, 115
Benowitz, Irving, TWAS copyeditor, 118
Benton, Rita, 61, 70, 71
Benton, Thomas Hart, Twayne projects, 56-72; lithographs, 59, 62, 214
Best-sellers, 9f.
Biblical Hebrew Grammar (Nakarai), 100
Birdsall, Caroline, Twayne editor, 264
Black poetry, 50f., 52-55
Blagowidow, George, 17, 183
Blagowidow, Ludmilla, 183
Blish, James, 74
Blocked funds, 136f.
B'nai B'rith, the Moscow Book Fairs, 198, 200
Boardman, Fon W., what sells books, 224

Bobbs-Merrill, 241, 242, 243
Book club, definition, 224
Book exchanges, 146, 159, 166, 167
Bookman Associates, 14, 49, 95, 100, 229-36
Book of Songs, The, Chinese classic, 174
Book reviewers, 114f., 119f., 224f.
Books, what sells? 225
Botha, Dr. Gyorgy, 151
Bowman, Sylvia E., the Authors Series, 16, 107-34, 240; and TWAS, 163, 173; annual round-up letters to authors, 220; illness and resignation as editor, 260
British writers, *see* Twayne's English Authors Series
Brookhouser, Frank, 62, 63
Brooklyn College, 27
Brooks, Bessie, Aunt Bessie, 21, 26
Brooks, Gwendolyn, 51
Brooks, Isidore, 26
Brown, Arthur W., 98
Brownsville, Jewish ghetto of Brooklyn, N.Y., 20
Bruskov, Vladimir, Novosti editor, 156f.
Buckley, William, 241
Bulgaria, literary explorations, 124, 148-51
"Burn, Witch, Burn," English film, 74
Butler, Ben, notorious Civil War general, 96

Cable, George Washington, 111
Call It Sleep (Roth), 102
Capouya, Emile, 17, 19*n*., 42
Cargill, Oscar, for wide lati-

tude in use of copyright material, 123

Case-Record from a Sonnetorium (Moore), 73

Cassell and Company, 56

Censorship, active private and public, 82; the role of the permissions editor, 120f.

Chang, Carsun, 172

Chase Manhattan, happy consequences of the loan not made, 185-87

Chiang Kai-shek, 12*n*., 36

"Childhood of Famous Americans," Bobbs-Merrill series, 243

China, Twayne's interest in, 13, 172-84

China's Red Masters (Elegant), 86ff., 172

China Weekly Review, charge of sedition, 179f.

Chinese language program in WWII, 34-36

Christian Problem, The...(Rosenberg), 131*n*.

Churchill, Winston, 51

CIA, book scandals of the 1960's, 135

Ciardi, John, Twayne's poetry editor, 11, 14-16; central to Twayne's early achievement, 41-95; on M.B. Tolson's poetry, 52, 53; Sidney Bechet's autobiography, 55f.; Benton projects, 56ff.; science fiction and fantasy publications for Twayne, 73-75; proposed volume of limericks with Gorey illustrations, 81f.; the Dante translations, 83; reverses field on poetry, 91; A.M. Lindbergh controversy, 92

Clinical Sonnets (Moore), 73

College and University Press Services, 108, 131-33

College English, 129

Columbia Encyclopedia, 28

Commins, Saxe, 79

Congress, U.S., book scandals of the 1960's, 135

Cooperative mailings, 129, 186

Cooper Union Gallery, 125-28

Copyright law, an author's proprietary rights *vs.* censorship, 120ff.

Cornell University, wartime Chinese language program, 12*n*., 34-36

Cousins, Norman, 64, 110

Crane, Hart, 53

Crown Publishers, 100

Cronbach, Abraham, 103, 104

Crawford, William, U.S. Ambassador to Romania, 140, 141

Current Chinese Readings (Wang), 172

Davis, A.R., *Tu Fu*, 175f.

Decker, Clarence, 61

deWit, D.J.J.D., efforts on behalf of Dutch literary works, 171

Dictionary of American Underworld Lingo (Goldin, *et al.*), 83-86, 224

Direct-mail promotions, 129, 185ff., 224

Doduck, I. Frederick, 132

Dream of the Red Chamber, 13, 42, 172, 173

Drew, Joseph, Moscow Book Fair delegate, 197

Durant, Will, *Story of Philosophy*, 10, 208

Dutch literary works, 171

Eastern Europe, literary diplomacy, 136ff., 167, 168

East N.Y. Vocational H.S., 28-31

Editors, and the author's ego, 115f., censorship role of permissions editor, 120f.

Elegant, Robert, *China's Red Masters*, 86-89, 172

Eliot, T.S., 53

Ellsberg, Daniel, 79

Eminescu Publishing House, 146

English authors, *see* Twayne's English Authors Series

English Journal, 129

Ethnocentric critics, 53

Evening Tales (Sadoveanu), 139

Exposition Press, 38, 233f.

Fairy Tales and Legends from Romania, 146

Fantasy literature, 73-75

Farrar-Straus, remainder policy, 244

Featherbedding and Job Security (Leiter), 96

Ferber, Edna, stops publication of TUSAS volume, 122

Flasch, Joy, 52*n*., 54

Flemish authors, 171

Flower, Desmond, 56

Foundation for the Promotion of the Translation of Dutch Literary Works, 171

Freedom at Issue, article on Moscow Book Fair, 193

Freedom House, 193

French, Warren, *John Steinbeck*, 9*n*.; section on film directors for TTAS, 259

Friis, Erik J., editor, 18, 170

Frost, Robert, 124

Fugitive group, 52, 72

Gannt, William Horsley, M.D., 152

Garvey, Bob, 195

Germany and American Neutrality (Trefousse), 96

Gillon, Adam, TWAS editor, 118

G.K. Hall, *see* Hall, G.K.

Golden, Harry, brouhaha with Twayne, 208ff.

Golden Age of Travel, The (Morrison), 83

Goldin, Hyman E., 83, 100, 101

Goldman, Robert I., at Moscow Book Fair, 200

Goldman, Sid, 132

Gore Vidal (White), TUSAS title gets lead review in N.Y. *Times*, 225

Gorey, Edward, early illustrations, 73

Great American Parade, The (Duteil), 68

Great Educators Series, 256

Great Histories Series, 97

Great Thinkers Series, 98, 256

Gregg Press, 249

Grove Press, *Lady Chatterley's Lover*, 15

Haldeman-Julius, Emanuel, 208ff.

Hall, Donald A., *Harvard Advocate Anthology*, 77-79

Hall, G.K., & Company, Twayne becomes a part of, 10, 238ff., 263

Hanscom, Leslie, on author-publisher relations, 219

Harlem Gallery (Tolson), 53-55

Harding, Walter, *The Variorum Walden*, 203f.

Harris, David, at the Moscow Book Fair, 200

Harvard Advocate Anthology (Hall, ed.), 77-79
Harvard University, 12*n*., 41
Hatem, George, 184
Hebrew Criminal Law and Procedure (Goldin), 101
Hadoar, Hebrew weekly,100
Helsinki Accords, the Moscow Book Fair, 194ff.
Hicks, Granville, 114
"Hidden" censorship, 120ff.
Hill and Wang, 56
Hill of Venus, The (Moore), 73
Hines, Alberta, "Taps," 134, 163
Hippocrene Books, 98, 103, 131*n*., 183, 235, 246f.
History of the Romanian People (Otetea), 146
Hoffa, Jimmy, 95
Holland, aid to Dutch or Flemish authors, 171
Honolulu *Star-Bulletin*, 12*n*.
Howells, William Dean, 114
Hungary, literary explorations, 151-52
"Hymn Singer, The," Benton litho, 57, 71

"If We Must Die," most popular Black poem, 50f.
Illegitimate Sonnets (Moore), 73
Immigrant Heritage of America Series, 98f., 256
Information Media Guaranty program, 136
Introductions Series, 124, 143, 159, 255; *to Modern Bulgarian Literature*, 148; *Modern Polish Literature*, 136, 151; *Romanian Literature*, 143-44, 152
Inventory shrinkage, 71, 214-18

Ion (Rebreanu), Romanian novel, 145
Irving, Washington, 116, 258
Isachenko, George, Soviet diplomat, 155
ITT, acquires Twayne for publishing unit, 238, 251-53, 267; sells publishing properties, 246; unwanted legal assistance, 262-63
Ives, Burl, subject of Benton's "The Hymn Singer," 60

Jaffe, Adrian, 144
Jefferson High School, B'klyn, 26
Jew in American Sports (Ribalow), 103
Jewish Book Council, 105, 200
Jewish Exponent, article on Jewish books, 99-102
Jews in Old China (Shapiro, ed.), 181, 182, 183
Jews in the Soviet Union, 169, 192-201
John Steinbeck (French), sales of, 9*n*.
Jones, Joseph, TWAS editor, 118, 238
Jones, Ralph, State Department official, 138
Journal of Ecumenical Studies, The, 131*n*.
Judaica, 99-105

Kansas City *Star*, 57
Katherine Mansfield (Daly), 177
Khokhlov, I., Novosti editor, 160
Kipling, Rudyard, 11
Kirilov, Nikolai, Bulgarian editor, 148
Kirk, Frank, editor, 148

Knight, Thomas S., series editor, 98
Knox, George, appraisal of TUSAS, 119f.
Korean War, 180
Kreymborg, Alfred, 49
Krispyn, Egbert, TWAS editor, 118, 171
Krzyzanowski, Ludwik, TWAS editor, 118
Kubik, Liz, Twayne editor, 262, 263, 264, 265

La Cucina (Sorce),77
Lady Chatterley's Lover (Lawrence), unexpurgated edition published, 15, 72
Lardner, John, 83*n*., 225*n*.
Lattimore, Owen, 12
Lawrence, D.H., 15, 72
Leary, Lewis, *Complete Works of Washington Irving*, 258
Lee Publishing, 246
Lehmann, John, 48
Leiter, Robert D., economics editor, 95f.
Lerner, Harry, Jewish books at Moscow Book Fair, 195
Levin, Martin, Jewish book exhibits at Moscow Book Fair, 200
Levinson, Bernard, Jewish book exhibits at Moscow Book Fair, 200
Lewenthal, Reeves, 57f., 67
Lewis, Sinclair, 10
"Lexicographers in Stir," *New Yorker* article, 83, 224
Libraries, royalties to authors in New Zealand, 177; advantages of standing orders, 252
Library of Classical Arabic Literature, 255

Library of Netherlandic Literature, 170-72, 255
Library of Russian and Soviet Literature, 153, 161
Library of Scandinavian Literature, 170, 255
Libretto for the Republic of Liberia (Tolson), 52f.
Lichtenstadter, Ilse, Twayne author and editor, 255
Lieber, Charles D., on the 7th Moscow Book Fair, 199, 200
Life in the Universe (Oparin and Fesenkov), 152
Limpus, Lowell, 225
Lincoln High School, Brooklyn, 29
Lindsay, Ann, Twayne editor, 162
Literary diplomacy, 135-84
Lithographs by Thomas Hart Benton, 56ff.
Littauer Foundation, Jewish books at the Moscow Book Fair, 200
Lodge, Henry Cabot, Jr., 94, 201
Logan, Joshua, 72
Lowell, Amy, 94
Lowell, Robert, 72
Lowengrund, Margaret, 66

McCarthy, Senator Joseph, 12, 139
McClellan, Anita, Twayne editor, 264
McDowell, Edwin, on timidity of big publishers, 148*n*.
McKay, Claude, great Black poet, 50f.
MacLeish, Archibald, 42
Macmillan Publishing Company, acquires G.K. Hall and Twayne, 10, 263; denies

permission to quote from E.A.Robinson, 123

McNaughton, William, study of *The Book of Songs*, 174

Mahoney, Margaret, 231*n.*

Mann, Milton, 126*n.*

Mark Twain, 11

Matthiessen, F.O., 42

Melvin B. Tolson...(Farnsworth), 55

Mencken, H.L., 83

Meridiane, Romanian publisher, 144

Merriam, Eve, 49

Meyerhoff Fund, Jewish book exhibits at the Moscow Book Fair, 200

Mid-Century American Poets (Ciardi, ed.), 44, 46, 47f., 90

Mid-Century British Poets, publication abandoned, 48

Mid-Century French Poets (Fowlie, ed.), 48

Milch, Robert, consulting editor, 156f.

Millay, Edna St. Vincent, permission fees affect teaching of, in colleges, 123

Miller, George, noted lithographer, 59, 60

Minnesota, University of, Press, 108

Mkrtchian, Anatoly A., Soviet diplomat, 165, 166

Modern Humanities Research Association, 171

Moore, Harry T., *Life and Works of D.H. Lawrence*, 72

Moore, Merrill, world's champion sonneteer, 72f.

Mordell, Albert, brouhaha with Harry Golden, 208ff.

More Clinical Sonnets (Moore), 73

Morgillo, Michael, 132

Moscow Book Fairs, Jewish book exhibits, 104, 169, 192-201, 241

Mud-Hut Dwellers, The (Sadoveanu), 139

Munowitz, Ken, retrospective review of his art, 125-28

Musicians and Petrillo, The (Leiter), 95

Nakarai, Toyozo W., *Biblical Hebrew Grammar*, 100

Nation, The, review of TUSAS, 119, 130

National Association of Book Editors, discussion on publication of the good ms. with little commercial value, 231ff.

National Conference for Soviet Jewry, the Moscow Book Fair, 200

National Council of Teachers of English, promotes Twayne series to members, 120, 129f.

National Histories Series, 147

Neider, Charles, 11

Neidle, Cecyle S., Immigrant Heritage of America Series editor, 18, 98f.

Nelson Atkins Museum of Art, Kansas City, 61

Netherlands, Dutch literary works, 171

Oahu, wartime service in, 37f.

Octagon Books, reprint program, 235f., 246

Official Guidebook to China, The, 183

Olivestone, David, Moscow Book Fair delegate, 197

"One of Two Thousand," Bowman's article on Authors Series, 109, 110-17

Paperbacks, "The Little Blue Books" as forerunner of, 208
Parker, Dorothy, 114
Paterson, Mark, 56
Permissions, editor's censorship role, 120f.; fees' effect on sales of author's works, 123; a perennial problem, 174
"Persephone," famous Benton nude, 61
Petrified Planet, The, science-fiction trio, 74
Phalen, Alice D., Twayne editor, 264
"Photographing the Bull," Benton lithograph, 57ff., 71
Pilpel, Harriet, 122
Pippett, Aileen, quoted, 124
Plagiarism, 202-05
Poetry, Twayne's early program in, 41ff.
Poland, literary explorations, 136f., 255
Powell, J.B., American journalist-hero, 179
Powell, John William, charged with sedition, 179f.
Pratt, Fletcher, 12, 68, 73
Publishers and publishing, an editor's credo, 110-17; role of the small firm, 111, 232, 239; clandestine government subsidies, 135; percentage of successful titles, 219, 231, 244; the subsidized book, 229-36; the problem of the good ms. with little commercial value, 231ff.; small editions can be profitable, 235; impact of large corporate ownership,

267f.; "publish or perish" dictum threatened, 119

Rawls, Walton H., Twayne editor, 17, 121
Rebreanu, Liviu, Romanian novelist, 145
Refugee Centaur, The (Antoniorrobles), 89f.
Reid, Joan, 55
Remainders, 226, 240ff.
Remini, Robert, *Andrew Jackson*, 96
Resko, John, self-taught artist, 86
Returns policy of publishers, 10, 227
Reviews and reviewers, 114f., 119f.; do they sell books? 224f.
Ribalow, Harold U., Judaica editor, 18, 99-105
Robinson, Edwin Arlington, excessive permission fees affect teaching of, 123
Rodman, Selden, 53
Roethke, Theodore, 44-46
Romania, literary explorations, 124, 138-48, 255
Roosevelt, Eleanor, 33
Rosenberg, Stuart, *The Christian Problem*, 131n.
Rosner, Eileen, 18
Rosset, Barney, 15
Rosten, Norman, *The Plane and the Shadow*, 49f.
Roth, Henry, *Call It Sleep*, 102
Royalty accounts, 227
Rukeyser, Muriel, 170

Sacco-Vanzetti case, 25
Sadoveanu, Mihail, Romanian writer, 139
Saltzman, Hilda, 14
Saltzman, Joel E., Twayne

principal, 14, 70, 76, 104, 132, 206f., 237; long illness, 91-93

Samizdat literature, 164

Saturday Review, 64f., 124n.

Scandinavia, literature of, 169-70

Schacht, Marshall, *Fingerboard*, 42

Scharfstein, Bernard, Jewish book exhibits at Moscow Book Fair, 200

Scharfstein, Sol, Jewish book exhibits at Moscow Book Fair, 200

Scholars, "publish or perish" dictum threatened, 119

Schultz, William R., TWAS editor, 118, 173ff.

Schuman, Julian, 178-80, 181

Schuster, M. Lincoln, 10

Science fiction and fantasy literature, 73-75

Selected Poems of Claude McKay, The, 49, 50f.

Selected Poems of Gunnar Ekelof, 170

Sex, Literature and Censorship (Lawrence), cited in judicial decision on *Lady Chatterley's Lover*, 72

Shapiro, Karl, on M.B. Tolson's poetry, 52, 53f.

Shapiro, Sidney, 180-84

Shapley, Harlow, 152

Sheffrey, David L., 58

Shinbaum, Myrna, Moscow Book Fair delegate, 197

Shirey, David, reviews the art of Ken Munowitz, 126-28

Shroyer, Frederick, book reviewer, 114

Sills, Stanley, head of ITT Publishing, 241f., 245, 246

Silverman, Mary, 14

Simo, Eugene, Hungarian publishing dignitary, 151

Siscoe, Frank G., State Department official, 138, 168

Sjoberg, Leif, TWAS editor, 170

Sloane, William, publisher, 231n.

Smith, Edwin, Am-Rus Agency head, 138, 139, 152

Smith, Maxwell A., TWAS editor, 118

Smith, Samuel, editor, 186

Soby, James, *Saturday Review* art editor, 65

Sokol, Yuri, Moscow Jewish Library, 199

Solomon, Sidney, book designer, 161

Southern Humanities Review, 109

Sovietskaya Kultura, critical of Jewish book exhibit at Moscow Book Fair, 197

Soviet Union, blocked funds, 51; Jewish books, 105 (*See also* Moscow Book Fairs); Twayne's interest in books from, 152-69; censorship, 164

Spector, Sherman D., 146

Spender, Stephen, 48

Stancu, Zaharia, *Barefoot*, 145

Stein, Aaron Marc, 35

Steinbeck, John, sales of TUSAS volume on, 9n.

Steinberg, Aaron, 14, 19

Steinberg, Brian, 18

Steinberg, Claire , 11, 31

Steinberg, Jacob ("Jack"), 14; books as objects of veneration, 19; parents, 21-23; first encounter with anti-Semitism, 23f., 25; at Columbia University Press,

28; per-diem teacher, 28ff.; marriage, 31; military service, 32ff; Chinese studies, 34-36, 38; Japanese cryptanalyst, 36-38; subscription plans for new writers and artists, 125ff.; literary diplomacy, 135-84; interest in China leads to founding of Twayne, 172; not a hands-off head of house, 174; world's best proofreader? 175n.; consultant to Hippocrene Books, 183, 246-47; Jewish book exhibits at the Moscow Book Fairs, 192-201; symposium on the good ms. with little commercial value, 231ff.; "Remainder maven," 240ff.; World Literature Book Club proposal, 242f.

Steinberg, Mary, 14, 19

Steinberg, Michael G., physician, 31

Stephanova, Ms. S., 149

Stilwell, General Joe, 12n., 35

Stone Avenue Children's Library, Brownsville, 19

Stone Avenue Hebrew School, 20

Subsidiary rights income, 220n.

Subsidized book, the, 38, 229-36

"Susanna and the Elders," famous Benton nude, 61

Sussman, Leonard R., 104

Swenson, May, 42

Synergy, corporate concept, 253

Tales from Gavagan's Bar (Pratt and deCamp), 74

Tales of War (Sadoveanu), 139

Tarr, Herbert, 10

Tate, Allen, on Tolson's poetry, 52

Teachers Union, 36

Teamsters Union, The (Leiter), 95f.

Tennessee Williams (Falk), flap over, 121

Theirs Be the Guilt (Sinclair), revised edition of *Manassas*, 108

Thomas, Rosemary, *Immediate Sun*, 42

Thompson, Douglas, 210

Thompson, Laurance, *Tilbury Town*, 123

Thunder Out of China (Jacoby and White), 231n.

Tikkun, 131n.

Time Magazine, erroneous attribution of McKay's "If We Must Die," 51

Titus, Ross P., State Department official, 168

Tolson, Melvin B., great Black poet, 52-55

Transcendentalism in America (Koster), 257

Translations, 157, 255; the Introduction Series, 124

Treasury of Jewish Holidays, A (Goldin), 86, 100

Trefousse, Hans Louis, history editor, 18, 95, 96-97

Treleaven, Phillips A., head of G.K. Hall, 256

Trevor-Roper, H.R., Great Histories Series, 97

Trial editions for new writers, 125

Tsurris (troubles), creative conversion of, 185ff., 250

Turner, Lady Dorothea, efforts on behalf of Twayne in New Zealand, 177f.

Twain, Mark, 11

Twayne Publishers, Inc.,
founding of, 10; origin of
name,11; original publishing plan,11; ownership, 14;
the early years, 41-105;
Thomas Hart Benton, 56ff.;
main business of, 73; at-
tempts at censorship, 85,
120ff.; authors series project, 107-34, 239, 260f., 264
(*See also below*: Twayne's
English Authors; Twayne's
United States Authors;
Twayne's World Authors Series); egalitarian thrust of
series books, 119; sale to
authors contemplated, 128;
consistent program of mailings to libraries, 129, 225;
the Bookman Associates imprint, 14, 49, 95, 100, 229ff.;
agreement with United
Printing Services, 131-33;
literary diplomacy, 135-84;
books of Polish interest,
136f.; Romanian book pro-
gram, 138-48; barter ar-
rangement for books, 146;
Bulgarian books, 148-51;
over-all publishing plans for
foreign literature, 158-60;
market for its books, 158f.;
porochnaya kniga incident,
162-65, 166; when disaster
strikes, 185ff.; Lifetime of
the Series Subscriptions
(TLSS), 187ff., 237; plagia-
risms, 202-5; brouhaha with
Harry Golden, 208-14; shipping and warehousing problems, 214ff.; author-
publisher relations, 219-27;
the end of Twayne, Inc., 237-
47; Twayne since 1972, 249-
68; why did ITT buy

Twayne? 251ff.; standing or-
ders, 252f.; the closed-end
series concept, 264; horror-
stimulus leads to explosion
of new series, 264ff.; be-
comes a Division of Macmil-
lan, 267
—Series Publications
American Women in the
Twentieth Century, 265f.
Twayne's Biography Series,
257
Twayne's Critical Editions
Program (TCEP), 257-59
Twayne's English Authors
Series (TEAS), 16f., 109,
251, 260
Twayne's Filmmakers Se-
ries, 259
Twayne's International
Studies and Translations
(TISAT), 255
Twayne Library of Modern
Poetry, 15, 42-49, 59
Twayne's Oral History Se-
ries, 266
Twayne's Rulers and States-
men of the World Series
(TROWS), 96, 256
Twayne's Theatrical Arts Se-
ries (TTAS), 259
Twayne's United States
Authors Series (TUSAS),
16f., 44, 107-34, 251; why
minor writers were in-
cluded, 109; a study in
depth of the American literary heritage, 111; in-
cluded books by young
scholars, 113; major objectives, 113; reviews, 119f.;
censorship and other barriers to publication, 120ff.;
USIA purchases and for-
eign language editions,

136; about 40% were first books on the subject authors, 174; Bowman's resignation as editor, 260

Twayne's United States Classics Series (TUSCS), 108

Twayne's World Authors Series (TWAS), 16f., 110, 112ff., 251; sub-editors, 117f; opens door to publication of translations, 124; Russian section, 157 (*See also* Soviet Union); Scandinavian section, 170; China section, 173ff.; crisis and tragedy, 261-64

Twayne's World Leaders Series (TWLS), 256f.

Uhlan, Edward, vanity publisher, 38f., 233

Under the Yoke (Vazov), 148

United Printing Services, 131-33

United States, cultural exchange agreement with Romania, 138ff.

United States Information Agency (USIA), book scandals of the 1960's, 135; book purchases and foreign language editions, 136

University of Chicago Press, plagiarism charge against Twayne author, 203-5

University of Kansas City, the Thomas Hart Benton-Twayne projects, 57ff.

Untermeyer, Louis, 73

Updike, John, 141

USSR, *see* Soviet Union

Valency, Maurice, 27

Vanderbilt, Kermit, "Publication Explosion," 119f.

Vanity publishing, 38f., 233

Variorum Walden, The (Harding, ed.), 108, 203f.

Vaslef, Nicholas P., TWAS Russian editor, 153ff.; *parochnaya kniga* incident, 164

Vassilev, Peter, 148

Vazov, Ivan, Bulgarian writer, 148, 149, 151

Vergelis, Aron, Soviet Yiddish editor, 196

Vickery, Walter, *Pushkin*, 163

Vidal, Gore, writes N.Y. *Times* lead review on TUSAS *Gore Vidal*, 225

Virtue, Hope McKay, 51

Voice of America, 142

Wade, Benjamin Franklin, 96

Wade, Gerald E., TWAS editor, 118

Wallace, Mesdames Eugenia and Lucie, 28

Wander, Meghan, Twayne editor, 264

Wang Chi-chen, trans. *Dream of the Red Chamber*, 13

Warth, Robert, books on Soviet leaders, 97

Washington Square Press, 97

Watson, Sir William, 117

Weisstein, Ulrich, TWAS editor, 118

Western Humanities Review, The, review of TUSAS, 120

What Happened at Pearl Harbor? (Trefousse), 51, 80, 96

What Happened in Cuba? (Smith), 80

What Happened in Salem? (Levin) 79f.

Whitman, Walt, 115

Wiesel, Elie, 102
Wilbur, Richard, 44
Williams, Joan Reid, 55
Williams, William Carlos, 47, 53
Winchell, Walter, 84f.
Winters, Yvor, refused permission to quote from E.A. Robinson, 123
Witches Three, science fiction collection, 74
Wood, Grant, 62
Workmen's Circle, Jewish books at the Moscow Book Fair, 200
World of Haldeman-Julius,
The (Mordell, ed.), brouhaha with Harry Golden, 208-14
World of Wonder (Pratt), 74
World's Greatest Boxing Stories (Ribalow, ed.), 102
Writers, *see* Authors

Yale Series of Younger Poets, 41
Year 2000, The (Bowman), 108
Yellow journalism, 25f.
Yugoslav literature, 124, 169

Zabriskie, Lilla Lyon, editor, 148